THE RUINED CITY

THE RUINED CITY

JOHN WILSON

ORCA BOOK PUBLISHERS

First published in North America in English by
Orca Book Publishers in 2018 as *The Ruined City: The Golden Mask.*

Golden Mask Book 1—The Arch
金色面具 第一部
Copyright © Sichuan Fine Arts Publishing House Co. Ltd., China
Golden Mask Book 1—The Arch originally published in Chinese Language
by Sichuan Fine Arts Publishing House Co., Ltd.

Library and Archives Canada Cataloguing in Publication

Wilson, John (John Alexander), 1951–, author
The ruined city / John Wilson.
(The golden mask)

Issued in print and electronic formats.
ISBN 978-1-4598-1970-2 (softcover).—ISBN 978-1-4598-1972-6 (PDF).—
ISBN 978-1-4598-1971-9 (EPUB)

I. Title.
PS8595.I5834R85 2018   JC813'.54   C2017-907967-0
C2017-907968-9

Library of Congress Control Number: 2018933713

Summary: Howard and Cate travel through time in this
fantasy novel for middle-grade readers.

*Orca Book Publishers is dedicated to preserving the environment and has
printed this book on Forest Stewardship Council® certified paper.*

Orca Book Publishers gratefully acknowledges the support for its publishing
programs provided by the following agencies: the Government of Canada through
the Canada Book Fund and the Canada Council for the Arts, and the Province of British
Columbia through the BC Arts Council and the Book Publishing Tax Credit.

Cover design by Teresa Bubela
Front cover image by Dehua Zhou
Author photo by Katherine Gordon

ORCA BOOK PUBLISHERS
orcabook.com

Printed and bound in Canada.

21 20 19 18 • 4 3 2 1

For Jen, who keeps me grounded in this dimension.

A WARNING:
DO NOT VOYAGE FAR!

Dear reader—whoever you are, wherever you are, whenever you are—it is my intention to fill the pages that follow with two tales so curious and singular that they will encourage you to believe in magic and monsters, lost cities and vanished worlds, and realities so fantastical they cannot be imagined in your wildest dreams. One tale happened thousands of years ago and is still happening now. The other happened now and is still happening thousands of years ago. Both will happen thousands of years from now. Time is not what you think it is.

These events I will describe occur in the world you surround yourself with every day and the worlds you visit in your most incredible fantasies. They involve people so like you and creatures so different that you will shiver just to think of them.

But beware, for it is also a tale of beings that were ancient before your world was born. A tale of monsters who are dead and yet dream, who are so powerful that humans are insignificant, and who are so frighteningly alien that simply to think of them can push a mind to the edges of sanity. As the great master of the macabre, H.P. Lovecraft, once said, "We live on a placid island of ignorance in the midst of black seas of infinity, and it was not meant that we should voyage far."

Is all that follows true? I cannot help you there. You must decide. But one thing is certain—it all began long ago in a place called Sanxingdui...

THE EMPEROR'S TEA

Kun Zhuang—emperor of Sanxingdui, the City of Masks, and all the surrounding lands that can be reached on a galloping horse in five days, lord of all creatures from the largest elephant in the royal menagerie to the tiniest mite in the straw bed of the poorest peasant, and keeper of the Golden Mask—sniffed.

A young servant boy, dressed in a gold-trimmed green uniform with a twisting imperial dragon on the front, scuttled forward from his position behind the emperor and offered him a silk handkerchief. Kun wiped his nose on the richly embroidered sleeve of his dressing gown and waved his arm dismissively.

"Thank you, Chen," he said, "but I would prefer if you brought Jingshen and me some tea."

The boy bowed and turned away, but he skidded to a halt when he realized the emperor was still talking.

"And make certain that foul-smelling dog is nowhere near the royal tea urn. Last time you served tea, it smelled as if you had drawn the water straight from the drinking trough in the imperial kennels."

The boy bowed even more deeply and fled.

"He's a good boy," Kun said to the tall, elegant woman seated cross-legged on the other side of the low table. "But his mind is always on either that kitchen girl, Ting, and her pet dog, or on his crazy dream of becoming a wushu master." He smiled at his guest.

"One day he will do great things," the woman predicted. Her snow-white hair hung straight over her shoulders, framing a gentle, high-cheekboned face. She returned Kun's smile with gray eyes that hinted she could read his most intimate thoughts.

"I would like that day to be while he still makes and serves my tea." The emperor's smile faded, and his brow furrowed. He pulled at his beard thoughtfully. "But we have more important things to talk of than tea. Are the auguries true?"

Jingshen nodded slowly. "The signs are all there. The time of danger threatens to unleash the power of the Golden Mask. Sanxingdui is facing doom."

"But how can that be? How can the City of Masks be in danger? It is the center of the world. It has endured for a thousand years. And are we not protected by the Golden Mask?"

"A thousand years is but a blink of the eye, and the Golden Mask does not simply protect us. It is not good or evil—it is naked power, and power can destroy as easily as create. We are safe from the mask's power only so long as it resides within the Chamber of the Deep."

"I know. The ancient prophecy clearly states"—the emperor closed his eyes to aid remembrance—"*The horrors of darkness may not endure the light while the Golden Mask resides in the Chamber of the Deep.*"

"This is true," Jingshen agreed.

"And you know as well as I," Kun went on, "that the Chamber of the Deep may be entered and the Golden Mask approached only by one of the three—you, me or Shenxian."

Jingshen sat silent for a long time, but she had a look of such worry on her face that Kun was scared to ask what troubled her. When she finally spoke, her voice was so quiet that the emperor had to lean forward to catch her words.

"Last night I dreamed that the Min Mountains fell, and that from their ruins arose a terrible demon of unimaginable power," she said. "The land vanished in great floods and fires, and the world was reduced to dust, ashes and rocks."

"The time of danger is coming?"

"Yes, and it is very close."

"Does Shenxian know this?" Kun forced himself to whisper.

"If I dreamed it, then so did Shenxian."

The emperor rubbed his temples as if to erase the terrifying thoughts running through his brain. "But still," he said at last, "Shenxian cannot act alone. Two of the three of us must recite the sacred incantation at the same instant to release the Golden Mask from its jade pillar."

"True, but you don't know *all* of the ancient prophecy." Jingshen clutched her hands together to prevent them from trembling. "'The horrors of darkness may not endure the light while the Golden Mask resides in the Chamber of the Deep. Yet at the time of danger, when the mountains fall in the reign of Skyfire, the courage of life-in-death may unlock the Arch until the return of the Ivory Ark.'"

"How can mountains fall?"

"The earth shakes when the gods are angry," she said simply. "Why not enough that mountains fall?"

Kun shrugged, unconvinced. "Even if that is possible, the sky cannot be on fire and the dead cannot live to be courageous."

"What happened the year you were born?"

For a moment the emperor was confused, and then he realized what Jingshen was asking.

"A great star fell to earth," he replied. "Its fall was so bright that it could be seen at noon."

"Do the chronicles not say that it was as if the sky was ablaze?"

Kun's voiced dropped. "They do. So the reign of Skyfire is when I am emperor?"

"Yes, and is Shenxian not the high priest who can speak with the dead as if they were standing beside him, alive? And has he not proven his courage in battle many times?"

Kun took a deep breath. "So when the mountains fall during my reign as emperor, Shenxian will be able to put on the Golden Mask without our aid?"

Jingshen nodded.

"But what is the Ivory Ark?"

"That I do not understand. But whatever it is, it is important."

The pair sat in worried silence as the sun rose and the shadows fled down the walls of the imperial tearoom. It seemed to Kun that they mirrored the darkness that was falling across his reign and the entire future of Sanxingdui. He had almost plucked up enough courage to ask Jingshen what could be done when the silence was shattered by a high-pitched yapping.

Kun leapt to his feet in surprise as a small brown dog shot into the room and tore around in circles. The dog had long hair, a shaggy tail, droopy ears and a squashed face that made it look as if it had run at full speed into a wall. Its pink tongue hung out, flapping wetly from side to side as it ran.

Kun spun around to the doorway, where a young girl, dressed in the same uniform as Chen, stood with her eyes and mouth open wide in horror.

"Ting!" he shouted. "How many times have I told you to keep that foul, smelly beast under control? Dogs are for work— to catch rats, to stand guard and to hunt—not to be pampered, overbred pets for kitchen girls who do not know their place. Remove it from the sacred tearoom immediately! We shall talk about what is to be done with it later."

Jingshen watched serenely as Ting chased the animal around the room, shouting, "Come here, Fu! Bad dog." At last she grabbed a leg, drew the protesting creature into her arms and retreated, bowing. As she disappeared out the door, she was replaced by Chen, who was carrying a tray with an ornate teapot and two cups on it. He shuffled across the room, bent forward, his eyes staring only at the mat in front of his feet.

"Chen! Have I not warned you enough about keeping that dog under control?" Kun demanded as he sat back down. "It cannot live in the palace if it disrupts everything."

Chen looked about to burst into tears as he bowed even lower.

As the boy reached the table, Jingshen said with a smile, "I understand that you have been studying wushu."

Chen nodded without looking up.

"Does wushu not promote fluid, elegant bodily movements?" she asked.

Chen flicked his eyes up to glance at Jingshen and mumbled, "It does."

"Then why do you move like an arthritic monkey? Does wushu not say, *Do not fight yourself—relax?*"

"I'm sorry."

"Don't be sorry. Simply move as you can."

Chen looked up at the emperor, who gave a nod. Slowly the boy unbent until he stood straight. He spun in a circle, raising the tray above his head as he did so. Balancing it on one hand, he performed an ever-faster sequence of complex twists and turns, then placed the tray neatly in the middle of the table. With a mesmerizing series of delicate hand moves, he poured the tea and placed a cup before each of the onlookers.

As Chen backed away, Jingshen said, "That was well done. I don't believe I've seen tea served that way before."

"I made up the moves myself," Chen said as he backed away toward the door.

"They're very graceful," Jingshen called as the boy disappeared. She turned to Kun. "Don't be too hard on Chen. To control Fu, he must first control Ting—and I'm not sure even *you* could do that."

The emperor grumbled and reached for his tea. "At least he didn't spill much," he said.

"He has talent," Jingshen asserted. "And I think his role in the struggle to come is greater than being the emperor's teaboy."

"And Ting? Will she have a role? Chen seems infatuated with her. Around the palace, it is almost impossible to see one without the other."

"I think she will," Jingshen said.

"But she is so quiet, like a mouse. Were it not for that annoying dog at her heel, she would be invisible."

"Remember the old saying: *There is greater depth in silence than a million words of senseless babble.*"

"That is true," Kun agreed.

"And," Jingshen continued, "do not be so ready to dismiss the annoying dog. There is magic in the number three."

Kun sputtered over his tea. "You cannot be serious. Chen has talent, yes. And Ting may well have hidden depths. But that dog! It's…it's…" Words failed him. He could find nothing to describe how he felt about Fu.

Jingshen smiled. "I understand. Fu is not the most lovable of creatures. But there is a story—a story that was ancient even when the first mask was cast in Sanxingdui."

She sipped her tea and began to tell the story. "When the world was young and newly born out of chaos, there were no people or animals. Heian, the god of darkness, and Guang, the goddess of light, decided to divide the world between them, but they could not agree which creatures to place in it. Heian saw the world as a playground for the gods and wished to populate it with mighty creatures from the beginning of time. Guang saw the earth as a garden where more modest creations could live peacefully."

"I know this," Kun said. "It is the tale of creation."

"But there is more to it for those who will listen," Jingshen said gently before continuing. "Unable to reconcile their differing ideas, Heian and Guang fought a war that brought chaos back and came close to destroying the world. Guang won, but she was not powerful enough to destroy Heian and his monsters. All she could do was banish his gods to a place of darkness far from the earth and lock them there with the power of the Golden Mask."

"Yes, yes," Kun interrupted. "So Guang and Heian made an unbreakable pact that never again would they fight each other and risk destroying the world. Then Guang created the first three—a man, a woman and an animal—and watched as they grew and evolved and populated the world. That is how we came to be living peaceably here."

"That is all true," Jingshen agreed. "Everything is peaceful, but what the chronicles do not tell us is that Heian cheated. He created a portal between the earth and the world of his monstrous gods. Normally the portal is closed, but at the time of danger, when the world of monsters comes close to ours, dreams and glimpses of that other world can seep through and disturb the minds of those who can see. At those times, there is a danger of the portal being flung open and the two worlds becoming one. Guang knows this, and so she has kept alive the spirits of her first three creations. In the time of danger, they can fight Heian and—if they win—save the world."

Kun stared at Jingshen. "Are you telling me that Chen, Ting and that foul dog are all that stands between us and an invasion of monsters that will destroy our world?"

She nodded. "As they have been many times in the past and will be many more times in the future."

"Jingshen, you are a powerful sorceress. Can you not put on the Golden Mask and defeat Shenxian yourself?"

"Because of the pact between Guang and Heian, I cannot intervene directly. I can only work through human agency. I can help and advise, but that is all. It is the same with Shenxian. If either of us dons the mask, the ancient pact will be shattered, and Heian and Guang will resume their age-old war. That would mean the destruction of not just our world, but of all worlds of creation for all time."

"Would Shenxian really risk the end of everything by putting on the mask?"

"Shenxian may think he will be able to control the forces he would let loose by putting on the mask. Ambition can blind us to many things, and Shenxian is very ambitious."

"I will talk with him," Kun said, without much hope in his voice. "Perhaps I can persuade him of the folly of his plan."

"I fear that he is determined and set upon his course. Already he has sent messengers across the mountains to seek an alliance with the Ma Zhang."

"The Horse Warriors!" Kun exclaimed. "But they are people of the flatlands. They've never crossed the mountains."

"Never is a long time, and we don't know what Shenxian has offered. If he seeks unlimited power, then he can offer much."

"But if all he needs to do to gain his power is put on the Golden Mask, why does he need the Ma Zhang?"

"Until he puts on the Golden Mask, he is still mortal. A powerful mortal, indeed, but still one who can be defeated.

I suspect he wishes to use the Ma Zhang to attack Sanxingdui in the time of danger. If they can occupy the city, even for a brief period, Shenxian will be free to open the Chamber of the Deep, release the mask and put it on. When he does that, nothing will matter. The world will be lost in a new chaos."

"But he must do this at the time of danger?" Kun asked, clinging to some hope.

"Yes," Jingshen agreed. "It must occur when the Min Mountains fall."

"But how can he know when that will be?"

"I don't know, but once it happens, I fear it will be too late for us."

"We must find out when."

"I agree," Jingshen said, "but how?"

As they sipped their tea and wondered about the future, neither Jingshen nor Kun noticed the tiny tremble that ran across the floor of the tearoom as the Min Mountains far to the west flexed ever so gently.

THE DREAMING DAWN

The sun hauled itself slowly into the narrow slab of clear sky between the eastern horizon and a strip of dark, rolling clouds. It announced its arrival by painting the undersides of the clouds a deep purple, but the first rays to illuminate Arkminster tinted the spires and office buildings an encouraging orange. Night fears were pushed aside, eyes cleared of sleep, breakfasts eaten, doors opened, vehicles retrieved from garages. The well-kept streets began to fill with the bustle and babble of another day.

Satisfied with its work, the sun swept on. Rays of light fired the tops of the Black Hills and found their way between the trunks of the fir trees and into the open spaces, where curiously carved, moss-draped stones stood in disturbing patterns, as if awaiting the arrival of someone—or something—to perform ancient rituals in their midst. The sharp line of dawn crept grudgingly down the treed slopes in a vain attempt to plumb the deepest reaches of the precipitous canyon where the dark water of the Bane River flowed endlessly over smooth rocks that were molten when the earth was young.

With obvious relief, the sunlight escaped the hills and raced across the southern plain, bringing the day to the pebbly beaches and the jagged black rocks of the Shipwreck Coast. Only one community, Aylford, huddled in the shadow of Knife Ridge, remained in darkness.

Aylford had once been a thriving port. Boats had navigated the Bane River and unloaded the ocean's bounty, passenger ships had delivered immigrants, and freighters had brought cargo from around the world. But a great storm had destroyed many of the waterfront warehouses and one of the largest Chinatowns on the west coast, the river had silted up, and the docks had emptied. The town's population declined as families moved to nearby Arkminster to seek opportunities and a better life. Now only the small Aylford College and the minor summer influx of tourists kept the town going.

At last the sun turned its attention to Aylford. It touched the gothic spires of the college, brightened the mansions on Hangman's Hill, washed over the portables outside Charles Dexter Ward High School and slipped along Arcton Street to number 194, where a shaft shone through the narrow gap in the curtains of Howard Peter Lawson's bedroom window. It skittered over the clutter of books and binders on Howard's desk and the pile of clothes on his floor, and climbed onto his bed.

Howard was restless. His eyeballs moved jerkily beneath closed lids, and his fingers clenched and unclenched spasmodically. Blankets had been thrown to one side, and only the twisted, sweat-soaked sheet remained. Howard was dreaming. He was sitting at his kitchen table across from Madison Danforth, the hottest girl in tenth grade.

Two things about this told Howard that he was dreaming. First, the real Madison was light years out of his league and acted as if he didn't exist. Second, they were talking about books, and as far as Howard could tell, Madison read nothing more than the instructions on bottles of hair products and the price tags in expensive clothing shops. Still, the dream was a pleasant enough fantasy until Leon appeared.

Howard and Madison were sharing a mutual love of Neil Gaiman novels when the beautiful girl across the table morphed into Leon Whateley. Leon was Howard's opposite in every way. Having been held back a year, he was the oldest kid in grade ten and the only one who had a full driver's license. Howard, having skipped a grade, was the youngest and had a beat-up bicycle. Leon had everything—rich parents, a flashy sports car and the beautiful Madison. Howard had a paper route.

Leon leaned across the table and leered. His watery blue eyes, rubbery lips and dramatically receding chin had earned him the nickname Fishman, but only Madison dared to call him that. Right now he looked particularly fishy—he was soaking wet, and strands of seaweed clung to his hair and draped over his shoulders. A hermit crab crawled out of his left nostril and scuttled over his pasty cheek.

"What do you want?" Howard asked.

Surprisingly, Leon laughed. He raised his right arm and pointed, tears of laughter adding to the salty moisture on his cheeks.

Howard looked down. He saw he wasn't wearing the aged sweatpants and Led Zeppelin T-shirt that was his usual night attire. Instead, he was dressed in shiny green pants with golden cuffs. His jacket had an intricately woven golden dragon on the front.

Puzzled, Howard looked back up. Leon had vanished. Sitting in his place was a Chinese girl wearing a costume identical to his. Howard was about to ask who she was when an ugly dog jumped onto her lap, tilted its head and stared at him.

The girl smiled, overwhelming Howard in a feeling of deep contentment. He smiled back, but the girl and the small dog grew dim and disappeared. Darkness began to slide in from the edges of Howard's vision, and the feeling of contentment was replaced by a sense of foreboding.

As the sunlight crossed Howard's face, the fitful motion of his eyes and hands ceased. He woke up, but his eyelids remained closed as he tried, unsuccessfully, to make sense of his dream. When the lingering feeling of dread had dwindled, Howard took a deep breath and opened his eyes. The sunbeam was scrambling across the wall, and he watched it flicker and fade as the sun was swallowed by the dark clouds covering the sky.

"Breakfast's ready," Howard's mom shouted from the kitchen. "It's your favorite—Smiley French Toast."

Howard groaned. He wanted to shout back, "I'm not five anymore!" What he said instead was, "Coming, Mom."

Howard grabbed some clothes from the floor, threw them on and headed to the kitchen. There it was on the table: a slice of bread, dipped in egg and fried. When Howard was five, his mom had struggled to get him to eat anything other than Cheerios. His dad had the brilliant idea of making a face on French toast using blueberries for eyes, a segment of orange for a nose and a line of chocolate sauce for a mouth. It had worked, and for weeks Howard had leapt out of bed in the morning to see what expression his dad had put on the face.

"Thanks, Mom," he said now, sitting down and popping a blueberry eye into his mouth. He had tried once to tell his mom that he didn't want Smiley French Toast anymore, but it hadn't ended well. Because Howard had been a sickly baby, and her only child, his mom had always been overprotective. As he'd grown, she'd continued to treat him like a much younger child, perhaps believing that babying him would keep him close to her and safeguard him against danger. Things had gotten worse after Howard's dad was committed to the Aylford Institute for Psychiatric Care. That was almost a year ago now.

Howard thought about his dad—and all the good times they'd had together—every day. He visited him once a week, even though his dad had no idea who Howard was. His mind had gone somewhere far away, and it didn't look like it was going to return anytime soon. Howard was convinced his dad would want him and his mom to move on. Unfortunately, his mom clung compulsively to the past, convinced her husband was about to recover and would be home in a week or two. She obsessively cleaned and rearranged his tools in the garage and his clothes in his closet. She even recorded every episode of his favorite TV show so that he could catch up when he came home. Not that Howard could criticize. He'd moved his dad's turntable, amplifier and vast collection of classic rock vinyl into his own room. Sometimes he spent entire evenings there, carefully playing odd albums by weird musicians with even weirder haircuts.

"What a lovely clean plate," his mom said, clearing the dishes and placing Howard's lunch bag beside him. At least she didn't make him take his old *Star Wars* lunch box to school. "I've packed you a nice healthy lunch today."

Like every day, Howard thought, but he said, "Thanks, Mom," and got up from the table. "Gotta go. I have some studying to do before class."

"That's good. Keep your grades up. Dad will be proud of you."

Howard grabbed his backpack, gave his mom a hug and headed out the door.

"I won't be home when you get back," she shouted after him. "It's Friday, so I've got my cosmic harmony group. But I'll put some vegan chili in the slow cooker, and we can eat when I get back."

"Okay, Mom," Howard shouted from the front gate. "I'm going to visit Dad this afternoon."

"That's lovely. He'll enjoy that. Have a good day, sweetie."

Howard scanned the street to see if anyone he knew was within hearing range. It was really unlikely that Leon would be in this part of town, but if he was and heard "sweetie," Howard might as well run away from home and join the circus.

AYLFORD

School Lunches

It was a typical lunch break at C.D.W. High. The cool girls were out in the open, giggling and preening where they were certain everyone could see them. The jocks were flexing their muscles and shooting hoops where they were sure the cool girls could see them. The 7-Eleven kids were wandering back with their slushies. And Howard was standing on his own beside a portable, worrying.

Worrying was Howard's specialty. Fearing that a single spot would burst into rampaging acne, that he'd turn over an exam paper and discover the questions meant nothing, that he'd forget which room his next class was in. None of these things had ever happened to him, but the possibility that they might could send him into an emotional tailspin.

He was also afraid of the dark.

There was a rational explanation for fearing what hides in darkness, of course. Thousands of years earlier, the dark could have been concealing a tiger, a deadly snake or a mortal enemy. None of that was likely to be outside Aylford's only high school, but for someone with anxiety, there was always *something* just out of sight—some lurking social horror hidden around the next corner.

Howard was used to this, but the darkness he feared most was different. It had started several months back. Howard would be having a perfectly ordinary dream, often about Madison, and darkness would begin to form at the edges of his vision. It would gradually thicken and move in—black tendrils overwhelming his dream with foreboding. Howard would wake up with a sense of dread but without any idea what was scaring him. He simply had a feeling there was something in the darkness that he should be very afraid of.

The feeling faded with the daylight, but Howard was an expert worrier, so he began to think the encroaching darkness was a sign he was having a stroke or an aneurism. He thought about telling his mom, but the last thing he needed was his mother freaking out. One day, as he watched everyone else getting on with their lives, Howard promised himself he would go to the doctor about it. Meanwhile, the possibilities for creative worrying were limitless.

Howard felt something rub against his ankle. He looked down to see bright green eyes staring up at him. "Hello...um, cat," he said, realizing he didn't know the animal's name. It was jet black and belonged to the Chinese girl who had entered his grade at the beginning of the semester. Her name was Cate— short for Hecate, she had said when she was introduced— and the cat followed her everywhere, even to school. It wasn't allowed into the buildings, but it hung around outside, doing whatever it was that cats did, and it was always by the door when the day ended. Howard bent to stroke the animal's head, but it darted under the portable.

A large raindrop thudded against the ground at Howard's feet. He looked up to see low dark clouds racing across the sky. A gust of wind rattled, bumped and bounced a cardboard coffee cup across the parking lot. Another storm coming through, Howard thought miserably. It seemed like there was one every few days, howling down out of the Black Hills.

"Hey, lonely boy! I've got a message for you."

Howard jumped at the voice and turned to see Leon lounging against the edge of the portable. He didn't look as fishy as he had in the dream, but he was no George Clooney either.

"Madison wants to talk to you." Leon inclined his head toward the school's west wing, where the beautiful and/or rich people hung out.

"Madison?" Howard squeaked as sweat broke out on his palms.

"Yeah," Leon said lazily. "You know, the good-looking blonde."

"Why?"

"God, you're such a dork. Why do you think? Maybe she wants to discuss the latest fashion trends."

Howard cringed at the sarcasm while Leon scanned his faded sweatshirt, torn jeans and scuffed runners. Leon dressed casually, but Howard knew that his designer hoodie had cost more than his own entire wardrobe.

"Why she would want to talk to you at all is beyond me," Leon drawled. "But she said, *Leon, go over and ask Howard to join us. I want to tell him something.* Now, I can never refuse a pretty girl, so here I am. I've passed on the message. The rest is up to you."

Leon flashed his perfect teeth in what was the most insincere smile Howard had ever seen and strolled back across the schoolyard as if the entire world bored him.

Howard's worry level skyrocketed. This was no dream—Madison wanted to talk to him. The girl with the perfect skin, every hair in place, clothing special-ordered from Italy and the most startlingly wide brown eyes Howard had ever seen had noticed him. Or was this some cruel trick of Leon's to suck him into their good-looking world just to mortally embarrass him? Should he take the bait? Should he stay where he was? What if Madison really did want to talk to him? His whole life could change.

Tendrils of darkness edged in at the corners of his eyes. Howard panicked. This had happened only in dreams before. The stroke was coming. He shook his head and blinked hard. The darkness withdrew, but Howard was unnaturally aware of his breathing and heartbeat. The raindrops hitting the roof of the portable behind him sounded like cannon fire. He had to make a decision. He inhaled deeply and took a couple of steps forward.

"Don't go," said someone behind him.

Howard spun around to see Cate leaning out one of the portable's windows, the black cat perched on the window ledge beside her. They both looked bored as they stared over at Madison and the others.

"Why not?" Howard asked.

Cate shrugged. "If you're too dumb to realize you're being set up, it's not my job to convince you." This was already the longest conversation they'd ever had.

Oddly, Howard didn't feel insulted by her comment. After all, she was probably right. "Why do you care if I'm being set up?"

Cate turned her head slowly and stared down at him. She wore heavy, dark eye makeup and peered out through a black fringe. She was Chinese, yet something about her reminded Howard of Chrissie Hynde, the lead singer of the Pretenders, an old rock band his dad was really into. He began to feel uncomfortable under this strange girl's intense gaze.

"I don't particularly care," she said at last.

At least, Howard *thought* that was what she said. He wasn't sure he'd seen her lips move.

Cate withdrew her head from the window. With a disdainful look at Howard, the cat disappeared after her.

Across the schoolyard, Madison and Leon appeared to be arguing. Howard made a snap decision and jogged around to the portable entrance. Cate was just coming down the steps.

"Thanks," he said.

Cate tilted her head in acknowledgment, and she and the cat walked past him.

"Hecate was a Greek goddess, wasn't she?" he blurted out at her retreating back.

As soon as the words left his mouth, Howard winced. He couldn't believe he had said something so cheesy—another opportunity for social interaction blown.

Cate continued walking, but after a couple of steps she turned back. "Yes, she was," she said. "And *Howard* in Middle English means 'sheepherder.'"

Those dark eyes were staring at Howard again. He knew he was supposed to talk into this silence, but his mind was a void. Then his dad came to his rescue with something he had once told Howard.

"It's also the first name of Duane Allman." Howard wanted to explain that Duane had been the lead guitarist with the Allman Brothers Band and had died in a motorcycle accident, but a tiny voice in the back of his head was screaming at him to shut up.

A faint smile softened Cate's face. "I knew that," she said. "Tell me something I don't know."

A direct question. An invitation to be a geek. Howard could handle that. "You know the story that Duane Allman crashed his motorcycle into a truck carrying peaches, and that's why the surviving band members called their next album *Eat a Peach*?"

Cate nodded.

"It's not true. It was a lumber truck. The album was actually named after something Duane Allman said in an interview: *Every time I'm in Georgia, I eat a peach for peace.*"

"Cool."

Cate's smile broadened, and Howard silently thanked his dad for his obsessive interest in classic rock.

"So," he said, "if you're Chinese, why are you named after a Greek goddess?"

"I've had an interesting life," Cate said. "Hecate is the daughter of Perses, the god of destruction, and Asteria, the goddess of nocturnal oracles. She's associated with cross-roads, doorways, poisonous plants, witchcraft, necromancy and sorcery, and she is one of the pre-Olympian deities of the underworld. She's often portrayed carrying a torch, a key and a dagger. To make an offering to Hecate, you have to dig a pit and slit a lamb's throat so that the blood runs into it."

"Okay, okay. This is getting too weird." It was not just the information that was weird but also the fact that Cate was speaking in the present tense, as if slitting a lamb's throat was part of her everyday experience.

"You asked," Cate said indifferently.

"I asked where your name came from, not an entire history of Greek mythology. And you didn't really answer me."

Cate shrugged. "Different cultures have different names for gods. Greek, Chinese—the gods don't care."

Howard had no idea how to respond to this, so to keep the conversation going he blurted out, "What's your cat called?"

"Heimao."

"Cool. What does it mean?"

"Black cat," Cate replied. "You'd better get inside—there's a storm coming." She spun on her heels and strode off toward the school's main door.

"Wait!" Howard shouted without thinking.

Cate stopped, turned back and looked at him.

His brain froze again. He had nothing. What did people say in situations like this?

"Do you want to hang out after school?" he spluttered.

For what seemed like an hour, Cate said nothing, and Howard felt as if he were dying inside. Then her smile returned.

"Sure. That'd be cool. I've got drama last class. See you in the theater."

With that Cate and her cat headed toward the main building. At the door, Heimao swerved off to the side and disappeared. Howard stood and watched, amazed that he had asked and thrilled that Cate had said yes.

His happiness evaporated as Leon and Madison's group passed by.

"Howie's hanging with the goth chick!" Leon shouted.

His companions burst out laughing. Madison threw Leon a look that could have started the next ice age.

WHAT BOOK?

Howard walked into the school in a daze and was twenty minutes into math class before he remembered that today was his day for visiting his dad. An insane asylum was probably not the best place to take Cate on a first date—if that was even what this was. What should he do, bail on Cate or not visit his dad? He knew his dad wouldn't notice if his son missed a weekly visit, but Howard would be wracked with guilt. Also, he'd have to handle his mother's obsessive questions about how his dad was doing. Howard's worry consumed the remainder of the class.

He searched for Cate between classes with no luck. He went into his last class wondering how he was going to survive to the end of the day and what he would do if he did.

The class—history—was normally Howard's favorite, but his worried mood was too entrenched to be lifted, even by the large A in a red circle at the top of the assignment that was handed back at the start of the class. The hour dragged by as Howard swung between joy at the prospect of meeting Cate and worry about how he was going to resolve the conflict.

The bell finally went. All he wanted to do was hurry off to meet Cate and end his torture, but the teacher, Mr. Campbell, had different ideas.

"That was a very good essay you wrote," he said as Howard passed his desk.

Howard hesitated. "Thank you," he mumbled, only half paying attention.

Mr. Campbell was an old-school teacher close to retirement. He dressed in tweed jackets and always wore a garish bow tie. He was considered a good teacher, but the story around school was that this was because he had actually lived through all the history he taught. He talked slowly and often headed off on tangents. Usually Howard found this interesting—when he wasn't stressed and in a hurry.

He took a tentative step back.

Mr. Campbell ignored Howard's hint and launched into a rambling reminiscence about his own history teacher, now long dead, and how the world and in particular the teaching of history had changed over the decades.

"Have you considered taking history at university?" Mr. Campbell asked, oblivious to Howard's discomfort. "I think you have a talent for it."

"Maybe," Howard said, taking another step back.

"There are many good schools to choose from. I wouldn't necessarily recommend our little college here in Aylford. Not that there's anything wrong with it per se, but it is a small school and that does limit one's options. I would suggest somewhere larger—perhaps even a European school. After all, they do have more history over there than we do. In fact, as someone once said, they have altogether too much history." Mr. Campbell chuckled at his little joke.

Howard coughed, to no effect.

"Of course, where you go will depend on what aspect of history you wish to study. Not all schools are equally good at all time periods. For example, some specialize in medieval studies, others in modern or ancient history. But perhaps that isn't something you need to worry about at the undergraduate level. Best to get a good grounding as broadly as possible. Plenty of time to specialize with postgraduate work."

"I have to go," Howard announced. "I'm meeting someone."

"Of course. Of course." Mr. Campbell seemed crestfallen at the abrupt end to his advice. "I didn't mean to keep you. But if you do decide on a life in history, come and see me. I'd be happy to pass on what little knowledge I have gathered on possible schools."

Howard forced out another thank-you and fled the classroom. He raced along the corridor, terrified that Cate had grown tired of waiting and gone home. His backpack seemed to weigh a ton, and the corridor stretched on to infinity. Then the blackness came. Howard's peripheral vision dissolved into seething tendrils of dark shadow that raced into the center of his vision until the corridor ahead narrowed. He had an overwhelming sense of falling down a dark tunnel.

He stumbled to one side and crashed into a row of lockers, causing a nearby group of eighth-grade girls to jump in surprise. He felt dizzy and nauseous and half expected a searing pain in his head or chest to announce a stroke or a heart attack.

He leaned on the locker, closed his eyes and forced himself to breathe slowly. The nausea and dizziness receded. When he opened his eyes, the world wavered back into normality and the darkness faded. Pushing himself off the locker, Howard smiled weakly at the staring girls and continued at a more sedate pace. He heard the girls giggle and say something about drugs. As he headed for the theater, he promised himself again that he would make an appointment to see the doctor.

Pushing open the main door, Howard had the impression that the theater was empty. He was too late, he thought, and resigned himself to an evening of wallowing in self-pity. Then he heard Cate's voice coming from backstage.

"Metamorphosis. Transformation. Evolution. Change. I am a teenage caterpillar."

Confused, Howard edged forward to stand in front of the stage.

"I will become a platypus."

He quietly climbed the steps and peered behind the heavy black curtain. As his eyes adjusted to the gloom, he made out Cate standing with her back to him, her black hair pulled into two bunches. She was wearing a black leather jacket, black fishnet tights, black boots and black lace gloves.

"I will remain in my cocoon until I change from a butterfly to a swallow, from a swallow to a duck and from a duck to a platypus."

With a flourish she pulled a brightly colored scarf from her pocket, wrapped it around her neck and spun around to face the worried face of Howard.

"Enjoy the show?" she asked, sitting down on a stage block.

"Yeah," Howard said. "What are you doing?"

"Acting," Cate replied, unzipping her backpack. "Want a granola bar?"

"Sure." Howard sat beside her and unwrapped the offered bar. "What was that you were saying?"

"I was rehearsing my big monologue."

"It sounded weird."

"It's from a play called *Dog Sees God: Confessions of a Teenage Blockhead*. I'm trying to persuade Ms. Irving to stage it as the school play this year. It's about the *Peanuts* characters when they're in high school."

"The *Peanuts* characters? Sounds cute."

"Not quite. It deals with bullying, homosexuality and death. It's pretty heavy stuff. Too strong for the C.D.W. High drama program, I think. Everyone else is keen on doing *Annie*. I think Madison wants the title role. Anyway, *Annie* will be much more popular with the parents and"—Cate smiled wickedly—"much more relevant for a bunch of high-school kids in the twenty-first century."

Howard grinned at her sarcasm. "So why bother rehearsing if everyone's going to do *Annie*?"

"Because it really unsettles Ms. Irving. You should see how uncomfortable she gets when I read the sex scenes."

"And you pick them deliberately."

"Yeah." The wicked smile returned. "I dreamed I was a platypus last night. When I'm dreaming I'm a platypus, is there a platypus somewhere dreaming it's me?"

Howard had no idea what to say, so he stayed silent.

Cate stood up. "So what do you want to do?"

Howard suddenly remembered his conflict and stammered, "I don't know. It's…I have to go see my dad. He's…um, in the hospital."

"I could walk with you."

"No," Howard said too loudly. "I'm sorry. I mean…" He swallowed hard and took a deep breath. "He's not in the hospital. Well, he sort of is. He's in the AIPC—the Aylford Institute for Psychiatric Care."

"I know where that is," Cate said cheerfully. "Give me five to change, and I'll see you outside."

Howard walked out of the school in a daze. In the few hours he'd known Cate, he felt as if he'd been caught up in a whirlwind that hadn't allowed his feet to land back on the ground. She hadn't even blinked when he told her his dad was in the AIPC. It was bewildering, but that was okay. Bewildering Howard could handle—it was normal conversations he had trouble with.

He shivered in the cold wind and pulled his jacket tighter around his shoulders. The sky was thick with heavy black clouds, and it was already so dark that the streetlamps had been fooled into switching themselves on. Heimao slunk out from beneath a bush to Howard's right and rubbed up against his leg.

The door behind Howard opened and he turned, expecting to see Cate. Instead, he was face-to-face with Madison. He stared stupidly. Wisps of her hair were caught by the wind and blown into a golden halo around her tanned face. Perfectly made-up eyes stared back at Howard from above sharp cheekbones.

Giving him a look of pity, Madison walked past him, trailing the faintest whiff of perfume. Howard watched her pass—the expensive clothes, the soft Italian-leather boots, the red satchel far too small to contain anything as uncool as homework. In a panic, he said, "What did you want to tell me?"

Madison turned and for an instant looked confused. Then her confidence reasserted itself. "What gave you the insane idea that I wanted to talk to *you*?" Her voice was loaded with scorn.

A wave of anger swept over Howard. He had agonized about talking to her, and now here she was, denying that she had asked.

"I can't imagine what we would have to talk about," Howard replied coldly, "but Leon said at lunch that you wanted to talk to me. I'm sick of you arrogant people who think you can do what you want and mess with anyone who isn't as rich or as good-looking as you. Either you have something you want to tell me or you don't. I don't care."

Instantly Howard's anger was replaced by the horrible sinking feeling that he had just destroyed any hope of getting Madison to talk to him again. On top of that, she had the power to make his life totally miserable for the rest of the year.

In the uncomfortable silence that followed, Heimao slunk over and rubbed against Madison's leg, letting out a loud, rumbling purr. Traitor, thought Howard.

Surprisingly, Madison's features twisted in confusion, and her hands clenched as if a sharp pain was passing through her body. It lasted only a second, and then her face calmed and her hands relaxed, and she stared at Howard with no expression at all.

"Are you okay?" he asked.

Holding Howard with her empty, unblinking stare, she said something that sounded like "*Ni yinggai kanshu*."

"What?" Howard asked. "That doesn't make any sense."

Madison repeated, "*Ni yinggai kanshu*," her voice strangely flat and emotionless.

"I have no idea what you're talking about," Howard said, "and repeating it doesn't help. You'll need to explain."

"You two friends now?" Cate asked from behind Howard. Heimao left Madison and hurried over to her owner.

Madison's stare flicked from Howard to Cate, and her face relaxed back into confusion. She seemed about to say something, but she was distracted by the throaty roar of a car engine. In the school turnaround, Leon was leaning out the window of his restored red Shelby Mustang.

"Maddy!" he shouted. "Let's go! If the party's going to last all weekend, we need to buy a lot of supplies, and I want to get it done before the storm hits. You can continue your charity work with the geeks later."

Madison flashed Howard a scornful look, shook her head in a cascade of blond hair and flounced over to Leon. Tires screaming, the Mustang fishtailed across the parking lot and out into the street.

"He'll get a ticket, driving like that," Cate commented.

"Daddy'll take care of it," Howard said. "Madison was acting really weird. I asked her what she'd wanted to say to me at lunchtime, and she blew me off. I got angry and called her arrogant."

"Wow! Way to go," Cate said admiringly. "Your life's finished, but I bet it was worth it just to see her expression."

"She didn't seem bothered by it. Then she went all—I don't know—flat, emotionless. Like a robot. And then she said something." He scratched his head as he tried to remember. "It was in a strange language, and yet…it sounded vaguely familiar."

"What did she say?"

Howard closed his eyes and concentrated. "*Nee yingie kanshu*, or something like that. I asked her what it meant, and she just repeated it in the same flat voice. But it seemed like it was really important."

When Cate didn't respond, Howard looked at her. She was staring at him intently.

"What?" he asked.

"It sounds Chinese," she said. "*Ni yinggai kanshu*. It means 'You should read the book.'"

"What book?"

Cate shrugged. "No idea. She didn't say?"

"No," Howard replied, "but it must be the Victoria's Secret catalog or something like that. It would be about her reading level."

"It's probably nothing," Cate said, ignoring his weak attempt at humor. "Maybe speaking a little Chinese is cool among the privileged these days. In any case, Leon was right about one thing—we need to get going if we hope to miss the storm. And we don't have a flashy car to shelter in."

As they set off through town, Howard couldn't shake the feeling that what Madison had said was important and that Cate didn't really think it was nothing. And why did it sound familiar?

SANXINGDUI

A SPY

"I'm sorry, Chen," Ting said. "Fu wriggled out of my arms. You know how excited he can become."

"That's because he has never been trained to do anything useful, like a proper working dog."

"He can't work, and you know that. He was the runt of the litter. He would have been drowned if I hadn't saved him."

"He doesn't look like a runt now," said Chen, looking down at the bundle of hair snoring on Ting's lap.

"That's only because I look after him so well. He's very intelligent."

"He's not intelligent enough to know not to run like a mad thing around the sacred tearoom. I've worked hard to become tea server to the emperor. This is my chance to rise high enough to be considered for admission to Master Duyu's school. Then I can become a wushu master myself." Chen's voice rose as he became more agitated and excited, his words tumbling out in a waterfall.

The two were sitting in one of the many imperial food storerooms behind the palace kitchen where Ting worked. It was a stone building with good air circulation, so it was pleasantly cool in the hot summer weather. There were only two problems: there wasn't much room between the racks of roasted scorpions and silkworms and the water-filled tanks of large warty toads and eels, and they would be in serious trouble if Zhifang, the imperial chef, found them.

"I've even invented a new move," Chen said eagerly. "I call it Scything the New Corn." He stood up and assumed a fighting stance, then leaped in the air, moving his left leg back and his right leg forward in a scissors motion. Unfortunately, his foot caught the neck of a hanging goose, and with a shout of pain, Chen landed awkwardly on the ground.

Ting choked back a laugh as Chen got to his feet. "The goose got in the way," he said sheepishly.

"There had better not be any geese around when you go into battle," she said.

"Okay, it needs work," Chen admitted, "but I'll perfect it. Then I'll be famous. Perhaps one day I can even lead the emperor's armies. I'll be—"

"Calm," Ting said. "Isn't that what wushu masters must be above all else?"

Chen looked abashed. "Of course. I forget sometimes. I must practice." He tucked his legs into the lotus position, placed his hands on his knees, palms up, closed his eyes and breathed deeply. The golden dragon on Chen's chest seemed almost alive as his chest rose and fell. Ting smiled at her friend's seriousness.

As Cheng meditated and Ting stroked the sleeping Fu, voices came to them from outside.

"But, sir, the Ma Zhang are disorganized and unmotivated." Ting recognized the voice of Fan Tong, Shenxian's arrogant, bullying and not very intelligent assistant. "Can they really hope to capture a walled city as big as Sanxingdui?"

"What?" Chen lost his focus at the sound of the voice. Fan Tong was jealous of Chen's position in the imperial staff, and the two had had a number of arguments.

Ting put her finger to her lips to quiet Chen. They heard Shenxian's reply.

"Don't worry. I shall cross the mountains and motivate them. As the prophecy says, *When the Min Mountains fall, the time of danger will be at hand.* That will be my opportunity."

There was a long pause before Fan Tong said anything. He sounded uncertain. "Sir, much could go wrong. What if Kun leads his army out to meet the tribes before they reach the city? What if the timing is wrong? What if—"

"You doubt my plan?" Shenxian's voice rose in anger. "Kun suspects that we are coming, but he does not know when. Even that sorceress of his does not know when the mountains will fall. Only *I* know that. The timing will not be wrong—it is everything. In any case, the tribes do not need to win the battle. They simply need to create a big enough distraction that I will be able to enter the Chamber of the Deep and retrieve the Golden Mask. But if you're frightened, I could always find another assistant."

"No, no. I'm not frightened. You can rely on me."

"Good, because there is much at stake here. Once I have released the power of the Golden Mask, I shall control the forces of the universe itself. Then you shall get your reward. Now, go and organize my loyal guard. Tell them to be ready to leave tonight at midnight."

"Yes, sir!" Fan Tong shouted loudly enough to wake Fu, who recognized the person who tormented him at every opportunity and began yapping frantically.

"Who's that?" Shenxian asked. "No one must overhear our plans. Go and see if anyone is there, and if they heard anything."

"Yes, sir!" Fan Tong repeated.

Footsteps headed for the door of the storeroom. Fu leapt off Ting's lap and shot out the door, yapping frantically. The yaps soon turned to growls.

"Get away from me, you horrible little beast!" Fan Tong shouted. "Ow! You bit my ankle."

Ting stood up. "I have to go and rescue Fu."

"It doesn't sound as if it's Fu who needs rescuing, but I'll come with you. I can beat Fan Tong."

"No. You must stay here in case there are others out there. Someone has to tell the emperor about Shenxian's plans."

"But—"

"No buts. Hide."

Ting rushed out the door. Chen hesitated, listening.

"Leave my dog alone!" Ting ordered.

"The little brute attacked me."

"And Fu is such a vicious beast that obviously your life was in great danger."

"What were you doing in the storeroom?" Fan Tong asked, changing topics.

"It's my break. I was having a nap before I have to help prepare the evening meal."

"What did you overhear?"

"Nothing."

Chen heard Shenxian join the conversation. "So! You have braved the demon dog and captured the eavesdropper!"

"Yes, sir," Fan Tong said. Chen imagined him standing to attention and saluting. "She claims she heard nothing of our plans to bring the tribes over the mountains to attack the city when the mountains fall."

There was a long silence, and then Shenxian said, "Have you always been stupid, or have you dedicated your life to learning the craft?"

"What do you mean, sir?"

"I mean that she may not have overheard our conversation, but she certainly knows our plans now."

"Oh."

Chen had to suppress a laugh at the embarrassment in Fan Tong's voice.

"I'm sorry, sir."

"Now I shall have to take her with me over the mountains. I cannot risk leaving her here with you, and she cannot tell the emperor what you blabbed."

"Sir, am I not coming over the mountains with you?"

"No, Fan Tong. You must stay here to look after things while I'm away. Can I trust you to do that?"

"Absolutely, sir."

"Excellent. Now bring her and the dog along—that is, if you aren't too scared of a girl and a hairy rat."

"No, sir…I mean, yes, sir."

Chen heard scuffling and a yap of pain from Fu. He almost burst out the door, but Ting was right—someone had to get the news to Emperor Kun. As soon as the sounds of movement had died away, he snuck out of the storeroom and ran through the bustling kitchen. Cooks jumped out of his way, and Zhifang yelled something and waved a ladle at him, but Chen ignored them all and dashed into the palace. He tore down the corridors past startled guards, skidded around a corner and almost collided with Jingshen.

"I see practicing calmness is not going as well as it could," she said as she dodged the flying boy.

"I have to speak to the emperor," Chen gasped. "We were hiding in a storeroom and Fu bit Fan Tong and Ting was kidnapped and the city's going to be attacked over the mountains and—"

Jingshen held up a hand. "Breathe. We will go and see the emperor together, but I suggest that you organize your thoughts before you open your mouth in his presence."

Chen followed her along the corridor, desperately trying to get his breathing under control and put all that had happened into a coherent story.

"Ah, Chen," the emperor said when the young man and Jingshen had been admitted into his presence. "Have you come to show me more wushu moves?"

Chen bowed deeply. "I am afraid not. I have come to tell you of an evil plot."

Now that he had calmed down, Chen found that the story flowed seamlessly. The emperor and Jingshen listened in silence as the tale unfolded.

When Chen had finished, the emperor turned to Jingshen and said, "And so it begins. How can Shenxian know when the mountains will fall?"

Jingshen shook her head. "I cannot imagine. But however he knows, we do not have as much time as we had hoped."

"We must try to discover the timing of Shenxian's plan."

"And we must rescue Ting!" Chen blurted out.

"Indeed," the emperor agreed, "although I doubt she's in any danger. Shenxian gains nothing by harming her. He simply wishes to keep her out of the way."

"I don't care. I'm going to rescue her." Chen turned and headed for the door.

"Perhaps there is a way you can do even more than that," Jingshen said.

Chen stopped in midstride and turned back. "How?"

"You want to keep an eye on Ting to make sure she's okay, and Kun wishes to have a spy who can find out Shenxian's plans."

"You want me to be a spy?" Chen asked.

"An informer," Kun said. "Shenxian's party will be small, going over the mountains, but it will still be large enough that you should have no difficulty tracking it. He will wait there until he knows the mountains are close to falling. That is the timing we need to know." He regarded Chen seriously. "Coming back, Shenxian will be leading an army. He will move slowly. If you keep watch and race back over the mountains as soon as he leaves the Ma Zhang lands, we will have time to take our own army out and ambush Shenxian and his men as they come through the narrow valleys that lead down from the mountains."

"I'll do it," Chen said without a moment's hesitation. What he didn't say was that while Jingshen and Kun were talking, he had been making his own plans. He would get the information to the emperor, but he would also rescue Ting and Fu from Shenxian's clutches.

AYLFORD

A First Date?

Howard and Cate walked in companionable silence past the mock gothic buildings of Aylford College, on to Arcton Street and up the gentle incline from downtown. Heimao took a less direct route, wandering under hedges and into people's yards, but never going far from her owner.

The Aylford Institute for Psychiatric Care lay on the other side of French Hill, and the route would take them past Howard's house. French Hill was not as prestigious as Hangman's Hill, but it was a step up from the rundown areas along the river.

"You live around here?" Cate asked as they strolled by the brightly painted clapboard houses that gave the town old-world charm and character.

"Aylford's small," Howard replied, feeling confident enough to try a joke. "Everyone lives around here."

Cate peered at him through her black fringe, and he suddenly didn't think his comment was so clever.

"I live a couple of blocks ahead along Arcton Street," he added quickly. "And you?"

"I'm renting a room in Crowninshield House on Old Ashton Road."

"You and your parents in one room?" Howard asked.

"No, just me."

"Your parents have another room?"

"No," Cate replied. "My parents aren't here."

"I'm sorry," Howard stammered when it became obvious that Cate wasn't going to add anything.

"Why?"

"What?"

"Why are you sorry that my parents aren't here? You don't know them, and we barely know each other."

Howard's newfound confidence vanished. "I don't know," he mumbled. "I guess I'm sorry that you're alone."

"Then you should have said so. Words are important, and people should think before they use them. But thank you." Cate looked down at Heimao, who had emerged from some bushes, before asking, "How long has your dad been in the AIPC?"

"About eight months."

"That must be hard for you. You must miss him a lot."

Cate's matter-of-fact response made him feel better than the uncomfortable or sentimental things most people said when Howard told them where his dad was.

"I do. He used to walk me to school down this street every day." Howard felt a lump form in his throat as the memories flooded back.

Normally, Howard's conversations about his dad petered out into embarrassed silence at this point, but talking to Cate was different.

"What happened to him?" She asked this in such a casual way that Howard had no difficulty answering.

"He was an archaeologist and taught at the college. He was a great storyteller. As a little kid, I never wanted a book at bedtime—I just wanted Dad to make up a story. They were always stories from the past, but he could make them come alive. I'd close my eyes and be an ancient hunter listening to saber-toothed tigers roaming nearby, or I'd be a Roman legionary cowering in the dark German forests, or an alchemist in a medieval workshop, convinced he was about to turn lead into gold. I used to have such wonderful, vivid dreams. No book could compete with my dad, and I hated when he had to go off to a conference for a few days.

"As I got older, the bedtime stories stopped, but I could always persuade Dad to tell me a new one when we had some spare time on weekends or on holiday. The stories got more complicated too, and I began to see history less as a series of exciting adventures and more as a real world where people struggled with the same issues and problems that I could see around me. The long-dead characters in Dad's stories inhabited a world just as complex, confusing and scary as mine."

Howard was walking slowly as he talked, but Cate didn't mind and simply adjusted her steps to stay beside him. When he paused, she waited in silence for him to continue.

"About fourteen months ago," Howard went on, "the stories began to get stranger. At first I didn't mind—they were still great stories—but there was less history to them, and fantasy elements started to appear. When Dad began going on about worlds before ours and hideous beasts that lived underground or deep in the oceans, I got worried. I asked him where these new stories came from, and he looked at me oddly and said they weren't new but very, very old."

Howard glanced at Cate to see how she was reacting. She looked deep in thought.

"I'm sorry," he said. "I must be boring you."

"Not at all." Cate looked up and smiled.

Howard didn't know why it seemed so easy to tell this person he barely knew such intimate details, but it was. He took a deep breath and continued. "One night shortly after Dad had come back from a trip to China, I woke up to the sound of thumping and Mom screaming. My first thought was that a burglar had broken in and was attacking my parents. I rushed to their bedroom. Dad was stumbling around the room like he was blind, waving his arms about, banging into walls and knocking over furniture. He was talking loudly to himself— sometimes calling my name or Mom's, sometimes babbling gibberish. Mom was hanging on to his arm, screaming in his ear to try to get him to stop, but he ignored her completely."

"That must have been terrible."

Cate slipped her hand into Howard's and squeezed. It was such a natural, comforting gesture that he squeezed back without thinking before going on.

"The rest of that night's a blur. It seemed to go on forever, but eventually Mom and I managed to get Dad to calm down. He couldn't remember wandering around or shouting. He tried to pass it off as just a bad dream, but he insisted he couldn't recall what it was about. He made light of the whole thing, but when it happened again the following week, Mom made him go and see a doctor."

"Did that help?"

"Nothing helped. Soon he was having these turns almost every night. I would lie awake in bed, waiting for the thumping or the shouting to begin. The later attacks were never as violent as the one that first night, but then he started having them during the day. He'd be sitting at the dinner table, telling us about his day, and suddenly he would get this glazed look in his eyes and start talking nonsense. One time, the dean of archaeology at the college phoned to say that Dad had started talking gibberish in the middle of a lecture to fifty students. He suggested a leave of absence.

"Having Dad home all the time didn't help. When he was having one of his turns, he had no sense of the physical world around him. He seemed to think he was somewhere else, where everything around him was totally different. He would walk into things—once he walked through our living room window and cut himself so bad he almost bled to death. He needed constant care, and looking after him almost drove Mom crazy."

"No one could work out what was wrong?" Cate asked.

Howard cleared his throat to hide how close he was to breaking down. Wisps of darkness teased the edges of his vision.

"We took Dad to every specialist we could think of, from psychiatrists to faith healers. There were lots of theories: A genetic disorder, but there was no history of insanity in his family. A tumor, but nothing ever showed up on any scans. A chemical imbalance in the blood, but all his tests were normal." Howard took a moment to blink back the tears and darkness. "We tried every drug and procedure suggested, from antidepressants to acupuncture. Nothing made any difference.

Dad's body was still with us, but his mind was moving into some different world that we couldn't understand. Eventually, we had to take him to the AIPC for his own protection. At least he's calmed down there. He doesn't seem to have violent fits anymore, but he's nowhere near back to normal. He just sits and stares. It's as if there's a wall between him and the world, and there's no way through to connect with him."

Cate was silent for so long, Howard worried he had told her too much. He had been so wrapped up in telling the story that he had missed pointing out his house as they passed it. Maybe she thought he was a loser with a really strange family, and she would never want to talk to him again.

But then she broke the silence with an odd question. "The gibberish he spoke. Did anyone ever work out if it was a language?"

"No, the doctors said it was made-up nonsense." Howard paused, remembering something. "But at first *I* thought it was a language. It sounded a bit like Chinese to me, but a Chinese doctor we consulted said it wasn't like any dialect he had ever heard. There was a rhythm, though, to the way Dad spoke. His voice rose and fell as if he was explaining something or asking a question."

"Do you remember any of it?" Cate stopped and looked at Howard. They had reached the AIPC gates.

Howard shook his head. "The sounds came from the back of his throat. It was almost as if he was choking. Just nonsense."

"I'm not so sure."

Cate spoke so quietly that Howard wasn't certain he'd heard her right.

"What?"

"Nothing," she said, shaking her head. "Thank you."

"For what?"

"For opening up the way you did. It can't be easy talking about this stuff. I feel privileged that you trusted me enough to tell me as much as you did."

Howard had no idea what to say. He wasn't good at emotional stuff, and he was already feeling self-conscious about everything he'd told her. He was saved by the embarrassing realization that he was still holding her hand. He let go as if it were on fire.

Cate didn't seem to mind. "We're here," she said, turning to the gates. "I'm looking forward to meeting your dad."

The Reading Room

The AIPC was an impressive building surrounded by extensive grounds where the patients tended vegetables and flowers or simply strolled in the open air. With dark clouds looming, thunder rumbling and the first heavy drops of rain from the second storm of the day splattering on the ground, no one was out taking the air. Heimao ran forward, settled under the porch at the front of the building and began carefully grooming.

The building itself was U-shaped. Its two wings stretched forward, drawing visitors to the flight of stone steps that led up to the imposing pillared entrance of the domed central building. Cate and Howard walked briskly toward that entrance. As they reached the base of the steps, the heavens opened as if someone far above had turned on a tap. They leaped up the steps just as a blinding light flashed and a thunderous roar shook the ground beneath them.

Howard's skin tingled, and his hair felt like it was standing on end. Dark spots swam across his eyes, and the solid world around him wavered. The pillars at the front door melted into a glutinous mass that began to pour down the steps toward him. He looked back and saw the building's wings swing around and come at him. Their sharp corners shimmered and smoothed, and they began to look like two arms moving in to embrace him, to draw him down into the heart of the building. Howard gasped and shook his head. Water sprayed off his soaking hair. The rumbling faded, the buildings solidified, and his vision cleared.

"What's the matter?" Cate asked.

"I don't know. Everything seemed to melt for a moment."

When they reached the shelter of the doorway, Howard stretched out and touched the cold stone pillars. They felt reassuringly solid. From her sheltered corner, Heimao stared at him with her piercing green eyes.

"Lightning can do odd things," Cate said, wringing water out of her hair, "and that strike was really close. I felt a tingling all over."

It sounded like a supportive, rational explanation, but Howard couldn't help noticing that she was looking at him oddly.

"It almost seemed as if the building was trying to hug me." Howard shivered. "I guess it must have been some kind of optical illusion caused by the electric charge in the air." He hoped Cate wouldn't think he was going crazy like his dad, but he didn't fully believe it himself. The sense of the building melting and coming at him had been incredibly real.

He and Cate dripped their way into the bright reception area of the institute. A smiling young woman behind the desk looked up.

"Hello, Howard. How are you this week?"

"Good," Howard responded as he returned the smile. "This is my friend Cate. How's Dad doing?"

"Much the same," the nurse said, as she did every week. "He's been a bit more restless the past couple of nights, but nothing violent—just tossing and turning and occasional shouts. The doctor says it's a good sign. Dreams mean that he's processing information, so maybe he's beginning to absorb more during the day."

"That's encouraging," Howard said without enthusiasm. His dad had had spells like this before, but they never amounted to anything.

"The doctor's running a bit late with his afternoon rounds," the nurse went on, "so he's still with your father. Shouldn't be long though."

"Can I take Cate up to meet the bibliognost and see the reading room while we're waiting?" Howard asked.

"Sure. Just be careful on the stairs."

"Who's the bibliognost?" Cate asked as they set off along a wide, brightly painted corridor.

"You'll find out soon," Howard answered with a wink.

Cheerful paintings of rural scenes and photographs of wildlife and sunsets lined the walls. Double doors on the right opened into a large lounge where several groups of people were sitting at tables, playing board games or watching daytime television on a large-screen TV.

"It's very relaxed," Howard said.

"Yeah," Cate agreed. "From the outside, I was expecting something a lot more Victorian."

"Apparently, this central part was a private house in the late 1800s. The wings were added when it was turned into the AIPC. Of course, it's been remodeled several times since then." He stopped at a widening in the corridor and pointed to a wrought-iron spiral staircase that rose to the floor above. "But they did keep some original fixtures, although there's a modern staircase at the back."

"Cool," Cate said, following Howard up the steep stairs. He led the way carefully, aware of the weight of his backpack, which was threatening to tip him backward. At the top Cate let out an involuntary gasp as they stepped into the reading room of the AIPC.

It was a large circular room with walls fully two stories high and topped by a glass dome. As Cate looked up, a flash of lightning flooded the room with colors from the dome's intricate stained glass.

"Wow!" she exclaimed as a roll of thunder echoed around the room. "You sure know how to put on a show."

"I arranged the storm personally," Howard said, thrilled to see Cate so happy.

The walls were floor-to-ceiling bookcases; an iron balcony encircled the room about halfway up. Heavy wooden desks surrounded a central circular counter where a striking Chinese woman sat. She lifted her head from a book as they entered.

"Well, hello again, Howard. Here to see your dad?" she asked with a slight American accent.

"Yes," Howard replied with a smile, "and I've brought a friend to see my favorite bibliognost. Cate, this is Aileen. She looks after this place and has probably read every book in it."

Aileen laughed and bowed to Cate. She had long snow-white hair that cascaded over her shoulders and striking gray eyes that sparkled above sharp cheekbones.

"I made the mistake of once telling Howard that I should be known as a bibliognost because it sounded much more mysterious and romantic than librarian."

"What does it mean?" Cate asked.

"It's simply a fancy name for someone who knows a lot about books. Sometimes I think I'm the last one. You young people have the world at your fingertips with your high-tech phones and computers. In an instant, you can find out things it would have taken me weeks to dig up in my dusty old library."

"I'm very pleased to meet a real bibliognost," Cate said, returning the bow. "This is a wonderful place. Do you mind if I take a few pictures with my new high-tech phone?"

Aileen laughed again, a light, tinkling sound. "Absolutely not. I wish I'd had one of those things when I was young. I could have captured all the places and people that exist only in my memory." She pointed an index finger at her temple. "That corner over there will give you the best views."

Cate stepped away from the desk and took a short video that, luckily, captured the burst of color from the next lightning flash. Then she wandered around the reading room, browsing the book titles and snapping occasional shots. When she reached the corner Aileen had indicated, she photographed Howard and Aileen standing at the central desk.

Cate was about to head back when she froze in midstep and gaped at a shelf beside her. She dropped her phone into her bag and tentatively eased a small red book out of its place on the shelf. She stared at the cover and flipped through a couple of pages as she slowly walked back to the desk.

"Can I borrow this?" she asked Aileen.

Howard squinted over her shoulder. The book was obviously very old. The cover was a deep red color with strange black characters in the middle—神的面具. The corners were worn and dog-eared, as if the book had been well read.

Aileen lifted the reading glasses that hung around her neck, adjusted them on her nose and peered at the book. "Ah," she said. "No one's read that one as long as I've been here. It's one of the original books. *Jinse de mianju*," she said, reading the title. "Of course you may borrow it. Tell me what it's about when you bring it back."

"Thanks." Cate placed the book carefully in her bag. "What did you mean when you said that it was one of the original books?"

"Do you have time for a good story?"

Cate looked over at Howard, who nodded. His dad would still be downstairs in his room whenever they got there.

Aileen leaned over the counter toward her visitors. "You know this used to be a private house before the AIPC took it over?" Howard and Cate both nodded. "It was built by a man named Wat Heely. Legend is he made a fortune in shipping in California during the 1849 gold rush. After the gold ran out, he brought his money up here when this was still the Oregon Territory. He ran his shipping fleet out of here, and he owned most of the warehouses and fish-canning plants in town. He used Chinese laborers from the goldfields or direct from China.

That's why at one time Aylford had one of the biggest Chinatowns on the west coast.

"I don't think he liked company, because this place must have been kind of hard to get to back then. He lived here alone, with only a single Chinese servant he'd brought up from San Francisco. Hardly anyone ever saw Heely. He spent all his time in this house and sent his servant down the hill into town to conduct his business and buy all his supplies. The only times he was seen was as a distant figure taking walks in the Black Hills.

"Seems he had a passion for learning. He kept in touch with scientists all over the world, and his servant used to give lists of books to ships' captains who traded with him. Heely wanted them to search out books in all the little-visited corners of the world where trade and tides might take them. He paid well when they brought back something he wanted. That's what built this library. It was the center of the original house and Heely's pride and joy."

Howard looked around at the bookshelves, expecting to see rows of dusty, leather-bound volumes like the red book Cate had found. Instead, he saw what looked more like the public library in town: the bright dust jackets of popular novels, the spines of large illustrated books and the dog-eared pages of paperbacks.

Aileen noticed Howard's look. "The only old book here now is the one that Cate found."

"What happened to the others? Some of them must have been worth a lot of money."

"Undoubtedly. Trouble was, Heely wasn't popular."

"Why not?" Cate asked. "Because of his money?"

"Oh no," Aileen said. "Heely was generous enough. He paid for a new schoolhouse when the old one burned down in 1885, and he put considerable money into the college. At one time there was even talk of calling it Heely College in his honor." She glanced around at the scattered readers. None were paying the group at the counter any attention. "There was talk that Wat Heely's curiosity led him to paths no one should venture along."

"What sort of paths?" Howard asked.

"Probably nothing. Like I said, Heely was a recluse. I suspect he was just a lonely, eccentric old man, but talk went around town of strange lights and noises coming from the windows in the dead of night—lights in colors that shouldn't be, and cries and screams not from any human or animal throat. People said there was ancient lore in some of Heely's books—spells and such that would summon creatures no sane man would want in this world." Aileen's voice dropped to a whisper. "They say he invoked the devil himself."

With perfect timing, lightning flashed outside and thunder rumbled.

Howard jumped.

Aileen laughed. "I told you it was a good story."

"Accusations of witchcraft and devil worship were common enough in small inbred communities," Cate pointed out. "As you say, Heely was probably just an old eccentric with a scientific turn of mind."

"But the tale's not done yet. On the night of the great storm of 1891, Heely and his Chinese servant disappeared."

"Disappeared?" Howard asked, drawn back into the story.

"Yup, disappeared. The storm was more violent than anyone could remember. The wind blew down most of the trees in town and ripped the roof off the town hall. The Bane River rose until it broke its banks and flooded most of the streets downtown. Destroyed many of Heely's warehouses and washed away most of Chinatown. No one knows how many people died that night."

"So why was Heely's disappearance so unusual?" Howard asked. "Maybe he and his servant went down to try to save his property by the river."

"Maybe." Aileen sounded unconvinced. "But this wasn't an ordinary storm. It came down, like most do, from the Black Hills, but instead of blowing through town, this one stopped. That's why there was so much flooding and destruction. The strange thing was, people swore afterward that the storm was centered here, over Heely's house. When dawn came, and the wind died down and the waters receded, a few brave souls ventured up here to investigate. Remarkably, the house was undamaged, but there was no sign of Heely or his servant anywhere. They had vanished, and no trace of them was ever found."

"They probably just went out in the storm and got lost," Howard suggested.

Aileen leaned back. "Perhaps," she said with a smile.

"So what happened to the books?" Cate asked, reminding Howard of why they were being told the story in the first place.

"There were tales that went around after that night of the curious things folks had seen in the house—unnatural creatures preserved in bottles, dried plants that no one could recognize.

They were probably just scientific curios, but people claimed there were other things, which they were reluctant to speak about, and the entire house was soaking wet. In the basement, where Heely had his laboratory, there was knee-deep water. Some people said it was as if the walls and the ceilings had been weeping, until there were a good two inches of water in every room."

"It must have been flooding from the storm," Howard suggested.

"Maybe," Aileen acknowledged, "but people said that when the water dried out, it left salt stains on the walls, as if it had been seawater."

Howard opened his mouth to suggest that the staining probably came from the chemicals in Heely's lab, but Aileen wasn't finished.

"Strangest thing, though, was that the library was untouched. It was completely dry. The other strange thing was that even though the house was allowed to lie empty for years after Heely's disappearance, and in that time there were many heavy rainstorms, the inside of the house, even the basement, remained bone dry."

Now Howard could think of nothing to say. He glanced at Cate, but she was staring intently at Aileen.

"Some months after the storm," Aileen carried on, "a bookseller came to town and bought up every book in old Heely's library. He got them for a song. Heely had no known relatives, so the townsfolk were happy to let the stranger take the books away for a generous contribution to the fund for fixing the town-hall roof. He removed the books in three cartloads.

Most were sold for good money in Arkminster or farther off. Made the bookseller a rich man. I reckon no one was interested in an old Chinese book though." Aileen smiled at Cate. "Anyway, with some of his money, the bookseller bought a mansion on Hangman's Hill."

"Which house?" Howard asked.

"The big red-brick one with turrets at the top. Family still lives there to this day."

Howard pictured the houses on Hangman's Hill. "What was the bookseller's name?"

"Josiah Whateley."

"Leon's family!" Howard exclaimed. "That explains where his money comes from."

"Indeed it does," Aileen said, "and there's plenty of tales attached to that lineage too. But that's enough stories for today. You'd better go and see your dad if you want to get home before it's late."

"Thank you for a great story," Howard said, "and for showing us the reading room." He nodded to Aileen and turned toward the stairs.

Cate remained by the desk. "Heely's servant," she said. "Did anyone record his name?"

Aileen shook her head. "People called him Hei, but whether that was his name or just what people shouted at him is anyone's guess. Why do you ask?"

"Just curious. Thanks for sharing your stories."

Cate joined Howard, and the pair carefully descended the spiral staircase.

A Breakthrough

Back in the main corridor, Cate and Howard stood and looked at each other. Howard broke the silence.

"Cool place, eh? Must have been incredible when it was filled with the original books."

Cate seemed preoccupied. "Aileen knows a lot about the town and its history," she said thoughtfully.

"Well, she is a bibliognost," Howard pointed out.

"Let's go and visit your dad."

Howard led the way toward the west wing of the institute. Closed doors lined the walls on either side of the corridor.

"This side's more like a hospital than the east wing is. Over there are the patients who can function fairly well, so there are a lot more common areas and activity rooms. The west wing is mostly for patients who need more medical care."

About halfway down the hallway he stopped in front of a door but made no move to knock or open it. Cate took his hand as she had earlier.

"This must be hard for you," she said gently.

"You're the first person I've ever brought to see Dad. Mom and I are the only visitors he gets."

"I'm honored that you've brought me." She squeezed his hand. "It's difficult to invite a stranger into such an emotional part of your life."

Howard surprised himself by saying, "You're not a stranger."

It was true. He'd known Cate only since lunchtime, and yet he felt as if she was an old friend. He was rewarded with a smile before the door opened and a man in a white coat stepped out. He was short and almost completely bald, and he wore small gold-rimmed spectacles. His round face was creased into a thoughtful frown, but it brightened into a broad smile when he saw Howard.

"Hello, Howard," he said. "Hope you haven't been waiting too long. Afraid I'm running a bit late. All the patients seem a bit restless today, and we've had a few minor crises."

"Is there a full moon?" Howard asked.

The doctor laughed. "I wish it were that simple, but that's just an old wives' tale. There are times when everyone seems to get upset, but I can never see a pattern to it." He nodded toward Cate. "I see you've brought a friend to visit."

"I have, Dr. Roe. This is Cate, a friend from school."

"Excellent," Dr. Roe said. "The more the merrier. As you know, mental stimulation is very important in cases like this." He turned to Cate. "Whatever was going on in Howard's dad's mind before he came here, it was so disturbing that his brain has blocked it out. Unfortunately, it overreacted and blocked out everything else as well. Our job is to try to stimulate the unthreatened part of his brain—talk to him, read stories, play music, sing. It's hard when you don't get any response, but I'm convinced that some things get through. When enough does get through, we hope it will unlock the safe memories, and we can bring him back."

"Are there any signs that it's working?" Cate asked.

"Hard to say. There are brief moments when we seem to get a response. Nothing much—a flicker of the eyes, a turn of the head—but it is a response. We mustn't lose hope. The brain is immensely complex, and for all our science, we understand only a tiny fraction of how it works." Dr. Roe turned back to Howard. "Anyway, I'll leave you to it. Your dad's in bed, but feel free to take him for a walk to the lounge."

"Thank you," Howard said, holding the door open for Cate.

The room was not large, but it looked nothing like a hospital room. There was a carpet on the floor, and the walls were painted a noninstitutional yellow and decorated with cheerful art prints. It was furnished with a closet in one corner, a coffee table with magazines on it and an armchair beside it, a bedside table with clock and light, and a bed with a wooden headboard and bright duvet, flanked on each side by a chair. One wall held a flat-screen TV. Out the window was a view of the institute's gardens. The storm had passed, and Howard could just make out Heimao's dark shape slinking across the lawn in the twilight.

The only hospital-like elements in the room were the guardrails to prevent his father from falling out of bed and a camera fixed high on the wall. Howard's father was propped up by a pile of pillows and staring at the TV, where a documentary about whales was playing with the sound muted.

He was dressed in paisley flannel pajamas, and he didn't react to the people entering his room.

Every time he came to visit, Howard was struck by how much his dad had changed. Even though he was not physically ill and physiotherapists worked on him every day, he was slowly wasting away. It was as though his muscles, deprived of any useful purpose, had simply given up. His hair was neatly brushed and his eyes were open, but there was no expression on his face. Sometimes Howard thought this wasn't actually his dad sitting before him.

"Hi, Dad," Howard said, forcing his voice to be cheerful. "How are you feeling? I've brought someone to visit. This is Cate. She's in my grade at school."

"Hello, Mr. Lawson," Cate said, stepping to the bedside. "I'm delighted to meet you. Howard has told me a lot about you."

Neither greeting provoked the slightest response from Howard's dad, whose only movement was the occasional blink of his eyes.

"Sit down." Howard indicated a chair beside the bed. He moved around to the other side and perched on the arm of a larger chair. "It's kind of strange talking and getting no feedback. I usually just tell him about my week at school, which is actually kind of relaxing. A little later we'll take him to the lounge."

"Can he walk?"

"Oh yes! If you slide him out of bed, he'll stand. If you move him forward, he'll walk. His mind hasn't forgotten how to do things—it's as if it's just gone somewhere else."

For a while Howard and Cate talked to his dad, telling him about their classes and what was going on at school and in the world in general. Eventually, without even noticing, they began talking to each other across the bed.

"Do you think Aileen's story about Josiah Whateley making his fortune selling the books was true?" Howard asked. "Could selling a few books make someone enough money to build a mansion and leave enough to pass down that Leon's dad could buy Leon a Shelby Mustang a hundred and some years later?"

Cate nodded slowly. "I'm certain of it."

"How can you be certain? It was a long time ago."

She delved into her shoulder bag and dug out a small notebook and pen. "What was the name of the guy who built this place?"

"Wat Heely."

Cate nodded, and Howard had the feeling she had remembered the name all along. She printed it at the top of a blank page in the notebook.

"Do you do cryptic crossword puzzles?"

Howard frowned at the wild change of topic and shook his head.

"You should. Many clues in cryptic crosswords rely on anagrams." Carefully she printed *Whateley* below *Wat Heely*. She held the notebook up over the bed so Howard could see what she'd written.

At first he was simply confused, and then the answer jumped out at him. "They're the same!"

Cate rewarded him with a smile. "Not quite the same, but you use the same eight letters to make both names. Whateley is an anagram of Wat Heely. The odds of that being a coincidence are astronomical."

"But if Wat Heely and Josiah Whateley are the same person, why didn't anyone recognize Whateley when he returned to town?"

"People see what they want or expect to see, and Heely was a recluse, remember. Most people only ever met Hei, his Chinese servant, and Heely could have changed his appearance when he returned as Whateley. Of course, it could have been someone else using the name. But why not use a different name?"

The two were pondering this when Howard noticed that his dad's arm was twitching as if he was trying to raise it.

"Dad, can you hear me? What's going on? What are you trying to do?"

Howard's father was still facing the TV, but his expression was changing. Surprise, worry and fear chased each other across his features, and his mouth moved as if struggling to form words. With obvious effort, he raised his arm and pointed at the TV screen.

Howard and Cate swiveled to look. The whale documentary was over, replaced by scenes of what looked like an archaeological dig. A Chinese scientist was talking at the camera and pointing at trenches that appeared to have been dug randomly across the landscape.

"He's never done that before. What's happening?" Howard asked worriedly. "Should we call a nurse?"

"You told me he was an archaeologist," Cate said. "Maybe this reminds him of his work."

Howard stared at his dad. His eyes were wide and more alive than Howard had seen them since the madness descended. He was struggling to say something, but only odd gurgling noises came out.

Just then a nurse bustled through the door, alerted by the camera on the wall. "Is everything all right?" she asked.

"Yes," Cate said without turning around.

"What are you trying to say, Dad?" Howard asked.

His dad was panting heavily, but between breaths he forced out a word: "Ma...sk..."

"Mask?" Howard looked back to the TV. The scene had changed to the inside of a museum. The scientist was still talking, but now he was pointing at a huge glass case in the middle of the room. Inside the case was a vast head, the size of a small car and with unnaturally protruding eyes, winglike ears and a wide, almost smiling mouth. "What's that?"

"Sanxingdui," Cate replied.

Howard was about to ask what or where that was, but before he could form the question, his dad turned, grabbed Cate's wrist and said, "Yes." Then he looked back at Howard and added, "Have...to...go."

"Go? To Sanxingdui? Cate, where is this place?"

"China."

"Dad, we can't go to China—" Howard began, but something niggled at his mind. "Wait! You went to China on an archaeological dig before you got sick. Did you see this...mask thing there?"

"Have...to...go," Howard's dad repeated. He was becoming more agitated.

"Shall I get Dr. Roe?" the nurse asked.

"Not yet," Howard said. He knew this was a breakthrough of some sort and didn't want the doctor interrupting whatever was happening. "Let's see where my dad wants to go. Maybe he just needs to go to the washroom." Howard lowered the sides of the bed and helped his father stand. He was shaky on his feet, but his jaw was clenched with determination. He pushed toward the door to the corridor.

"Okay," Howard said, "let's try the lounge. But you're going to have to put your bathrobe on if we're going out in public."

As he helped his father into his robe, he looked over at Cate and shrugged. This was all immensely confusing, but Howard's heart was racing. He hadn't heard his dad speak or seen him move purposefully in months. Did this mean he was coming back?

With Cate on one side, Howard on the other and the nurse following behind, Howard's dad led them along the corridor to the old center of the building. Progress was slow, and he needed help to stay on his feet, but there could be no doubt that he was leading the way. Howard was close to tears and grinning broadly.

"He's never done anything like this before?" Cate asked.

"No, never."

Howard expected his father to head for either the lounge or the reading room. Instead, he led them toward the back of the building.

"There's nothing down that way," the nurse said.

"Then there's no harm in us taking a stroll there," Howard said over his shoulder.

At the end of the corridor they came to two doors that led onto a stairwell. Howard's dad kept stumbling forward until he bumped into them. Howard tried the handle of one, but it didn't move. There was a small keypad on the wall to one side.

"These doors are kept locked," the nurse explained. "We should probably take Mr. Lawson back to his room."

"Where do the stairs lead?" Cate asked.

"They're the back stairs to the reading room. They also head down to the basement—a furnace room and storage."

"Maybe he just wants to avoid the difficult spiral staircase to the reading room," Howard suggested. "Maybe he wants to look up a book about the TV show he saw. Do you know the code?"

"Yes, I know the code, but I don't know if we should be doing this." The nurse sounded uncertain. "Patients aren't usually allowed through here. I should check with Dr. Roe."

"Dr. Roe said stimulation was good for Mr. Lawson," Cate pointed out. "And it's clear he wants to go through these doors. I don't think Dr. Roe would be very happy if Mr. Lawson sank back into lethargy while we waited for permission to open a door."

While Cate was speaking, Howard's dad began slowly and rhythmically bumping his forehead against the door.

"There's three of us here to look after him," Howard pointed out. "As soon as we've got him to the reading room, one of us can go and find Dr. Roe."

The nurse sighed, but she reached over and punched five numbers into the keypad. There was a loud click, and the door handle turned in Howard's hand. His father pushed forward and, to everyone's surprise, ignored the wide stairs leading to the reading room and headed for the narrower stairs that led down to the basement.

As the group slowly descended the stairs, the light from the landing above faded. The stairs led to a corridor that disappeared into gloom. Howard was uncomfortably reminded of the creeping darkness of his dreams. Maybe following his dad down here wasn't the smartest idea after all. He was about to suggest that they turn back, but as he stepped off the last step onto the bare concrete floor of the corridor, the world suddenly exploded into intense light.

Howard stumbled backward in fright, almost pulling his dad and Cate with him.

"Easy," Cate said, steadying the trio. "It's just a motion sensor. It saves power in places that aren't visited much."

"Good idea," Howard said, recovering his composure. He was looking along a concrete tunnel lit by a series of long, flickering fluorescent tubes. Silver ducting, black pipes and multicolored cables ran along the ceiling on either side of the light fixtures. The walls were painted an institutional green, and the floor was dirty gray. There were doors off either side at irregular intervals, and the one at the far end was open, revealing a room full of machinery.

"That's the boiler room," the nurse explained. "The rooms are either storage or electrical."

Howard's father was making no attempt to go down the corridor. He seemed content simply to be in the basement. Howard felt sad. The surprise of the lights going on had pushed his dad back into his catatonic state.

"There's nothing here," the nurse said. "We should go back up. I'll go and tell Dr. Roe what happened. I'm sure he'll have some ideas about how we can build on these developments. Can you bring your dad back up to his room?"

"Okay," Howard agreed. If his father wasn't leading the way, there was no point in taking him down the corridor.

The nurse climbed back up the stairs.

"Come on, Dad," Howard encouraged. "Let's get you back to your room. This has been enough of an adventure for one day."

Howard grasped his father's arm and tried to turn him. He was surprised to meet resistance. Then his father's whole body tensed. Both Howard and Cate looked at him. He was still staring down the corridor, but there was a frown on his face. He began to speak, and this time Howard recognized what he was saying. "*Jinse de mianju.*"

"Isn't that the name of the book you found upstairs?"

Before Cate could answer, the husky voice continued, "*Jinse de mianju. Zhe ben shu zai zheli. Ni yinggai kanshu. Xiaoxin sizhe shei mengxiang.*"

Howard recognized the phrase in the middle that Madison had said to him earlier. But before he had a chance to tell Cate, dizziness swept over him, and the solid concrete walls of the corridor wavered and began to melt. Darkness rushed in from the edges of his vision, forming a tunnel that led to the door at the far end of the corridor. The door was filled with a long, narrow smiling Chinese face that looked vaguely familiar. A voice echoed inside Howard's head: *Welcome. I have waited long for you.*

A feeling of dread overwhelmed him. Howard was anxious, scared and alarmed all at once. His breath was coming in short, urgent gasps, and he was breaking out in a cold sweat all over. He felt like he was about to throw up, so he reached out blindly, searching for something to hold on to—something solid to counteract the spinning nausea. The air was suddenly numbingly cold. Time seemed to stand still. Was he having a seizure or a stroke? Panic hurtled at Howard like an express train. He tried to take a step forward, but the blackness was closing in. The tunnel of his vision was getting narrower. The door and the face were getting smaller and smaller and moving farther away. Howard screamed, "Cate!" Then the blackness overwhelmed everything, and he fell to the ground.

ACROSS THE MOUNTAINS

"It's beautiful." Ting had almost forgotten that she was being dragged against her will across the plain toward the Min Mountains. Shenxian, Ting, Fu and twenty of Shenxian's soldier bodyguards had been traveling since midnight. At last the sky was brightening behind them, and Shenxian had ordered a halt for the day at a temple a mile or so off the main route. Half of the soldiers were already asleep, and the other half were keeping watch, including one whose job it was to carry the small cage with Fu in it. He had strict orders from Shenxian to drop the cage and the dog down the nearest deep well should Ting attempt to escape.

Ting was exhausted, but Shenxian had insisted that she follow him down a long flight of stairs to a room deep beneath the temple. The room was brightly lit, and an old monk sat to one side. In the center, standing on a stone pedestal, was a huge bronze egg. Its surface was covered with intricate carvings and swirling writing. Eight golden dragons were arranged around the fattest part of the egg, their tails intertwining as they wound to the top of the egg. Their whiskered faces looked down to the bottom of the egg, where eight copper toads sat with wide-open mouths. In the mouth of each dragon lay a small copper ball.

"It is beautiful," Shenxian agreed. "But it is also practical."

"Is it magic?" Ting asked, despite having promised herself she wouldn't say a word to her kidnapper on the journey.

"It's magic only to those who don't understand," Shenxian said. He turned to the old monk and asked, "How many balls have been fed to the toad since yesterday?"

The monk took out a string of beads and counted. "Fifty-two," he said.

"Excellent," Shenxian said. "And always the same toad? You are certain."

"Yes."

"And do the shakes in the ground become stronger?"

The monk shrugged. "Some do. I felt more through my sandals than the day before."

"How can you feed copper toads?" Ting interrupted.

As if in answer, a ball dropped from the closest dragon's mouth into the mouth of the toad below it. Ting jumped back.

"It is magic," she said. "How else can a golden dragon spit a ball into a copper toad's mouth?"

"It is magic only because you cannot see what is going on inside the bronze egg. There is a pendulum in there, and even the faintest vibrations in the earth will set it swinging. If the vibrations last long enough, the pendulum will hit a dragon, tilting it so that the ball in its mouth is released to the toad below."

"But I didn't feel any vibrations," Ting said.

"That's because the pendulum is much more sensitive than your feet. It can detect vibrations from hundreds of miles away.

"When I see which ball falls," Shenxian went on, pleased to show his captive how clever he was, "that tells me where the vibrations come from. This one"—he lifted the most recent ball from the toad's mouth and gently replaced it in the dragon's mouth—"tells me that the vibrations are coming from the Min Mountains. The frequency with which this ball has been falling tells me that the vibrations are increasing in number, and our friend here"—he waved at the monk—"says they are getting stronger."

Ting gasped as she suddenly understood what Shenxian was telling her. "So *this* is how you know when the Min Mountains will fall!"

"Clever girl. There are more vibrations every day. When they run together, the mountains will fall, and the Golden Mask will be mine."

Without warning, Ting spun away from Shenxian and leaped high into a perfect wushu move. Her right leg flashed out and connected with the bronze egg just below the closest dragon. For a moment the entire machine teetered, balls falling from the dragons' mouths and bouncing onto the floor, and then the huge contraption crashed to the ground at the feet of the startled monk, shattering into a dozen pieces.

"There," Ting shouted triumphantly as she landed on the floor. "Now you won't know when the mountains will fall. The emperor and Jingshen will defeat you."

Shenxian stood calmly to one side, a faint smile on his lips. "You stupid girl," he said. "It is a shame that you have destroyed a thing of such beauty, but how did you think I was able to see what it was doing when I was with the Ma Zhang on the other side of the mountains? I have been watching and recording my machine for months. I don't need it anymore. I already know exactly when the Min Mountains will fall."

><o

"How much time do we have?" Kun asked.

"Shenxian has been gone a day," Jingshen replied. "The journey to the mountains and then across them will take another eight or nine days. With all their carts and baggage, the Ma Zhang soldiers will need at least that long again to get here, so we have seventeen or eighteen days—more if we are lucky."

"Will the plan work?"

"Chen will be able to travel faster than the tribal army, so we will have warning of their arrival. How are our preparations coming along?"

"Not well," Kun admitted. "Our army is small, and it has not had to fight a battle since our soldiers' grandfathers were children. They are brave, but the Ma Zhang are a warrior people. Fighting is their life, and they ride on those mysterious beasts they call horses. I don't think our soldiers will do well against such an army."

Jingshen rubbed her chin thoughtfully. "It probably won't matter. If all the elements of the prophecy come together, then it won't be an army that will stop Shenxian. Did you feel the earth shake this morning?"

"I did. Does that mean the Min Mountains are falling?"

"Not yet, but soon. The shaking will be much greater when they fall."

Kun rubbed his forehead. He had lost weight, and his eyes were red with tiredness. "Is Sanxingdui doomed?"

Jingshen nodded sadly. "I fear so."

"Then there is no point in organizing our army to fight the tribes from across the mountains?"

"None."

"So why do we try?"

"Because even if Sanxingdui is destroyed, our culture and people must go on."

"Are you saying we must abandon the city?"

"Yes. It is the only chance for our people."

"Where will we go?"

"Jinsha."

"But Jinsha is only thirty miles to the south," Kun pointed out. "Shenxian's soldiers could get there in two days' hard marching."

"But they will not. Shenxian gains nothing by destroying our cities. The Chamber of the Deep and the Golden Mask are his goal, and they will always remain here."

"So we must all flee to Jinsha?"

"Not we. Our people must, and they must take our most treasured possessions with them so they can begin once more. Our soldiers are enough to protect them. What cannot be taken must be broken and buried in the sacred pits."

Kun nodded sadly. "But we cannot remove the Golden Mask."

"No," Jingshen agreed. "It must remain here in the Chamber of the Deep."

"Then we are giving it to Shenxian. You said that if he dons the Golden Mask, he will achieve the power he desires."

"And in doing so, he will open the way to the realm of monsters."

"And that will mean the end of the world."

"Yes," Jingshen conceded. "That is why you and I must remain here to stop him."

"Just us two against Shenxian and his army?"

"I suspect we will not be alone. But take heart—this is a battle that has been fought many times before and, I suspect, will be fought many times in the future," Jingshen said enigmatically. "Remember the ancient prophecy.

When that which is far comes near,
That which is closed may open.
When worlds bleed one through the other,
That which cannot is.
Doors that the power of the moon may open,
The power of the sun shall close.

Chen trudged along a narrow path above the huge Min Lake. He had been walking for days, and he was exhausted. Shenxian was not moving fast, and it was easy enough to follow the track that he and his men had left. They weren't worried about being followed and had left plenty of signs. Besides, there was only one real road through the mountains.

Chen looked down at the expanse of water below him and wondered, not for the first time, how such a thing could exist in the middle of a mountain range. He remembered the first time he'd seen it. He'd climbed a broad, grassy slope and been confronted by a seemingly limitless sea of blue. It had seemed magical then, and it still did.

He raised his eyes to where the head of the valley cut a sharp line against the blue sky. It was at least a day's walk away. He had never been this far into the mountains and assumed that across the ridge was another valley—this one leading to the plain of the Ma Zhang. He hoped this was the case. He longed for Shenxian to stop and give him a chance to rescue Ting and Fu.

As he slogged up the path, he had the strange sensation that the air between him and the ridgetop was shimmering. Then the ground beneath him bucked and threw him off his feet. He dropped his bag and landed painfully on the slope. As the shaking continued, rocks bounced down the slope around him.

Fortunately, no large boulders hit him, and he had only a few extra cuts and bruises when the shaking stopped. The clear view was gone, and the air was dusty. A few larger pieces of rock still trundled down the slope, splashing into the waters of Min Lake.

Chen breathed a sigh of relief and stood up. For a moment he had thought that this was the mountains falling, but it was only a small earthquake. Still, it was probably a sign that the fall was not far off.

AYLFORD

BASEMENT DREAMS?

The darkness was so thick that no light could ever pierce it. Yet Howard was aware, so he wasn't dead.

Was he mad? Was he lost in a dream world, just like his father? But Howard could remember, think and reason.

Maybe he was in a coma. Perhaps a slowly exploding blood vessel in his brain was dooming him to lie for years in a hospital bed, hooked up to medical devices, alive but unaware of anything around him. Yet Howard was standing—he could feel the ground beneath his feet—and he was cold.

He stretched out his arms to find walls on either side. They weren't the smooth painted walls of the basement corridor, however; they were rough and wet and slimy. Howard shuddered at the feel of them. He stretched an arm above his head and discovered a dripping roof. Streamers of repulsive feathery slime wrapped themselves around his fingers. Disgusted and terrified, he tore his hand free. He reached behind and found another wet wall.

In a sudden panic Howard lurched forward, scared to death that he was trapped in a tiny, foul cave. But there was no wall in front of him, and he fell to his knees. He let out several gasping sobs. He wasn't dreaming, dead, mad or in a coma— he was alive and aware in a gross stone tunnel. But how had he gotten here, where was he, and how could he get back? Where were Cate and his dad?

Howard called their names as loudly as he could. He yelled. He screamed. It was hopeless. The darkness and the walls swallowed all sound. In frustration he struck out and scraped at the walls around him. It did no good, but the pain at least confirmed that he was alive. Exhausted, he slumped on his haunches and wept.

He sat for seconds, hours, days, years—time meant nothing in this darkness. At last his tears ceased. He took a deep breath of the dank air and stood. He had never been so afraid. He listened hard, praying for a noise of some sort—then praying that there was nothing in the darkness to make a noise. The silence was as complete as the darkness, and Howard's mind filled both with barely imaginable horrors.

What was this place? It was real—Howard had no doubt about that. It felt like no nightmare he'd ever had. The walls, the sloping floor, the slime—they all felt too real, too solid, too genuine. And everything was consistent. Nothing changed the way it did in dreams. Howard was rational. Could he even think this way in a dream? In a dream, could he question that he was in a dream?

Was his physical body somewhere other than the AIPC basement? Had he blacked out, and was he now awake somewhere else? If so, where? When? Why? Had he been abducted by aliens? There were no answers.

A wave of anger overwhelmed him, pushing aside the rising terror. "This is impossible!" he yelled into the silent darkness. "It's not real. I can't be here. I'm *not* here. I'm standing beside Cate and my dad at the end of a corridor leading to the boiler room in the basement of the Aylford Institute for Psychiatric Care." His voice rose. "There's a slow cooker filled with vegan chili simmering on the counter at home. My mom's somewhere with a bunch of flakes learning how to get in touch with her inner self through cosmic harmony." He was screaming now. "I'm about to wake up in the institute basement or in my bed at home—I really don't care where. Just let me wake up. Pleeeeeeeease!"

Howard opened his eyes...to darkness, cold walls and dripping slime. He felt overwhelmed, helpless, powerless. But as he calmed down, he became aware of cold air against his face. It was coming from the tunnel ahead. Was this a way out?

Shuffling his feet, he stumbled forward. What else could he do? He kept his arms out, feeling his way along the repellant walls on either side and the roof above. Gradually he noticed that the walls were edging in and the roof was lowering. Howard had to crouch to prevent the tendrils of slime from dragging across his face. What if the walls and roof narrowed so much that he had to crawl? What if he got stuck? He'd be trapped in this hideous tunnel until he died of thirst or starvation—or lost what little sanity he had left.

He heard a soft, rhythmic rattling sound, and there was a smell, faint but unmistakable. Aylford and the AIPC were miles from the coast, but Howard could smell the salt tang of the sea and hear waves breaking gently on a beach.

He had the strange feeling that the tunnel walls were gone. Gingerly he straightened and stretched. He took several steps forward and found himself standing on a rocky beach, his feet sinking into the round, wet stones, his view illuminated by a low full moon. Small waves broke with a whisper.

Howard gaped at the inky expanse of ocean. To his right a dark peninsula stretched out to sea. It appeared to be pointing at a vague white blotch near the horizon. A movement there caught Howard's attention. As he stared, the surface of the ocean seemed to bulge. It rose to impossible heights, and then violent, white torrents of water cascaded off, revealing a black island.

In the bright moonlight, Howard could make out the shattered remnants of a colossal ruined city scattered over the slopes of the hill that formed the center of the island. Massive blocks of polished black stone, cut in intricate shapes that seemed to defy geometry, lay everywhere. The smooth stone surfaces were covered with deeply incised hieroglyphs that he somehow knew were words in an ancient language that no human voice had ever uttered.

In the center of the awful wreckage, several of the blocks were interlocked, each fitting exactly to its neighbor along mortarless joins and surrounding an arch of impenetrable blackness, out of which blew an icy wind.

As he watched, mesmerized, Howard noticed movement. The fallen blocks and pillars were covered with a host of loathsome sea creatures, many crawling on all fours, their disgusting swollen bellies dragging over the stone. Others were slithering into the water and swimming toward him with powerful strokes, the crests on their heads and backs cutting through the waves like shark fins.

Unable to tear his eyes away, Howard watched in horror as the repulsive fishmen swam closer. A cloud swept across the moon, plunging the view into blackness. Frozen in terror and shivering in the icy wind blowing off the sea, Howard gradually became aware of a sound, just audible above the hissing waves. It was a soft, piping sigh at the very extremity of hearing. Howard stared harder but could see nothing. The unearthly whistling was rising and falling, and getting louder, drowning out the sound of the waves on the shore. Then another noise joined the chorus. It was deeper than the whistling, almost more felt than heard. A dragging, scraping sound, as if something—or some *things*—grotesque and monstrous was slithering and crawling over the cold, slimy stones.

A wave, larger than the others, crashed over Howard's feet. From it a hand reached out and grabbed his ankle. Howard screamed and kicked out wildly. His foot connected with something, and the hand let go. The force of the kick made his other foot slip on the shingle, and he fell heavily to the ground. Something lurched upright out of the shallow water and loomed over him.

A painfully bright flash of light illuminated the scene. It lasted for only an instant, but it imprinted on Howard's mind a vision he would never forget. The creature was vaguely human but covered with coarse scales. A fin ran along the crown of its head and down its back. The head was hunched forward, and a pair of large, bulging, sickly eyes stared at Howard. The face had no nose, but there were lines of slit-like gills pulsing on either side of the neck. The wide-open mouth revealed rows of razor-sharp teeth and a red, slobbering tongue, which licked eagerly over drooling rubbery lips. It was a creature from a nightmare, and it wasn't alone. The flash had revealed hordes of the hideous beasts trudging from the surf, dripping and seaweed draped, all reaching their eager webbed hands hungrily forward.

Howard thought his thumping heart was about to explode from his chest, and he had to fight to drag air into his lungs in short, painful gasps.

The whistling rose to a crescendo, and the crawling noises intensified. For a dreadful moment, Howard thought the things were rushing at him, but the noises faded. They were fleeing.

"What were those?" said a voice.

Howard turned to see a rectangular light bobbing toward him.

"They were utterly gross," the voice continued. "Did you see those mouths? And that smell. Ugh!"

"Who are you?" Howard gasped.

The light tilted up to reveal the face that had haunted many of his dreams.

"Madison! What are you doing here?"

"That's a stupid question," Madison said as she came over and stood beside him. He rose unsteadily to his feet. "If I knew what I was doing here, I wouldn't be wandering around in the dark. This is the craziest dream, eh? One minute I'm at Leon's, getting stuff ready for the party. Next thing I know, I'm here.

I mean, like, it doesn't make sense, right? Okay, maybe I've had a couple of drinks, but Leon's being such a jerk these days. Do you think he spiked my drink? If that idiot put something in my drink, I'll kill him. Hey, what are you doing in my dream, anyway?"

Howard stared at Madison, her face lit by the pale glow from her cell phone. He felt the urge to both laugh and cry. Her inane babble was so ordinary compared with the situation they were in. On the other hand, she had thought of using her cell phone as a light source, something that had never occurred to him.

"This isn't a dream, Madison," he explained.

"What are you talking about? Is this one of those nerdy online games you lonely people spend your lives playing? I just want to get back to the party. I'm outta here." She turned away from him.

"Wait!" Howard shouted. "How will you get back?"

Madison stopped, shuddered and slowly turned back. She was wearing the same blank expression she'd had outside the school.

"*Chuanguo gongmen*," she said.

"What does that mean?"

Madison's brow furrowed with the effort of trying to think. Then her face relaxed. "No idea. It must not be important." She began to turn away again.

"Is it Chinese?" Howard asked. "Like what you said before, when you told me that I should read a book?" His voice was rising in frustration.

"What? Chinese? You're *too* weird."

"What book was it? And why should I read it?"

Madison shook her head. "You're the geek—you decide. This is getting too creepy. I'm going back to kill Leon for spiking my drink." She turned and strode up the beach.

"How will you get back?" Howard repeated.

"Duh. Through the door."

He rushed after the fading glow of Madison's cell phone. "What door?"

"The one I came through. God, you're such a dork."

In front of him, the glow from Madison's phone disappeared. He yelled again for her to wait, but there was no reply. He struggled up the shingle in the darkness and crashed into a stone wall. There was no door.

Howard worked his way to the right and the left but found only cold, wet stone. He slumped exhausted onto the beach and wondered what to do. The view brightened as the clouds moved away from the moon. The island was still there, but there was no sign of the creatures. The white blur was now closer and had resolved itself into an old-fashioned sailing ship.

What could he do? He was trapped here in this dark and terrifying world.

Just then he heard a voice: "*Huilai! Xinglai! Huilai! Xinglai!*"

He dragged himself to his feet and spun around, trying to locate the voice. "Help me!" he howled. "Where are you? Help me. I'm lost."

Howard was beginning to feel dizzy, but he kept turning, searching for assistance. Sparks of brilliant white were exploding like a thousand suns behind his eyes. He was stumbling, staggering, falling. His shoulder made painful contact with a concrete wall, and he landed on his back.

He looked up to a face hovering over him. It was the same long, narrow Chinese face he'd seen at the end of the basement corridor just before he blacked out. It wore the same unsettling smile as before. Howard wasn't sure if he was still in the nightmare world.

"I have found you at last," the voice in his head said.

Ancient Chinese

Cate helped Howard to his feet, and they fell into an embrace. Despite his pain and fear, Howard had never been so happy to see anyone in his life.

"What happened?" he asked when they separated.

"You cried out, beat the walls a few times with your fists and collapsed."

Howard looked down. The backs and knuckles of his hands were seriously scratched—no deep cuts, but enough to bleed and sting. One of his fingernails was broken, and there was dirt under the others.

Howard noticed his father standing motionless behind them, staring blankly down the corridor. But he also sensed a third person nearby. He looked around and saw a man. That same face! "Who's that?" he asked quietly.

"I think he's the janitor," Cate explained. "He saw you fall and came along to help."

"You had a fit," the janitor said in a voice that suggested he didn't particularly care. The man was tall and incredibly skinny.

90

His grubby overalls hung off his frame, and his face looked like a skull with pale, grayish skin pulled tightly over it. "You shouldn't be down here. This is not your place. There are things here not for your eyes." He turned away and headed back down the corridor into the boiler room.

"Creepy guy," Howard said. "His skin looks so pale, like he never sees sunshine. And what did he mean about things here not for our eyes?"

"Probably doesn't want us messing with the furnace or his machinery," Cate said, shrugging. "He's not the most charming person I've ever met."

"I wouldn't be either if I spent my life down here." Howard shivered. "But he looks sort of familiar."

"You've probably seen him around on visits to your dad."

"I guess so." Howard was uncertain.

Cate was staring at him with an odd expression. Concern dominated, but under that there was something else. Curiosity?

"What?" he asked.

"I thought you were dead, but your eyeballs were moving under your lids."

"How long was I unconscious?"

Cate shrugged again. "Not long. Thirty seconds at most. Just enough time for the janitor to come along the corridor."

"It seemed much longer." Howard thought about his journey down the dark slope to the beach. It had seemed endless.

"Do you remember anything?"

"Darkness and a long sloping tunnel." Howard hesitated to give more detail. Something about Cate's question bothered him.

"What made you think I had something to remember? I don't think people usually remember things after they have a fit."

"Your eyeballs were moving like people's do when they dream."

"But I wasn't asleep," he said. "I was unconscious or having an attack of some sort. It was too real to be a dream. It doesn't make sense." Something else pushed itself into his mind. "I heard words before I came to. *Wheee...*something?"

Cate nodded. "Two words—*huilai* and *xinglai*."

"Chinese again?" Howard guessed.

"Yes."

"What do they mean?"

Cate took a deep breath. "*Huilai* means 'come back,' and *xinglai* means 'wake up.'"

"Why did you say those things, and why in Chinese?"

Cate looked Howard straight in the eyes. "I didn't say anything."

"What? Who then?"

"When you collapsed, your father threw his arms wide and said, '*Huilai! Xinglai!*' He repeated it over and over, like a slogan or a mantra. As soon as you opened your eyes, he stopped, and his arms dropped."

They both looked at Howard's dad, who stood like a statue, totally oblivious to everything around him.

As Howard stared at his unresponsive father, something else struck him. "What he said down here and what Madison said outside the school—that's all Chinese, right?"

Cate nodded.

"And it's just like the words my dad was babbling before he came into the AIPC. So why didn't the Chinese doctor recognize it?"

"There are many different dialects and languages in China—Mandarin, Wu, Min and so on. Most of them are mutually unintelligible."

"But he still would have recognized them, right?"

"What your dad spoke is not a common language in China. It's very ancient, and pronunciation is very different. But maybe we should get your dad back to his room before we get into that."

"I guess you're right." Howard was confused and scared, and his brain was a chaotic muddle of thoughts, ideas, emotions and impressions. Nothing was solidifying enough to help explain what had just happened. "There's not much point in staying here."

"Yes," Cate agreed. "Are you feeling okay?"

"Honestly? No. My head's really messed up. I felt dizzy and nauseated when I passed out, but that's gone now." He noticed that Cate was chewing her bottom lip, like she was trying to make a tough decision. "What?"

She blinked, and her face relaxed. She shook her head as if she'd made a choice she was not particularly comfortable with. "Dr. Roe is going to want a detailed report on what happened."

"I suppose so."

"I don't think we should mention what happened to you."

"I hadn't thought about it, but why not? Maybe he can tell me what's going on."

"I doubt it," Cate said. "Is there a cafeteria here?"

"Cafeteria?" Howard was thrown off by the abrupt shift in the conversation. "Yes. In the other wing."

"Good. There's something I need to explain. It might help you understand. Let's get your dad back to his room, and then I'll buy you a Coke and fries in the cafeteria."

The pair led the unresisting patient back up the stairs and down the hallway to his room. Howard was looking around nervously, examining everything to reassure himself that the world around him was real. He was horribly aware of his peripheral vision, terrified that the blackness would return to hurl him back into the nightmare from which he had just escaped.

As soon as they had gotten his dad settled back in his bed, and he was staring vacantly at the TV, Dr. Roe showed up.

"The nurse tells me we had a bit of a breakthrough," he said, briefly examining Howard's dad, who paid him no attention whatsoever. "Want to tell me what happened?"

Together, Howard and Cate related his dad's reaction to the TV documentary and the walk down to the basement. They kept silent about Howard's fit.

"Interesting." Dr. Roe scratched his chin. "Once patients like your father begin to respond to stimuli, one of the most difficult challenges is working out exactly which ones cause the response. It's not uncommon for something to trigger a reaction once, but then never again."

Dr. Roe went on to explain some of the psychology around his work, but Howard had trouble focusing. He was glad his dad had shown some reactions, but he was confused by their strangeness, and the whole episode was overshadowed by his frightening experience in the basement. He wanted to hear what Cate had to say, hopeful that she would be able to calm his confusions and fears. Maybe even offer some kind of rational explanation and help him toward a decision about what to do next.

Eventually, Dr. Roe drew his monologue to a close. "Well, at the very least, we know there's *something* that can trigger a response in your dad. I'll see if I can chase up a copy of that documentary. Maybe it'll provoke a reaction again. In the meantime, I think we should let him rest."

Cafeteria Confessions #1

The cafeteria was designed like a large 1950s diner. A curving stainless-steel counter, complete with gleaming soda fountain, ran along one wall. Red-leather-topped stools lined the counter, and booths were set against the other walls and clustered in groups in the center. A huge jukebox sat in solitary splendor beside the door.

Howard and Cate ordered two drinks and a side of fries from the bored woman behind the counter, paid and chose a booth by the wall. The only other customers were a pair of doctors and a table of four nurses. When Howard's dad had first been admitted, the young man who took Howard and his mom on a tour of the facility explained that the retro cafeteria was meant to represent a different world—somewhere staff members and patients' families could escape their stress for a short time. It seemed to work: Howard began to relax in the comforting setting. He dipped a fry in ketchup, almost ready to believe that the world was normal again. Then Cate started talking.

"What do you remember?" she asked, grabbing a couple of fries for herself.

Howard wanted to forget, not remember, so his first instinct was to pass the question off with some flippant comment. But Cate looked far too serious for that. Besides, she was the only person in the world he *could* talk to about this. On the walk to the cafeteria, he'd considered his decision to seek professional help. A part of him thought that doctors would be of no more use to him than they had been to his dad. At least Cate would understand something of what had gone on. She'd been there in the corridor and seen Howard's attack and his father's strange reaction.

"I was in a black tunnel," Howard began. Once he'd started, he found it impossible to stop. He told Cate about everything: the impenetrable blackness of the disgusting sloping tunnel, the slick beach, the island with its ruins and arch, the ship, the monsters and Madison's sudden appearance. He described the confusion and horror he'd felt.

"Did Madison say anything?" Cate interrupted.

"Yeah. It sounded Chinese, like what she said outside the school." He tried to remember. "*Chungo gong men*, or something like that."

"*Chuanguo gongmen*," Cate said.

"That's it. What does it mean?"

"It means 'go through the arch.' What else happened?"

Howard finished telling Cate about his conversation with Madison and her insistence that she was going back to Leon's party. As he talked, he realized he had been a lot more worried about what was happening to him than he'd been prepared to admit to himself. It was a huge relief to be able to talk to someone he trusted. Throughout, Cate sat in silence, demolishing the rest of the fries.

"I'm terrified that I'm going crazy like my dad," Howard admitted. "And you know, the thing that worries me most is what my dad had to do with it all. That weird TV show did something to him. He led us down to the basement, and he brought me back by chanting those Chinese words. What does that have to do with what happened? Why is everyone speaking some ancient version of Chinese? Why is Madison telling me these things? What book was she talking about? And why did she want me going through that arch?"

"It's complicated," Cate said. She smiled and slurped down the last of her drink. "First off," she said, "you're not going crazy—at least, not in the way you think you are." Howard didn't find that particularly encouraging, but he said nothing. "What I'm going to tell you will seem really strange and complex. You won't understand it all, but I don't either. Just try to keep an open mind, okay?"

"I'll try," Howard agreed. He was prepared to work hard at anything that might explain what was happening to him.

"Okay. Some of it is easy to explain. That TV show was a documentary about a real place. It's called Sanxingdui now, but it's had many names over the centuries. You mentioned that your dad had been to China. Did he go to Sanxingdui?"

"I don't know. He went to some high-powered conference at a place called Cheng...something."

"Chengdu?" Cate suggested.

"Yeah, that's it. Chengdu. He was really thrilled about going, said all the top names in archaeology would be there." Howard took a sip of his Coke, and Cate waited for him to go on. "Dad would come back from those trips all excited. He would tell Mom and me these cool stories about the digs he'd been on and show us photographs of the stuff that had been found." Howard smiled. "He could be a bit of a geek. I guess it runs in the family."

Cate smiled encouragement, and Howard continued. "But when he came back from Chengdu, he said very little about what he'd done. He told us about the great food and about visiting a panda research sanctuary, but he said nothing about the archaeological work he'd done there. Odd, huh?"

"Especially since Sanxingdui is one of the most extraordinary archaeological sites in the world, and it's only an hour's drive from Chengdu."

"So he recognized Sanxingdui in the documentary?"

Cate nodded. "He *must* have gone there."

"But why did he never talk about it? And why did he have such a reaction to seeing it again? Is Sanxingdui a part of this? If it's so famous that they're making documentaries about it, thousands of people must visit it every day. Are they all going crazy?"

"Sanxingdui is the key, but not the Sanxingdui of today. It's about something that happened there long ago."

"If it happened long ago, how can it have an effect now, and why only on my dad?"

"It's not only on your dad. What happened at Sanxingdui is having an impact on you as well."

"So I *am* going mad."

"No." Cate reached across the table and took Howard's hand. "But what I'm going to tell you might make you wish you were. It's a long story, and if you believe it, it will take you places where madness will seem like a hoped-for escape. Should I go on?"

"Do I have a choice?"

"Not if you want to understand."

Howard nodded his agreement.

"We humans like to think that we're rational and in control of our world. Sure, there are earthquakes, tsunamis, volcanic eruptions—many natural, sometimes deadly events that we can't control—but we think we're in charge of most of what shapes the world and our place in it. We think we're important, but we're very, very wrong."

Cate paused as if expecting a response.

"But we do have some control," Howard said. "We can mess up the world through deforestation, pollution, climate change and wars, or we can make it better through recycling, reforestation and peacekeeping. My mom says the world is a living thing, and we're placed here to be its custodians." He couldn't believe he was quoting his flaky mother, but it seemed appropriate.

Cate didn't agree.

"You and your mother are both wrong. You both think like humans."

"How can we not? We *are* humans."

"The trouble with being human is that we can only talk to ourselves, and that's never a healthy thing to do. We can't

communicate with other species. If you could have a conversation with a whale, for example, you would have a very different
view of the world. And what if we could talk to a dinosaur
or a trilobite? Creatures from times in the earth's geological
history—they would have told you that *they* were in control."

Howard had no idea what a trilobite was, but he doubted
that was important. "But we're in control now," he pointed out.

"To some degree," Cate acknowledged. "But what if there's
something else? Something that we—or the whales, dinosaurs
and trilobites—can't imagine. Something so powerful that it
makes our idea of being in charge seem as stupid as an ant in
your backyard thinking it is controlling you."

"God?"

"Not in the way you mean," Cate said, shaking her head.
"Imagine you're an ant, happily helping your colony build
tunnels, look after eggs and collect food. You comfortably
believe that you are in charge of your world. One day you're
out dragging back a bit of dead fly. It's a nice summer afternoon, so the human owner of the backyard comes out to have
a barbecue on the patio. They notice your colony and go back
inside to put the kettle on. While you're still struggling with
the dead fly and wondering what it all means, a torrent of
boiling water descends on your colony and wipes out your
world and everyone you have ever known, from the queen on
down to the lowliest worker. As you recoil in horror, desperately trying to hold on to your sanity, the world darkens as
the sole of a shoe descends. In the last second of your exist-
ence, you realize that you live in a universe of immeasurable,
uncaring forces, populated by beings of incalculable power

and malignancy who dwarf anything you could ever have imagined."

"Whoa," Howard said, his brow furrowing. "The ant story's cool, and I'll never step on one again, but…"

He waited as Cate stared down at the tabletop. When she looked up, her eyes were hard. "What if *we're* the ants?"

It took Howard a moment to work out what she was saying. "You mean, there's something out there much more powerful than us? Something that doesn't care about us and could destroy our world?"

Cate nodded slowly.

"So why don't we know about it?" Howard asked, vaguely wondering if his new friend was as crazy as his dad.

"Perhaps because it hasn't come out on the patio yet." Cate smiled, but Howard didn't feel like responding in kind. "Look," she went on, "we know the world only through our five limited senses. To many creatures, the world appears radically different—ants can 'taste' chemicals in the air, snakes can 'see' heat, some insects can detect ultraviolet light, dogs smell a world we know nothing about. And we're not even getting into what other senses there might be."

"So you're saying there are monsters out there that we can't see?" All hope he'd had of Cate providing a rational explanation for what had happened was fast disappearing.

"If they only reflected ultraviolet light, we would never see them." She hurried on before Howard could point out that they could still bump into them. "But the real problem is that we cannot see what we cannot imagine."

"What do you mean?"

"Have you ever lost your phone?"

"Sure. Everybody has," Howard said, instinctively feeling in his pocket to make sure it was there.

"Okay, so you can't find your phone. You usually put it on your bedside table, so you go look—not there. Then you remember you went to brush your teeth, so you go look in the bathroom—not there. You were watching TV, so you look on the couch—not there. It *must* be on the bedside table. You look again, and this time you search the floor in case it fell off—not there."

"Okay, I get the point."

"The point is that you imagine places your phone usually is and look there. In fact, what really happened was that your mom found your phone in the bathroom and didn't want it to get wet, so she put it on the kitchen counter. It's out in the open, and you've walked past it three times on your search, but you didn't see it because you weren't imagining it there."

"Okay, I've done that. But I would see a monster sitting on the kitchen counter."

"What if it was made of a material that you couldn't detect with your five imperfect senses? What if it existed in a different time?"

Cate tilted her head and looked at him. Howard tried to imagine a monster living in another time but still sitting on his kitchen counter—and failed.

"This is really weird." The idea that Cate might be crazy was getting stronger, but Howard decided to humor her. "I get what you're saying, I think, but what does that have to do with Sanxingdui and what happened to me in the basement?"

"What if the monsters existed in different dimensions from ours?"

"Then we would never see them. We can't travel between dimensions—if other dimensions even exist."

"What if some of us can? What if there are places in our world of great power—points where our dimension or time rubs against another one? What if those places are gateways where things can pass from one dimension into another—where someone or something can exist in two realities at once?"

Howard stared at Cate, his brain spinning. How had they got from backyard ants and lost cell phones to gateways in time and space? He'd followed the path Cate had led him on, but he couldn't believe where they'd ended up.

"It's impossible," he said at last, hoping against hope that Cate was about to laugh and say that all this came from some strange play she was learning or...something.

"Okay, what's *your* theory for what happened in the basement?"

"Look," Howard said. "What happened was really eerie and frightening, and I admit it didn't feel like a dream—I could think clearly and act on the decisions I made, and nothing changed for no reason, the way it often does in dreams. I was exactly as I am in the real world, even down to my backpack, but that doesn't make it a trip to another dimension. It was just a weird dream that proves I'm going mad. I really appreciate your trying to explain it away, and you've been incredibly creative, but what you're saying about other dimensions and monsters is insane."

"So how do you explain your dad's reaction to the TV? What about his speaking ancient Chinese and calling you back from wherever you went when you had your fit?"

"My dad's insane!" Howard said, so loud that the woman behind the counter turned and stared at him. "And clearly I'm going insane too. There are no incredibly powerful monsters waiting to step on us. I'll go to the doctor tomorrow and he'll order a bunch of tests that will show nothing. Meanwhile, the attacks will get worse and more frequent, and two months from now, I'll be in the room next to Dad's, not even able to recognize you or Mom."

Saying it out loud was much worse than thinking it. Howard was within an inch of breaking down completely. Blinking back tears, he stood up and reached over to lift his backpack.

"I have to go."

Cate grabbed his wrist. "One last thing," she said, picking a toothpick out of the holder on the table and offering it. "Clean under your fingernails before you go."

"What?" The request was so bizarre that Howard sat back down. "Clean under my fingernails?"

"Yes. That's all you need to do."

He looked at his hands. His nails were filthy, and he wasn't sure how they got that way. He scraped some green dirt from under each nail onto the tabletop. As he stared at the tiny pile of greenish slime on the table, it hit him. "Oh my god!" he said in a voice barely above a whisper. "It's the slime from the walls and roof of the tunnel."

"Now look at your backpack," Cate said.

There were damp greenish streaks running all along the outside.

"Now smell your runners."

It was an odd request, but Howard was not about to question Cate at this point. He lifted his leg and smelled the runner on his right foot. It was damp. That could have been from the rainstorm they had run through, but that wouldn't explain why it smelled of seawater and a beach.

"A wave that washed over my feet when the creature grabbed my ankle!" Howard couldn't have left now even if he'd wanted to. "It actually happened," he whispered. "How, how, how?"

In an instant, everything that Howard believed in—everything that he and everyone else in the world accepted as normal and stable—had become fluid, uncertain and hideously frightening.

"I'm not crazy?" he asked softly, his shoulders slumping.

"I told you that you weren't," Cate said.

"How do you know all this stuff?"

She grinned broadly. "I'm a witch."

CAFETERIA CONFESSIONS #2

"No!" Howard exclaimed. His mind desperately wanted to reject everything Cate had just said. It was all totally unthinkable, unimaginable, inconceivable. But so was the green slime beneath his nails and on his backpack, not to mention his runners smelling of the sea. In desperation he focused on the last thing Cate had said. "You can't be a witch! There's no such thing. It's impossible."

"Oh, I wouldn't rush to say things are impossible," said Cate, her grin firmly in place. "Would you?"

Howard had to admit that his definition of impossible was broadening.

"Anyway, I'm not really a witch. I don't fly around at night on a broomstick. I'm a *wu*."

"And that is?" Howard asked.

"It's an ancient Chinese spirit medium. Probably more like a shaman than a witch, but we've been called many things: prophets, seers, magicians, lunatics. I prefer the term *Adept*."

"And you're…an Adept?"

Cate nodded. "Throughout history, there have been people who are sensitive to things outside normal day-to-day reality. Where do you think Lewis Carroll got all his strange ideas for Alice's adventures, Edgar Allan Poe his horror stories and Hieronymus Bosch the images for his paintings? But right now, what's more important for you to realize is that *you* are an Adept—and your father too, I think."

"So his fits—which everyone is assuming are related to mental instability—are the same as what's happening to me?"

"Not exactly the same. Different people see different things and react in different ways."

"Like how I remember every detail of my fits and he can't remember a thing?"

"Yeah. Whatever your dad saw was so strange or terrifying that his brain couldn't handle it. It blocked his memories as a defense mechanism."

"But he's started talking again," Howard pointed out. "He said *mask* and *have to go* before he led us downstairs. Is he beginning to remember things?"

"I think all the things he saw in his dreams are still there in his head—he's just locked them away. Somehow a tiny corner of those experiences was opened up by the pictures of Sanxingdui on the TV."

"He also said something before I had my fit in the basement. What did that mean? Was that Chinese as well?"

"Yes. He repeated the name of the book from the reading room, *Jinse de mianju*. Then he said, *Zhe ben shu zai zheli,* which means 'The book is here,' and then *Ni yinggai kanshu*, which means 'You should read the book.' The same thing Madison said to you."

"So we should read the book you found in the reading room?"

"Probably." Cate looked worried.

"What is it?"

"It was really quite extraordinary to find *Jinse de mianju*, Chinese for 'the golden mask,' in the reading room. There are only a few copies anywhere in the world, and mostly those are only badly translated fragments. What excited me was that this copy seemed to be complete."

"So why should that worry you?"

"Because it might be very dangerous. The original *Jinse de mianju* was translated from an ancient text written thousands of years ago in an unknown language. I assumed that the book I found was a relatively recent copy, but now I'm not so sure. Unlikely as it seems, both Madison and your dad keep telling us to read the book—and *Jinse de mianju* is the only one they could be referring to."

"I agree that's weird, but what's the problem? The book's in Chinese, so you can read it, right?"

"The problem is that it might be an accurate copy of the original."

"So?"

"The original copy of *The Golden Mask* is said to have had immense power. People believed they could open portals to other dimensions, particularly the Realm of the Elder Gods, simply by reading aloud certain passages from it."

"What's that?" Howard had the uncomfortable feeling that what she was saying was drawing him deeper into a place he wasn't particularly keen to go to.

"There are places in our world where it is easier to move not only between dimensions but also times. The dimensions swirl around in space and time, and when two are close together, it's easier to move between them. We are almost at a time when the Realm of the Elder Gods will be very close to our world."

"What's so terrible about that?"

"If we're the ants in the backyard, the Elder Gods are the homeowners about to come out for a barbecue."

Howard stared at Cate. "How do you know it's the Realm of the Elder Gods that's coming close?"

"Partly from your dad. In the basement, after he told you to read the book, he chanted, *Xiaoxin sizhe shei mengxiang*— 'Beware the dead who dream.' It is written in some ancient texts that the Elder Gods are the sleeping dead who dream, and that those dreams can sometimes leak across into our world and inform our thoughts when we're asleep and our guard of rationality is at its lowest."

"Nightmares?" Howard asked.

"Yes, and if an Adept is particularly sensitive, he or she can sense other elements. As the dimensions swirl closer together, the dreams become more realistic and stronger. They can become so powerful that they form a different reality."

"Powerful enough to happen during the day—like my attack in the basement?"

Cate nodded. "You're a very strong Adept. That's why all this stuff with other Adepts is happening around you."

"Okay, let's say I accept that you and my dad are these so-called Adepts. But Madison? I have a hard time believing she's smart enough."

"Intelligence doesn't have much to do with it," Cate said with a smile.

Howard finished his drink and thought long and hard about what Cate had told him. It all sounded crazy, but it did explain some of what was going on. But even if it was all true, it wasn't going to help Howard escape from his dreams. And from what Cate had said, they were only going to get worse.

"You said there were other elements to being a sensitive Adept," Howard said. "The dreams and what else?"

"You're not going to like it."

"As opposed to realistic daytime nightmares of monsters coming to get me?" But Howard was relieved to see that Cate was smiling.

"The other element is that Adepts can share dreams."

"Like Madison was in my dream?"

"Yes," Cate said, "and you were in mine. I came to Aylford to find you."

"Find *me*?"

"Yeah. I've been dreaming about you for months."

Until a few days ago, Howard would have given his right arm to hear a girl say that to him. Now he wasn't so sure.

"My first dreams of Aylford were confused—images of streets, houses, the college, the psychiatric institute. Then they gradually became more focused. I saw through someone's eyes as he moved around his house, went to work, lectured to students—"

"Lectured to students?" Howard interrupted. "When did you begin having these dreams?"

"A little over a year ago. At first they were very ordinary, but then they started to become more fractured. Large parts of them would just dissolve into blackness. I knew I was still dreaming, but I couldn't see or hear anything. All I had was a sense that I wasn't alone. Then the scenes of home and work were replaced by a hospital of some sort. Often I had a feeling of being restrained, tied to a bed or something, and then the dreams stopped."

Another silence—this one much longer.

Eventually Howard managed to force out some words. "My dad. You were dreaming about my dad going insane."

Cate nodded. "I think I was. After those dreams stopped, there was nothing for a while, and then, about three months ago, the dreams started again. This time they were different. I had no sense of seeing the world through someone's eyes. Instead, I was an observer, watching fragments of a specific person going about his daily life."

"Do you know who it was?" Howard asked, dreading the answer.

"It was you."

It was shocking to think that for weeks someone—even someone as nice as Cate—had been watching him. He couldn't stop his mind from running through all the stupid, embarrassing, private things he had done.

"You were watching me. That's so freaky."

"Don't worry," Cate responded quickly. "The bits of your life I saw were really boring."

"That doesn't make me feel a whole lot better," Howard said. "So you were stalking me in your dreams."

"No," Cate said. "I had no more control over my dreams than you have over yours."

Howard considered this. Cate was right: he couldn't get upset over something she had no control over.

"Do you still dream about me?"

"No. The dreams stopped when I arrived in Aylford."

"If I'm so boring, why did you come here?"

"The dreams began to change. I started to get the feeling that I wasn't the only one watching you. There was something else—something malevolent and evil. But I also had a weird impression that there was glee."

"Glee?"

"Yes. A feeling that whatever else was watching you was glad to have found you."

"What was it?"

"I have no idea, but the thought that it might have somehow discovered you through my dreams bothered me, so I came to Aylford."

"And found out that I was just as boring as your dreams had shown you."

Cate didn't laugh at Howard's nervous attempt at a joke.

"When I came here, the dreams of you stopped," she said, "but they were replaced by vague dreams of a threatening blackness."

"What is it that's causing our dreams? Is it evil?"

Cate thought for a long moment and then said, "Evil, yes. Probably. As to what it is, I'm not sure. There are many Elder

Gods and many tales of them. Some say they ruled the earth before there were people—perhaps even before there was life as we know it. Others say they arrived from the stars at different times."

"Stop!" Howard said. "You're making my brain hurt. You've given me enough information to last a lifetime. I just want the dreams to stop."

"So do I," Cate agreed, "but I don't know how to make that happen. Obviously, you and I are linked in some way, and I think your dad is as well. And we're all linked to the book."

"But we have the book, so we should be all right."

"We have to be even more careful now that we have the book."

"Why? How can a book be so powerful? It's just a collection of words."

"Words are immensely important." Cate spoke softly, but there was an intensity in her voice that made Howard pay attention. "Some ancient religions believe that the uttering of a single word created the universe. In Judaism there are seventy-two names for God, and manipulations of those names created the world and can destroy it. Even in the New Testament, the Gospel of John begins with *In the beginning was the Word, and the Word was with God, and the Word was God*. Think about it. John's saying the word is actually God. It's possible that words can open portals between different dimensions and realities. During your episode, your father's words brought you back to the basement."

Howard knew Cate was right about that, but it was all so confusing.

"So what's real?" he asked.

"That's the million-dollar question. We rationalize what we see around us, but that doesn't make it real. There are countless cults and fringe religions with some very strange ideas about reality and our place in it. Some of those ideas, maybe most, derive from distorted or perverted versions of tales told by Adepts."

"I guess. There are people in Mom's cosmic harmony group who believe they are channeling messages from the lost island of Atlantis."

"Exactly."

"So if my dad's words could actually bring me back from the beach to the basement, can saying the right words unlock the gateways between these realities you talked about?"

"Maybe not unlock, and certainly not for someone who isn't an Adept, but perhaps certain phrases and combinations of words can act as a trigger, alerting whoever or whatever is on the other side. It's best to be careful."

"Kind of like sending an email into a different dimension."

"Kind of," Cate agreed. "But it's an email you don't really want an answer to."

"So what's the other side like?"

Cate stood up. "I think we've covered enough impossible things for now. It's getting late, and we should probably head back into town. Heimao will be worried about us."

They walked in silence along the AIPC corridors. Howard's mind was a confusion of monsters, dreams, magic books and other dimensions. He was still not certain whether he was going mad or was involved in something so vast and frightening that insanity seemed like a better choice. On the plus side, his dad seemed to be making progress, and whatever Howard was going through, at least he was with Cate. He was so wrapped in his thoughts that he barely noticed as they passed the reception desk.

"Is that black cat yours?" the receptionist asked Cate. "We don't allow pets in here."

"Heimao's not a pet," Cate replied, "and she wouldn't have come in here if I didn't ask her to."

"Well, she did," the receptionist answered. "One of the doctors was heading home, and she shot in the instant he opened the door."

Cate looked seriously puzzled. "Where did she go?"

"Headed straight up the steps to the reading room. She was too quick for me, and I can't leave my desk, so you'd better go up and get her. Here, I'll write down the code for the door."

By the time the receptionist had finished speaking, Cate was already halfway to the stairs. Howard was at her heels. In the reading room, they found Heimao curled on the central desk and being stroked by Aileen.

"What happened?" Cate asked.

"She came in here like devils were chasing her," Aileen explained, "and then jumped on the desk and settled down as if she'd always lived here."

"I'm sorry. This isn't like her."

"No problem. We're close friends now. We've had a good conversation, haven't we, Heimao?"

"How do you know her name?" asked Howard.

Aileen's smile broadened. "It just seemed right. How was the visit with your dad?"

"Encouraging. He seems to be responding more."

"Any change is good, I understand," Aileen said. "You were here a long time."

"We went down to the basement," Cate said. Howard tensed, thinking she was going to tell Aileen about his fit, but she merely said, "We met the creepy janitor."

"Creepy janitor?" Aileen looked puzzled. "Admittedly, Jim's got a strange sense of humor, but we excuse that because he's Scottish. I don't think anyone would call him creepy. But that's weird—he doesn't usually work Fridays."

"What does Jim look like?" Cate asked.

"Short ginger hair, a bit overweight."

"Maybe we saw his assistant?" Howard suggested. "A tall, pale Chinese guy?"

Aileen stared at him. She looked worried. "Jim doesn't have an assistant, Chinese or otherwise. Not a huge staff here, and as far as I know, I'm the only one you could mistake for Chinese."

"You saw him too, right?" Howard asked, turning to Cate, but she was already on her way to the stairs to the basement.

Heimao jumped off the desk and followed her.

Howard looked back at Aileen in confusion. "Excuse me. I've got to go now," he mumbled and set off after Cate.

The two hurried down the steps to the basement. Howard was nervous at returning to the scene of his incident, and he jumped again as the overhead lights came on with the same unsettling flash. The basement corridor was exactly as he remembered it, but the door at the end was closed. Howard ran down the corridor, turned the handle and pulled open the door.

The light from the corridor illuminated a boiler and a mass of pipes and electrical lines.

"What's going on?" he asked Cate. "There's no one here. The Chinese man wasn't just a part of my nightmare. You saw him too, right?"

Cate stood at the far end of the corridor. "I saw him too," she replied.

"How can that be? What's happening?" Howard said as he rejoined her.

"I'm not sure. I need to think."

Not certain he liked the things Cate thought about, Howard followed her up the stairs and out into the night.

ESCAPE

As the sun rose above the mountains behind him, Chen got his first good look at the Ma Zhang camp. It was much larger than he had expected—a vast, sprawling mass of colored tents, banners and piles of weapons, alive with busy warriors cooking over open fires, fetching water from the river and loading equipment into high-sided two-wheeled carts.

Chen couldn't see how Sanxingdui's army had a chance against such a horde, but that was not what made him gasp in shock. To one side of the camp, hundreds of horses stood in long lines, tethered to ropes strung between posts driven into the ground. They were restless, moving like a single strange creature. In the still, cold morning air, Chen could hear them snorting and stamping, and he could see the steam rising from their nostrils.

Chen had heard of horses. He had even seen a couple that had been captured when the Ma Zhang attempted a small raid across the mountains. But he had never dreamed of numbers like this. It was said that horses were very fast and could carry a warrior great distances in a single day. They were also faster and more efficient at hauling wagons than the placid, plodding oxen that the farmers and traders around Sanxingdui used. An army mounted on these beasts would be unbeatable.

Worse, the idea behind Chen's spying mission was that if he headed back to Sanxingdui as soon as he saw the tribal army getting ready to cross the mountains, he would travel much faster and be able to give the emperor plenty of warning of the enemy's approach. That would not be the case, however, if the soldiers were on horseback. They would overtake a boy on foot in a few hours, and he would never get home in time.

Chen had no idea how he could overcome this problem, but he was determined not to let it prevent him from carrying out the task he had set himself—to rescue Ting and Fu. That part of his plan had called for sneaking into the camp at night, but it didn't seem as if even that would work. Judging by the activity below, the army was preparing to move that very day.

For a moment Chen considered turning around and heading back to Sanxingdui as fast as possible, but he soon discarded that idea too. He would never get there in time, and besides, he couldn't leave Ting behind. Glad that he had swapped his servant's clothing for nondescript peasant's clothes, Chen headed down the hill.

Everyone was busy loading wagons and taking down tents, so no one gave a second glance to the scruffy peasant boy heading for the center of the camp. A couple of soldiers shouted at Chen as he passed. He didn't understand their coarse dialect, but it was obvious they were ordering him to help them load a cart. Chen kept going, waving his satchel at them and pointing ahead as if he were in the middle of performing some important task.

Chen was nearing the center of the camp and wondering how he was going to find Ting when a soldier shouted, "You, boy. Come over here. I've got a job for you."

Chen was so surprised to hear someone shout something he understood that he stopped. "I have an important message to deliver," he said.

"Never mind about that."

A hand grabbed the collar of Chen's grubby shirt and dragged him to one side. The man pointed at a cage sitting on the ground. In the middle sat a forlorn, bedraggled Fu.

"I've been looking after this stupid brute for ten days. To tell the truth, I'd have dropped it down a well long ago if anyone other than Shenxian had told me to look after it. He ain't someone I want to mess with. Anyway, with no warning, we was told this morning that it was time to leave. If I don't get a chance to pack my kit on a wagon, it'll either get stolen or left behind, or I'll end up slogging over those mountains with it on my back. So stay right here and watch this ugly dog for me. If you or it ain't here when I get back, it'll be you going down the well. Understand?"

Chen nodded, not trusting himself to speak.

"Good." The soldier let go of his collar and left.

Chen approached the cage. "Hello, Fu," he whispered.

At the sound of his name, the dog looked up and wagged his tail feebly.

"They haven't looked after you very well, have they? Don't worry! I'm here to rescue you and Ting."

At the sound of Ting's name, Fu stood up and put more energy into the wagging tail.

"That's a good dog. Do you know where Ting is?"

The tail wagging increased, and the pink tongue flopped from side to side.

"Okay. Let's go find her."

Chen looked up to make sure the soldier wasn't returning and opened the cage. With surprising agility, Fu jumped out and disappeared around the side of the nearest tent. Chen had to hurry to keep up. He managed to skid to halt and take cover as Shenxian and a rough warrior dressed in a thick sheepskin jacket emerged from a large red tent in front of him. Fu seemed to recognize Shenxian and scuttled under the flap of the tent just in time to avoid being stepped on.

"We must be across the mountains by midnight tonight," Shenxian said.

"It is seventy miles to the far end of Min Lake. That's a long way for a single day's travel," the warrior said.

"That is why we must leave the wagons behind and travel light. Each warrior must take only his weapons, a bag of food and a water bag. Timing is everything."

"The road over the mountains is good, but the horses will collapse if we push them too hard, and horses are valuable."

"What is the value of a few horses compared with the gold and riches that will be yours when you take Sanxingdui? But you will not take Sanxingdui if you do not get your army over the mountains by midnight tonight."

The warrior considered this. "I don't understand your magic, but you have convinced me that it is powerful. We will be camped below Min Lake before today turns into tomorrow. I will give the orders."

"Very good. I must see to my bodyguard."

The two men walked within six feet of Chen, but they were so engrossed in their conversation that they never saw the boy huddled in the tent's shadow. As soon as they were gone, he scuttled out and crawled under the tent flap where Fu had disappeared. The instant he was through, a figure hurled itself at him. Chen managed to push the figure off and assume a fighting stance before he realized it was Ting.

"I've found you!" he said.

"No," Ting said with a laugh, "Fu found me. You just followed." Then she became serious. "But there's no time to talk. We have to get back to Sanxingdui."

"There's no point. Shenxian's men are leaving on horseback right now. They'll be across the mountains by tonight."

"I know. Shenxian had a machine that calculated the Min Mountains would fall tomorrow. But we have to try. Maybe his machine made an error. And anyway, we have to escape. Our lives won't be worth anything here once Shenxian leaves, and he does not intend to take us with him."

"How do we escape?"

"On horseback."

"What?" Chen asked, horrified. "I've never been on one of those things. They're dangerous. We could be—"

He was interrupted by the low growl of Fu at the tent flap.

"Shenxian's coming back," Ting said. "We have to go."

The three dove through the flap and ran. Outside was chaos. Soldiers shouted orders and rushed about collecting weapons and getting their horses ready. No one paid any attention to two children and a small ugly dog.

Chen had no idea where they were going, but he trusted Ting and followed her. Occasionally he looked back over his shoulder, but he knew that even Shenxian would have a hard time pursuing them through the pandemonium of the army getting ready to march.

Eventually, they arrived at the edge of the camp, where the horses were tied. The animals were not as big as Chen had feared, but he was still horrified at the prospect of trying to stay on the back of one as it galloped over the mountains.

Ting was heading for a black-and-white pony with a long flowing mane when a tribesman dressed in a rough leather jacket and pants stepped forward and grabbed her by the shoulder. He shouted something Chen didn't understand, but it was obviously threatening.

With visions of being a heroic wushu master flashing through his head, Chen leaped forward. He planted his left foot and began what should have been the devastating Scything the New Corn move. But his left foot slipped on mud, and Chen twisted clumsily and landed in an untidy heap at Ting's feet.

The tribesman looked surprised and then burst out laughing. He also relaxed his grip on Ting enough to allow her to turn and deliver a painful kick to the back of his knees. At the same time, Fu sank his teeth into the man's ankle. With a cry, he fell heavily into the nearest horse, which reared in surprise and began lashing out at its tormentor.

As the tribesman cowered, covering his head to protect himself from the flying hooves, Ting yelled, "Come on!" and leaped smoothly onto the back of the black-and-white pony. She pointed to the brown pony beside hers. "It's not that difficult," she said.

Chen jumped to his feet and scrambled awkwardly onto the beast's back. The horse shuffled nervously, sensing Chen's incompetence.

"Grab hold of the long hair in front of you—it's called the mane—and hold on," Ting called as she turned her pony and headed away from the camp.

The tribesman who had attacked them was back on his feet and shouting. Fu had let go of his ankle and was racing after Ting. Chen leaned forward, grabbed a handful of hair, yelled "Go!" as loud as he could, then closed his eyes and hoped for the best. His mount was happy to follow Ting's pony and charged off through the mess of men and horses. Chen was vaguely aware of angry shouting voices, but he concentrated on hanging on. By the time he felt brave enough to open his eyes, they had already left the camp behind.

Chen bounced up and down painfully as Ting increased the pace. The view of the ground rushing beneath him almost made him throw up, so he tried to look ahead at the approaching mountains.

After a while Ting stopped, lifted Fu up beside her and asked Chen if he was okay. When he nodded and grunted a reply, she laughed and said, "That was a brilliant idea to distract the man with your fall. It was spectacular."

"Yeah," Chen agreed, although all he wanted to do was crawl into a hole and hide in embarrassment.

"We have to keep moving," Ting said, turning her pony back along the road. "The army will be setting off soon, and we don't want them to catch us."

Getting caught and not having to go any farther on the back of this terrifying animal seemed like quite a good idea to Chen, but he said nothing, tightened his grip on his pony's mane and set off after Ting. He occupied himself by praying to every god he could think of to help him survive the day.

Cosmic Harmony

The two friends walked back toward town in silence. Heimao walked beside them, delicately stepping around the puddles left by the rain. The clouds had broken up, and a crescent moon left its silvery reflection on the wet sidewalk. The air still felt damp and cold, and a chilling wind gusted down the side streets, shoving soggy pieces of garbage along the gutters. Howard and Cate both pulled their jackets tight as they trudged down Arcton Street, deep in thought.

Every few steps, Howard came up with new questions, but Cate had given him more than enough to think about already, so he remained silent. His mind instinctively wanted to reject the unbelievable things she had told him, but the more he went over it, the more he realized that Cate's explanation was the only one that made any sense. He was about to ask her what she thought they should do when his phone rang.

"Thank heavens. Are you okay? Where are you?" It was his mom. "I got home and you weren't here. I was so worried. I thought something dreadful had happened to you."

Something fairly dreadful *had* happened to Howard, but he wasn't about to mention it to his mom.

"Sorry, Mom. I forgot to call." He realized that he had spent far longer than usual at the AIPC. "I'm fine. I went out to visit Dad, and I guess time got away from me. A friend came with me, and we hung out in the cafeteria for a bit. We're just heading out. I'll be home soon."

"Okay. Be careful."

"My mom worries," Howard told Cate as he slipped his phone back in his pocket.

She took his hand as they walked through the dark. "Are you going to be all right? I've thrown a lot of stuff at you."

"No kidding," Howard said, trying to sound more confident than he felt. He was worried about going home and about what dreams might come when he went to sleep. "I'll be fine."

"You sure?"

"Honestly—no. But you've been great." He squeezed Cate's hand. "It's just that I'm having trouble wrapping my head around some of the things you've told me. I know it explains what's happening to me, but I feel like the whole world— everything that I've always believed and taken comfort in—is melting. I'm really scared."

"Of going to sleep?" She seemed to be reading his thoughts. "You're worried about whether you'll have nightmares tonight?"

"Yeah, that's part of it."

"I might be able to help with that." Cate reached into her satchel, brought out a small green statue and handed it to him.

The statue felt smooth and vaguely greasy, like the Inuit soapstone carving Howard's mom had on their mantel. It was of a squat man with a wide beard and prominent cheeks and ears. The carving was about the length of Howard's thumb and fitted snuggly into the palm of his hand.

"Who's this?"

"It's Bes," Cate explained. "He's a very old god. No one knows for sure how old, but he was a favorite of the ancient Egyptians. He's the protector of homes, the guardian of everything good and the enemy of everything bad. He's also good at killing snakes."

"So I'm fine if a python crawls in my bedroom window. What do I do with Bes?"

"Place him under your pillow tonight. He'll keep the bad dreams away."

"Awesome," Howard said, and he meant it. Already Bes felt like an old friend. "Thanks."

"We need to come up with a plan," Cate said as they reached his house.

"To defeat the monsters from the other dimension?" Howard joked.

"At least not to let them defeat us." She was perfectly serious. "I'll think about it tonight. Why don't you come round to Crowninshield House tomorrow? I'm in the attic room. We can hang out and decide what to do."

"Sure. I'd like that. Thanks."

"I'm not sure you should thank me, but it's probably better to have some idea of what's going on than to be totally in the dark."

"It's certainly less scary."

"Perhaps," Cate said. Before Howard could ask her what she meant by that, she squeezed his hand and then let go. "Don't forget to put Bes under your pillow."

Howard almost made a stupid comment about the tooth fairy, but Cate's serious expression stopped him. "Thank you for explaining everything," he said instead. "I'm going to have to think about it all. Visits to other dimensions will take a bit of getting used to. Still, it's been cool to hang out with a witch."

He was rewarded with a smile and a punch on the shoulder.

"Adept," Cate corrected. "Sleep well."

Howard stood and watched as she and Heimao disappeared into the darkness. The idea of spending Saturday with Cate thrilled him. She was very weird, and he wasn't certain he believed everything she'd told him, but he felt comfortable and safe when he was with her, and those feelings were increasingly rare these days. He shivered and turned toward his house.

"I'm so glad you're home." His mom hugged him the moment he walked through the door. "Your dinner's on the table. Come and eat and tell me all about your day."

"Just let me drop my backpack in my room," Howard said. He was starving, so dinner was a good idea, but he wasn't about to tell his mom what his day had really been like.

"Who's the friend you were hanging out with?" she asked when they sat down to piping-hot bowls of chili.

"Just someone from school."

"Invite him around for dinner one night. I like to meet your friends."

"Sure." Howard had no intention of telling his mother that his friend was a girl. She'd be picking out a dress for the wedding before he'd finished the sentence.

"So what did you two do?"

"We hung out at the cafeteria," he said. And before his mother could ask more, he added, "Dad was good. He even said a few words."

"What? What did he say?" his mom asked eagerly.

"They were just random words, Mom. They didn't mean anything." Howard couldn't very well tell her what had really happened, but when he saw the disappointment on his mother's face, he added, "Dr. Roe thinks it's a very good sign. He called it a breakthrough and said it was common in cases like Dad's for a recovery to begin this way."

It was stretching the truth a little, but Howard was happy to see how his mother immediately brightened up.

"That's wonderful news. I'll go out and visit him tomorrow. Maybe he'll be able to come home soon."

To keep his mother from getting totally carried away, Howard quickly asked, "How was your meeting?"

It was an old trick he used to sidetrack his mom, but it never failed. And while normally Howard didn't care about his mother's flaky groups, his interest in things different and weird had increased dramatically in the past few hours.

"We learned about the universal life stream, which in our world takes the form of the honeybee," his mom said. "Did you know that the ancients in Atlantis used the honeybee as the symbol for the sun god Solareh? Hardly surprising, since honey bees are the purest form of solar angelic energy in our world."

Once his mom got started, she needed nothing more from Howard than an encouraging nod between mouthfuls of chili. Normally he zoned out when she got going about her latest fad, but this time he realized that what she was saying was not any weirder than what Cate had told him that afternoon. Even so, Howard was more inclined to believe that his new friend was a witch who could access other dimensions than that his mom's group was able to communicate with inhabitants of the lost island of Atlantis. Maybe if his experience in the basement had involved light and honey bees instead of darkness and terror?

"Of course, that's just mainstream cosmic harmony," his mom was saying. "Our group in Aylford broke away many years ago. Our full name is the Cosmic Harmony of the Light of Atlantis and the Nine Dimensions—Aylford Chapter—the CHLANDAC."

Howard nodded, awed by the name and the idea that there was such a thing as mainstream cosmic harmony.

"We understand the Atlanteans," his mom continued happily. "They could travel cosmically to distant stars and between the different dimensions."

This caught Howard's attention. "They could travel to different dimensions?"

"Oh yes." His mom beamed at her son's sudden interest. "There are some places on earth where the barriers between the dimensions are thinner: Atlantis before it was destroyed; Göbekli Tepe in Turkey; Nazca in Peru; Callanish in Scotland; the City of Masks in China; and, of course, Aylford."

"Aylford?"

"Absolutely. There's a lot of cosmic power right here, all around us. If we could access the ancient knowledge, we could even travel back and forth through time. Sometimes I dream of finding *The Golden Mask* in an old bookstore somewhere."

Howard choked on a mouthful of chili and collapsed in a fit of coughing.

His mom leaned over and patted him on the back. "Are you all right, dear?"

"*The Golden Mask?*" he gasped out eventually.

"Yes. Walt—he's the leader of the CHLANDAC—says *The Golden Mask* was the most important book to the Atlanteans," his mom told him. "Of course, it would be a translation. The original would have been written in Enochian—that was the Atlantean language—or maybe even something older than that. Anyway, it was copied into many different languages over the ages. It was lost centuries ago, but we all dream of finding a copy somewhere. That would be so thrilling!"

"*Jinse de mianju,*" Howard couldn't help whispering under his breath.

"What, dear?"

"Nothing," he said.

"The Atlanteans had many ancient books of spells, and their high priests knew which ones to recite so they could journey back and forth at will. Apart from fragments, they were all lost long ago. The names were in old languages, and I'm not very good with languages—unlike your father. He can read books in French, Spanish, Latin. He even knows some Russian, I think."

His mother went off on a rambling tale about how Howard's father used to go to archives around the world to read old documents for his archaeological research. But her son wasn't listening. He was wondering how it was possible for his mother's weird friends to know about the same book he'd been told to read by Madison and his father and that Cate knew as a lost work written by Adepts. Was there a link, or was it all just coincidence?

"What dimensions could the Atlanteans visit?" Howard asked.

"There are nine dimensions," she explained. "The medieval alchemists knew this, but we seem to have forgotten. The CHLANDAC tries to keep this ancient knowledge alive." A wistful look came over her face. "Sometimes I think I was born five hundred years too late. How I would have loved to sit with the great magus Dr. John Dee in his alchemical laboratory in Mortlake and communicate through crystallomancy with the angels of the Enochian dimension."

Howard shook his head to clear the jumble of words his mother had just thrown at him, then asked, "Do we know anything about the other eight dimensions?"

"We know a tiny bit about the Enochian through the wonderful work of Dr. Dee—even though almost all his work was destroyed after he died. Five other dimensions are alternative versions of our own world or worlds that existed or exist on Venus and Mars."

She stopped talking, and her face sagged into an expression of unutterable sadness.

"What are the other two dimensions?" Howard prompted.

"It's such a terrible tragedy," she said. "In the last age of the Atlanteans, there were two high priests—Amshu, which means 'light,' and Claec, which means 'dark.' Amshu was filled with the bright energy of the sun, but Claec followed the darker forces of the moon. In an attempt to increase his power, Claec journeyed to those last two dimensions. They were places that priests in a time ancient even to the Atlanteans had decreed were never to be visited. From those hellish places Claec unleashed horrors that destroyed the gentle Atlantean civilization. All that wonderful truth and knowledge lost."

Howard's mom seemed to have wandered away from talk of *The Golden Mask*. Howard tried to steer her back. "So if the Atlanteans were destroyed and their books lost," he asked, "how does your group know so much about them?"

"A few traders and travelers survived the cataclysm, and they wandered throughout the world, telling tales of their vanished continent. Of course, the tales have become horribly corrupted over the centuries, but the ones that were written down long ago may contain a germ of truth. We must be careful though." She looked at Howard seriously, as if she were telling him to wear his helmet when out on his bicycle. "It was not just the solar knowledge of Amshu that was preserved. Some of the survivors were followers of Claec, so there are dangers in the knowledge too." She closed her eyes and concentrated. "We learned an incantation this evening."

Filleadh abhaile.
Duisg.

Filleadh abhaile.
Duisg.

His mom opened her eyes and smiled at Howard as if this was supposed to mean something. When he looked blank, she said, "It's a charm that will protect you and get you home from wherever you are."

"Wouldn't a taxi be easier?" He couldn't help himself. His mom had looked so serious as she chanted that nonsense.

"Very funny," she said. "I thought you were interested."

"I'm sorry, Mom," he said. "I *am* interested in the Atlanteans and their culture, and I'm glad you have something to protect you from...Claec."

"Thank you." His mom brightened again. "Of course, the only true way to understand more about the Atlanteans is through the CHLANDAC. You should come along to a meeting."

This was a step too far. "I'll think about it," he said.

He had no intention of joining his mom's group, but he would talk to Cate about all this and find out if there was a link to what she knew. Maybe what his mom had said could help them find a way through to his father's hidden mind.

Standing up from the table, Howard said, "Thank you for sharing all that stuff. It really is fascinating, but I've got a history essay due on Monday. I should get started on it."

"Okay, sweetie." She began to pile up the dinner dishes. "Don't forget to invite your friend around for dinner soon."

Howard smiled at an image of Cate at the dinner table, dressed in her goth outfit and telling his mom that she was turning into a platypus. Actually, his mom would probably be totally fine with the other dimensions/witch thing.

"Okay," he said over his shoulder as he retreated to his room.

Instead of firing up his computer, he sat and thought about what his mom had said. Her group was flaky, for sure, but the similarities to all the other stuff he'd discovered that day were striking. Howard looked forward to talking to Cate about it the next day.

As he sat staring at the top of his desk, the bouncy little incantation his mom had told him ran insistently and annoyingly around his brain.

Filleadh abhaile.
Duisg.
Filleadh abhaile.
Duisg.

Without knowing what language it was in, let alone how the words were spelled, there was no way to look up what it meant. Howard pushed it to the back of his mind and went over all that had happened that day. The day before, his only worries had been a few disturbing dreams and the complexities of daily life at school. Today he had met an extraordinary person, and she had turned his world upside down.

No, that was not quite true. The inexplicable things that had happened to him would have happened even if he had never met Cate. In fact, she had helped him a lot. He shuddered at the thought of experiencing the horror of the basement without her calm support. Howard didn't *know* what was happening, but it seemed there were only two choices: either he was going insane, like his dad, or Cate's story about other dimensions was at least partly right.

The former was the explanation any normal person—or any doctor—would go for, but it terrified him more than being in the tunnel had. And it didn't explain the physical evidence he had brought back from the experience.

On the other hand, to accept all that Cate had told him, he'd have to completely rethink the world he lived in and almost everything he had ever learned. Howard smiled at the thought of joining his mom's group—communicating with ancient lost civilizations, exploring other dimensions alongside reality, accepting the idea that some people can be in two dimensions at once and that monsters that can control dreams. Howard would have to be insane to believe all that, wouldn't he?

He sighed. Maybe a good night's sleep would help him see things more clearly. He dug Bes out of his backpack.

"Will you keep my dreams away?" he asked.

Bes just smiled as Howard slid the small idol under his pillow.

AYLFORD

An Invitation

Bes kept out the bad dreams but let in the good, so the first one Howard had was a world away from the darkness he'd become used to. He was cheerfully walking through Aylford on a delightful sunny day. There was nothing in the world to worry about, and he was so happy he felt he could fly. Thinking about it, he decided he *should* be able to swim through the air just as he could swim through water. His hands grew bigger and flatter, and as he began to sweep them around as if he were swimming the breaststroke, he slowly lifted off the ground. By moving his arms faster and kicking his legs, he gained height, sped up and learned how to swoop and dive.

It was a superb, glorious, sublime feeling, and he soared high into the atmosphere, banking, spiraling and wheeling between puffy white clouds. Aylford looked tiny below him, and he could see the cliffs of the coast and the white swell of the ocean waves to the west, as well as the dark forested landscape of the Black Hills and the spires of Arkminster to the east. He flew faster and faster, laughing wildly as the fresh air rushed past his face and ruffled his hair. He shouted hello to a startled V formation of geese beside him and zoomed over the surprised, earthbound humans below. He spotted his parents walking arm in arm through the park beside the Bane River. They both looked up, smiled and waved.

Then Madison was flying beside him, swooping and diving elegantly. "Follow me," she said with a laugh, and dove back toward Aylford.

Soon they were flying over C.D.W. High. There was Leon, driving around in his little sports car like a Lego character.

"Let's scare Leon," Howard suggested.

Madison just smiled and banked around over the other side of the school. There was Cate below them. She was waving frantically. For a moment Howard felt a twinge of guilt at being so happy with Madison, but he pushed it away. "Come up and join us!" he shouted. "It's easy. Just like swimming."

Cate shook her head. Her lips were moving, but he couldn't hear what she was saying. It didn't matter—he was having such a wonderful time that he never wanted to stop.

"Let's see the world," Madison said, taking his hand.

Holding hands didn't prevent them from flying. As long as they kept moving their other arms, they soared higher and higher. Howard could see everything. The whole of North America was below him. Europe was across the sparkling blue ocean in one direction, and Japan and China in the other. He could see how Africa and South America had once fitted together, and in the hazy distance he could make out Australia and the white of Antarctica. It was incredible, fabulous. Howard felt like a god.

Madison turned to look at him. She was so beautiful. "Isn't this wonderful?" she said.

Howard could only agree. "It's the best day of my life."

"And mine. I hope you can come to the party at Leon's this weekend. It's the event of the year, and I'm really, really looking forward to getting to know you."

"There's nothing I would like more in the world."

"Good," Madison said.

Howard's world was perfect—his dad had recovered, there were no more dark dreams of threatening dimensions, and he was not going mad or having a stroke. There was nothing to worry about, and he was going to the party of the year with the most popular girl in the school.

Still smiling, Madison let go of Howard's hand and waved at him. He began to fall. As Madison became a smaller and smaller figure above him, Howard's sense of blissful euphoria dissolved, and he hurtled through the air. He moved his arms harder, but he kept falling, faster and faster. He thrashed wildly, but his hands had shrunk back to their normal size. What had ever made him think he could fly?

Terror grew as he tumbled down. It was taking forever, but North America was growing, until finally it filled Howard's view. Suddenly, Aylford, his street, his house—all were rushing toward him at horrifying speed. He wanted to scream, but he couldn't. His dream had become a nightmare.

He hit the ground—and woke up, soaked in sweat, on his bed at home.

Howard's arms ached, and he had kicked his sheets and blankets into a tangled pile at the foot of the bed. As the sweat on his body cooled, he hauled up his bedclothes, wrapped them around himself and wondered why Bes had allowed his pleasant dream to become a night terror. Then, in an instant, he fell back into a deep sleep.

Suddenly Howard was on the same terrifying beach he'd visited that day in the basement of the AIPC. He could smell the ocean, hear the waves breaking and feel the cold wind on his skin. He was dressed in his baggy sweatpants and T-shirt, immobile in the frigid air, shivering with more than the cold. He knew what would come next: the sickening, crawling noises of creatures edging toward him through the shallow water.

He looked up to see the white ship, now close to the end of the peninsula. Out in the ocean, the island with the mysterious ruined city and the threatening dark arch was still there, even larger than before. To Howard's dismay, a horde of the disgusting sea creatures rose from the surf in front of him.

He tried to step back, but he couldn't move. He looked over his shoulder, hoping Madison would come to his rescue again. But she was nowhere to be seen. Then he had an idea. To stave off the approaching horror, Howard started to recite the words his dad had used to rescue him in the basement. "*Huilai! Xinglai! Huilai! Xinglai!*"

Nothing happened.

He repeated the words—almost screaming them this time. Still nothing. Perhaps he was remembering them wrong. He tried once more. A cold, clawed hand pawed at his ankle.

Annoyingly, in the middle of what could well be the last moments of his life, the ditty that his mother had told him popped into his head. He pushed it away. Another foul hand grasped at his waist. Breath that smelled of rotting fish wafted over his face. Without fully understanding why, Howard shouted out:

Filleadh abhaile.
Duisg.
Filleadh abhaile.
Duisg.

He awoke, wrapped in his tangled bedding.

With a hand still shaking from fear, Howard reached up and switched on the light. His messy room looked wonderfully normal. His heart rate slowed, and he murmured, "Thanks, Mom. I'll never laugh at your odd friends again."

But Howard was confused. His first dream had been wonderful, his second a horror. Why hadn't Bes protected him? He felt let down. Cate had promised. He reached for his pillows and discovered they were both on the floor. He must have thrown them off the bed while he was doing the breast-stroke above Aylford. A small green statue was nestled between them. Was that why Bes hadn't worked?

He crawled out of bed and scooped up both pillows and Bes. As soon as he held the little smiling god, he felt calm and unutterably tired. He crawled back under his blankets, Bes clutched in one hand. A disturbing thought crossed Howard's mind. Was the flying dream sent so that he would knock Bes away and allow the darkness back in? If so, by whom? He shook his head. Anything was possible these days.

AYLFORD

ARCHES

The next morning Howard slept late and woke up more refreshed than he'd been in days. The sun was streaming through his window, and he felt good as he got dressed. On the kitchen table he found a note from his mom, saying that it was such a beautiful day she couldn't resist going to tai chi in the park on her way to visit his dad. Howard grabbed a bowl of cereal—healthy stuff with dried fruit, nuts and lots of whole grains—and a glass of milk. He wolfed them down as he texted Cate. She replied almost immediately, inviting him over. He scrawled a cryptic note for his mom, saying he might be gone all day, threw on his hoodie and left.

Crowninshield House was large, with two stories and an attic, and set in rambling grounds at the end of Old Ashton Road. It had been a boarding house as long as Howard could remember, but it was once the home of the victim in Aylford's most notorious murder, Edward Derby. A man named Daniel Upton had been convicted of and eventually hanged for shooting Derby six times in the head.

As Howard walked up the curving drive, Cate leaned out one of the attic windows. "I'll be right down!" she shouted. She answered the door wearing a paint-stained smock over her clothes and holding a cup of coffee. "Want a cup?" she asked. "I've just made a pot."

As Cate led the way through to the kitchen at the back of the house, Howard, eager to show off his knowledge of local history, asked if she knew about the murder. When she nodded, he asked, "Aren't you nervous living in a house where a gruesome crime was committed?"

"When you've been around as long as I have, you discover that most buildings have something dark in their past," Cate replied.

When they got to the kitchen, Howard accepted a mug of coffee that Cate poured from the silver coffee percolator on the stove and helped himself to milk and sugar at the table. He was about to point out that he and Cate were the same age when she gestured toward the front of the house.

"Let's go upstairs. I'll show you where the coven meets."

"What?"

"Joke," Cate said. "The really creepy bit about the Derby story is that when Upton was being dragged up the scaffold steps, he claimed he wasn't Daniel Upton at all. He said that he had been possessed by a ghostly spirit."

"I'd probably say strange things too if I were about to be hanged."

"The odd thing is that Upton made his claim in a voice that, according to the townsfolk, sounded exactly like that of Derby's long-dead wife."

"Enough," Howard said. "Now you're telling me ghost stories."

"*There are more things in heaven and earth, Horatio—*"

"*Than are dreamt of in your philosophy.* Yeah, I know. *Hamlet.* I'm in the same English class as you."

They both laughed.

"There aren't many people here at this time of year," Cate said as they climbed the narrow stairs to the attic room, "so I got to choose my room. I took the attic. The ceiling's full height only in the middle, and because the dormer windows are small, there's not as much light as some of the other rooms get. But it's the full length of the house, so I have three times as much space."

Howard banged his head on the top of the door frame.

"Watch out for the low ceiling," Cate said.

Rubbing his forehead, Howard entered the room and straightened up. If he stayed in the center, where the ceiling peaked, there was plenty of room to stand. The space was indeed huge. Two dormers on the front of the house and a small window at each side let in enough light to see by, but the shadows were deep, and it took Howard's eyes a minute to adjust. The bed, a small bookcase and a bedside table were below the window at one end. At the other end was a low desk covered with papers and Cate's computer. A single chair stood next to an artist's easel with a large square canvas turned toward the wall. Several large multicolored cushions were scattered along the walls. Heimao was occupying one and regarded Howard with a bored look.

"Keep Heimao company," Cate said, putting her cup down the floor. "I'll be back in a minute."

Howard settled himself on the cushion beside the cat. "What's it like being a witch's familiar?" he asked, reaching over and stroking Heimao. The cat stretched luxuriously and began purring. "Doesn't seem like such a hard life. Maybe I should get a familiar. Then I'd have someone to talk to. The trouble with talking to humans is that they react. Cate's not bad—I feel I can say most things to her, although sometimes her responses are a bit odd. On the other hand, I have to be really careful with what I say to my mom."

As Howard stroked Heimao he let his thoughts drift back over the previous night's dream. "I suppose if I had a conversation with Madison in real life, she'd just say something dumb."

Heimao purred more loudly, as if she agreed.

"Actually, I had a conversation with Madison in my dream last night," he told the cat, "and she didn't say anything dumb. I was really happy, but I think I'll skip that bit when I tell Cate about it. I don't want her to be jealous that I'm dreaming of someone else." He fell silent when he heard Cate ascending the stairs.

"You two seem to be getting on all right." She settled onto a cushion.

"These are really comfortable," Howard said, working his body deeper into the cushion's softness.

"They're much better than regular furniture in an oddly shaped room like this," Cate said. "Sometimes I just spend the whole night on them."

"The room's not what I expected."

"What did you expect? Vials of potions and dried bat wings hanging from the ceiling?"

"Of course not. But for someone as smart as you, I *did* expect more books."

"I've got all I need here." Cate pulled a tablet out of her satchel. "Besides, I can't lug around too many books when I travel as much as I do. Did you put Bes under your pillow last night?"

"I did," Howard answered, "and I had two dreams." He told Cate about flying and seeing the world and how wonderful it felt, but he edited out Madison's appearance.

Cate was staring intently at him. "That was it? That was the dream?"

"The first one," Howard confirmed. "I guess when I was moving my arms around in the dream, I knocked Bes to the floor. In the second dream I was back at the same beach I went to during my fit at the AIPC. The only thing different was that the white ship was closer to the end of the peninsula." He hesitated. Just talking about the dream brought back the numbing fear of being on the beach.

"Was anything different on the island?"

"It might have grown a bit, but the arch was there and so were all the weird stone blocks with the inscriptions on them. I felt a sense of dread when I looked at the ruins. The blocks of stone and the fallen pillars were wrong somehow, like the buildings in ruin shouldn't have been possible. I can't describe it, but I was sure no one should have been able to build that city."

"No one human," Cate said softly.

"And there was something odd about the arch too," Howard went on, the memories flooding in faster now. "It was black inside, and not just shadow. I got the feeling the darkness was solid, yet a cold wind was blowing out of it. I could feel it on the beach." He shivered at the memory.

"No creatures though?"

"Not on the island. They were all coming for me on the beach."

"Wow! Scary."

"No kidding. They were rising out of the sea. It was terrifying. Their webbed hands were clutching at me, and I was sure they wanted to kill me. But I had a much deeper sense of fear when I looked at the island. What I couldn't see through the arch was terrifying."

Howard fell silent. He was emotionally drained, as if he'd just lived through the dream again.

Cate stared at him for a long time. Then she stood up. "There's something I think I should show you," she said, moving over to the easel at the end of the room.

Howard stood by her side as she turned the canvas around.

"I'm not happy with it," she said. "The proportions are wrong, and it's too bright. It should be much darker than this."

In fact, the painting was remarkably dark. It was completely black around the edges. Then fragments of ruined buildings began to appear as half-seen, ghostly shapes. At the center of the painting was a well-defined black arch made of massive interlocking stones.

Howard gasped. "That's the arch from my dream!"

"I thought it might be."

"The only difference is that the arch in my dream was covered with marks and hieroglyphs, and it was on an island out in the sea."

"Mine could be on an island." Cate reached out and gently touched the black shape in her painting. "I never saw a white ship. Everything around the ruins and the arch was black. The darkness could have been hiding anything. You're certain it's the same arch?"

"Yes, absolutely. It has the same feeling of strangeness. When did you paint it?"

"After a dream I had almost a week ago."

"You saw it in a dream before I did? Have you dreamed about it since then?"

Cate shook her head. "Just that one time, and I didn't see it clearly. We're dreaming about the same arch, but you're seeing it and its surroundings in much more detail. It's almost as if someone tried to show me the dream, but when I couldn't see it clearly, they tried showing it to you."

"That's a creepy idea, but I guess anything's possible," Howard said.

"How did you get out of the dream?"

"I tried using the words Dad said in the basement, but they didn't work. Then I remembered something my mom told me she learned at her cosmic harmony group."

"What was it?" Cate asked eagerly.

Howard closed his eyes and recited his mother's little chant. "That doesn't sound like Chinese though."

"It's not. It's one of the Celtic languages."

"Is it the language they spoke in Atlantis?"

"They spoke many languages in Atlantis. Supposedly Enochian was the most common, but no one's sure it's even a real language. It might have been made up by medieval alchemists."

"Mom also said the Atlanteans had a book called *The Golden Mask*," he said. "That can't be a coincidence, right?"

"No. No coincidence," Cate said. "Can you remember anything else your mom told you?"

"Yeah, she said there were two high priests in Atlantis, one who followed the light and one who was dark. I can't remember their names."

"Amshu and Claec."

"That's it. Mom said the chant would ward off the bad guy, Claec. Does this mean she's an Adept of some kind as well?"

"Probably, but she has no idea."

Cate absentmindedly scratched Heimao's ear. The cat looked up at her, and Howard had the odd feeling that they were talking to each other.

"When you told me about your episode in the basement, you said you thought the Chinese guy looked familiar," she said.

"And you said I'd probably seen him around when I was visiting Dad."

"But he wasn't the real janitor, so you couldn't have seen him at the AIPC."

"So who was he? Where did he come from? Where did he go?" Howard had too many questions swirling around his brain.

Cate ignored them all and said, "Think hard. Where did you see him before? It might be very important."

Howard closed his eyes. He could picture the face he'd seen in the door, but where had he seen it before? Then it came to him.

"Leon!" he exclaimed.

"Leon's not Chinese," Cate pointed out.

"No, no! Last summer Leon lost his license for reckless driving. For the first week or two of school, he was driven in by someone I assumed was a family servant. The driver never got out of the car, so I only caught a glimpse of him a couple of times, but it was definitely the Chinese guy from the basement. I'm certain of it. He had the same long gray face. But how can that be? Why was Leon's driver in the basement of the AIPC?"

"You say you first saw the face just before you had the fit?" Howard nodded.

"And it spoke to you?"

"Yeah. It said, *Welcome. I have waited long for you.* What did that mean?"

Again Cate ignored his question. "When you came to, the face said something else?"

Howard nodded. "*I have found you at last.* What's this all about, Cate?"

"I think Leon's driver is more than he seems. What if he somehow woke your dad and got him to lead you down to the basement so you could have your attack?"

"But what would be the point of terrifying me?"

"He was testing you. Searching for someone who can help him."

"That's ridiculous. I'm not going to help Leon or his driver."

"You may not have a choice. Look, something tested your dad—something immensely powerful. He beat it by shutting it out, by closing down his mind. Now something is sending you dreams to test you. It's looking for someone it can use."

Howard shivered. The words *I have found you at last* suddenly had a much more sinister meaning. He was still struggling with the implications of what Cate was telling him when she went off on one of her tangents.

"What did Madison say to you in your dream last night?"

"She said—" And then it hit him. He hadn't mentioned that Madison was in his dream. He stared at Cate. "How did you know she was in my dream?"

"Heimao told me," she said matter-of-factly.

"What?" Howard stared at the cat.

Heimao stared back at him with green eyes that seemed so deep he felt he was being drawn into them. Howard looked back at Cate, who was almost smiling at him. "You're joking, right?"

Cate shrugged. "Okay, how about this? Madison was in your last dream, so I assumed she would be in this one as well. Is that a more comfortable explanation?"

"Okay," Howard said grudgingly. "She *was* in my flying dream. She invited me to the big party this weekend at Leon's house."

Cate frowned, and Howard worried that he'd offended her. But she just said, "I think we should accept her invitation and go to Leon's party."

"What? We're not members of that crowd, and in real life we weren't even invited. There's no way we could fit in with those people, even if we're allowed through the door. Besides, the party was last night."

"Yeah, but at school Leon said it was going to be an all-weekender. It'll definitely be on tonight as well. That might make it easier to get in. And think about it. Everything is leading us to Leon's house—Aileen's story about Wat Heely and Josiah Whateley, the Chinese guy who appeared during your attack, and now Madison in your dream."

"What do you think we'll find there?"

"I don't know, but I do know one thing we should do before we go. We need to read the book."

EARTHQUAKE

"We won't make it." It was evening, and Chen and Ting were on the hillside high above the eastern end of Min Lake. They had stopped to drink and water the horses where a small stream crossed the road.

"They're getting closer," Chen agreed, looking back at a dust cloud that was nearer every time he checked. He stretched. Every bone in his body hurt, and it felt as if his insides had been shaken and rearranged.

"The scouts ahead of the army are only a mile or two back, and they're moving fast," Ting said with urgency. "They will overtake us on the open stretch of road sloping down to the plain."

Chen had trouble caring. He felt so miserable after the long day on horseback that capture and torture almost seemed like something to hope for.

"It's too open ahead," Ting went on. "We'll have to find somewhere to hide. Do you see that cliff up there?"

Chen grunted in reply.

"If we follow the base of it around the shoulder of the mountain, we might find a cave or a wide overhang. We'll be out of sight of the road, but we should still be able to see what's happening out on the plain. Come on."

Ting led her pony off the road and up the hillside, with Fu, happy to be let go, frolicking at her feet. Chen forced his stiff muscles to move and stumbled behind her.

"Come on," she repeated. "We have to hurry!"

With Ting's encouragement and Fu rushing back to see what was keeping him, Chen forced himself to increase his plodding pace up the slope. He had never felt less like a wushu master. Every step hurt. But the more that he took, the more his stiff joints eased. By the time they'd reached the foot of the cliff, he could almost believe he would be able to move normally again one day.

"Here they come," Ting said, looking back at the road.

Chen turned to see the first mounted riders in the distance. "I hope there's a big cave," he said as he tried to hurry on and ignore his pain.

"I think we're far enough around now," Ting said after a few minutes. "We can't be seen from the road, but we'll be able to see the army when it comes out of the valley and onto the plain."

"That won't do us or Sanxingdui any good," Chen said wearily. "We needed to stay in front of them. We've failed."

"We have no choice," Ting said. "We've done our best, and who knows what will happen tomorrow. Let's at least make ourselves as comfortable as possible." She led the way to an overhang that was already in deep shadow. They encouraged the horses in with coarse grass pulled from the hillside and collected enough to build a small pile in front of each animal.

"I wish I ate grass," Chen said wistfully as he watched the horses eat. "I've had nothing but a few berries for days."

"At least Fu and I got fed. We can go days without food, and we've had plenty of water today, so we'll be okay."

"If being incredibly hungry and in great pain is how you define okay, then yes, we are."

Ting laughed. It made Chen feel happier than he had in days. "At least we're together and away from Shenxian," he said.

"Yes," Ting agreed. She clasped his hand. "Thank you for coming to rescue Fu and me."

Chen blushed in the cool evening air. "The emperor suggested that I follow Shenxian and spy on him, but I saw it as a chance to rescue you. How did you learn to ride a horse so well?"

"I didn't grow up in Sanxingdui," Ting explained. "My parents were Ma Zhang. All the Ma Zhang learn to ride almost before they can walk."

"How did you end up in Sanxingdui?"

Ting hesitated. "When I was six years old, my father got into an argument over a horse with the clan leader. There was a fight, and my father was killed. My mother took me and my brother, Jian, and fled across the mountains."

"I didn't know you had a brother."

"Jian was older than me and never settled in Sanxingdui. One night he just disappeared. Mother said he went back over the mountains to avenge Father's death, but I don't know. We never heard anything from him again."

"That must have been hard."

"It was, but I grew to love Sanxingdui—and I got to meet Fu and you."

Ting squeezed Chen's hand, and they sat in companionable silence, listening to the comforting sounds of the horses chewing and Fu snoring. Soon the more distant sounds of the army passing on the road became audible. Later, in the darkness before the full moon rose, they saw the flickering lights of fires being lit on the plain below. The army was setting up camp beside the river flowing down from Min Lake.

Chen was thinking of asking Ting if they should try to sneak past the army in the dark, but he fell asleep in a huddled heap before he had a chance to put his thoughts into words.

>○

He was woken by Fu, who was yapping insanely and running around in circles outside their overhang. Chen rolled over and stretched, noticing a few new aches from sleeping on the ground.

"What's the matter, Fu?" Ting asked as she stirred beside him. "What's upsetting you?"

Chen hauled himself upright and stepped out onto the open slope, worried that Fu had sensed some of Shenxian's soldiers approaching. But in the pale predawn light, he could see that the slope was deserted in all directions. The army camp was too far off for anyone to hear the noise Fu was making, but Chen could see activity as soldiers prepared for the march on Sanxingdui.

"There's no one here," he said. He had just taken a step toward Ting when the horses whinnied loudly and bolted out from the overhang, knocking him aside. They set off at a gallop across the slope. Fu stopped yapping, stared for a moment at Ting and Chen and then set off after the horses.

"What's the matter with them?" Chen asked.

"I have no idea, but we should go after them. They're our best hope of getting back to Sanxingdui."

The pair set off to retrieve the fleeing animals. They hadn't got far when Fu returned at top speed to see where they were. He led them to a flat area on the hillside where the horses were shuffling about nervously and whinnying.

"What's the matter with them?" Chen asked.

"I don't know." Ting moved forward to try to calm the jittery animals. "I've never seen this kind of behavior for no reason."

As Chen followed Ting to the horses, he began to hear a low, grumbling roar. It seemed to be coming from the ground below him—and it was getting louder. He only had time to ask, "What's that?" before the ground beneath his feet dropped away. He lurched forward and fell, colliding with the ground as it jumped up to meet him.

Chen tried to get to his feet, but it was impossible. It was as if waves were passing through the solid ground. He began to feel seasick. He saw Ting curled into a ball with Fu beside her. The horses looked as if they were dancing as they struggled to stay on their feet.

The noise was deafening, and the air was becoming thick with dust. Chen was convinced he was going to die. The earth was trying to kill him. He had done something to offend the gods, and now the mountains were about to shake him off.

Then it stopped. The roar died away to a low grumble, and the ground returned to doing what it normally did—nothing.

Breathing hard, Chen stood up. The horses were standing still. For a few moments they looked around and sniffed the air, and then they began placidly cropping the grass at their feet. Fu was lying on his belly, panting.

Chen stepped over and helped Ting to her feet. "What happened?" he asked.

"Earthquake," Ting said.

The pair looked down the slope through the settling dust. The army camp was a chaos of collapsed tents, panicked men and stampeding horses.

"This is our chance," Chen said. "It'll take them a while to catch their horses and get organized."

When Ting didn't answer, he looked at her. She was staring, openmouthed, over his shoulder. "The mountain's falling," she whispered.

Chen spun around to look at the mountain across Min Lake. It *was* falling. A huge wedge of earth and rock was sliding in slow motion down the mountainside, leaving a raw scar of bare rock above it. Large trees were being snapped like matchsticks and carried along as the slide grew and sped up. Rocks splashed into the lake. Then the main body of the landslide hit it.

The blue surface of Min Lake foamed white, and an enormous surge of water swept across it. As more earth and rock crashed down, the surges became bigger. They crashed against the ridge blocking the valley and holding the lake in place. Soon the surges overflowed the ridge, cutting great gouges through it. Immense jets of muddy water, thick with rocks and trees, ate away at the gouges until they joined to form a single thundering torrent that hurtled down the valley toward the plain—and the army camp.

The soldiers had seen the landslide and the water spilling over the ridge. Chen and Ting watched in silence as those who could grabbed horses and fled. The rest ran for their lives away from the river. The flood tore through the abandoned tents, creating a deeper river valley and sweeping far out onto the plain.

"I think the mountain just saved Sanxingdui," Chen said when he had recovered enough to speak.

"I think we've been given a chance," Ting agreed, turning back toward the horses. "We must take it."

AYLFORD

READING LESSONS

Kun Zhuang—emperor of Sanxingdui, the City of Masks, and all the surrounding lands that can be reached on a galloping horse in five days, lord of all creatures from the largest elephant in the royal menagerie to the tiniest mite in the straw bed of the poorest peasant, and keeper of the Golden Mask—sniffed.

A young servant boy, dressed in a gold-trimmed green uniform with a twisting imperial dragon on the front, scuttled forward from his position behind the emperor and offered him a silk handkerchief. Kun wiped his nose on the richly embroidered sleeve of his dressing gown and waved his arm dismissively.

"Thank you, Chen," he said, "but I would prefer if you brought Jingshen and me some tea."

The boy bowed and turned away, but he skidded to a halt when he realized the emperor was still talking.

"And make certain that foul-smelling dog is nowhere near the royal tea urn. Last time you served tea, it smelled as if you had drawn the water straight from the drinking trough in the imperial kennels."

The boy bowed even more deeply and fled.

"He's a good boy," Kun said to the tall, elegant woman seated cross-legged on the other side of the low table. "But his mind is always on either that kitchen girl, Ting, and her pet dog, or on his crazy dream of becoming a wushu master." He smiled at his guest.

"One day he will do great things," the woman predicted. Her snow-white hair hung straight over her shoulders, framing a gentle, high-cheekboned face. She returned Kun's smile with gray eyes that hinted she could read his most intimate thoughts.

"This is just a story," Howard said. He and Cate were sitting side by side on her cushions. Cate was translating the brittle yellow pages of *The Golden Mask.*

"What were you expecting?" she asked.

"I don't know...spells and things? It's supposed to tell us ancient secrets about other dimensions and the Elder Gods, and it's a cute little story."

"What better place to hide secrets?"

Cate resumed reading, but Howard was after more than a simple tale of emperors, sorcerers and serving boys. "Okay, I get the gist of the story, and I'm kind of fond of Chen, Ting and Fu, but it happened thousands of years ago on the other side of the world. What does it have to do with us?"

"The Golden Mask on the jade pillar beneath the city was incredibly powerful—powerful enough to keep the portal to other dimensions closed."

"Or to open it," he suggested.

"Exactly. When the Realm of the Elder Gods swirled close to our world, Kun and his city were safe only as long as the Golden Mask was in the Chamber of the Deep and protected by spells."

"But Shenxian was powerful enough to break the spells."

"Yes, and if he had succeeded in wearing the mask, the Elder Gods would have come through the portal and destroyed our entire world."

"Okay, but it still happened thousands of years ago. The people in the story are long dead, and the Golden Mask's lost. What does this have to do with us?"

"We live in a time very similar to that in which the book is set."

"How so?"

"I think someone—or something—is trying to get the mask today, just as Shenxian tried all those years ago."

"To open the portal?"

Cate nodded.

"But that would mean the end of the world!"

Cate nodded again.

"Why would anyone want to do that?"

"Power has a way of seducing people into doing stupid things. The book told us that about Shenxian."

"What does all this mean for us?"

"Remember when I told you that I'd been having dreams about you? That I sensed there was something malignant hiding in the darkness, watching?"

"How could I forget?"

"I think that whatever is watching is trying to manipulate you through your dreams."

"Why me? I'm still just a high-school kid who's scared of the dark. I have no control over any of this. There's no point in anything manipulating my dreams."

"Chen and Ting were just a couple of kids with an annoying dog, and yet they saved the world."

"You're saying that you, me and your cat have to save the world?"

"Maybe," Cate said. She was staring so intensely at Howard that he was beginning to feel uncomfortable. "Actually, I think you're the key to everything that's happening. I think you have much greater power than you imagine."

"I don't!" Howard shouted. "I'm not the key to anything. I'm just an ordinary kid who doesn't want to go crazy like his dad." He jumped up from the cushion and started pacing up and down the room. "I don't believe you. We're not ants. There are no other dimensions or monsters. The world's not in danger. It's just the same place it has always been. The Golden Mask is just part of a story. I don't have special powers, and I'm not a superhero. Leave me alone!"

Howard's outburst drained him and left him shaking. He collapsed back on the cushion and stared at Cate, who looked at him calmly. Heimao stretched, slid off her own cushion and settled herself on Howard's lap.

"*Be calm, Sheepherder,*" a voice inside Howard's head said.

"What?" he asked, staring at Cate.

Her lips hadn't moved.

"*Be calm,*" the voice repeated.

Howard looked down at Heimao. The cat stared back with those unsettling eyes. "No," Howard said.

"*Yes,*" the voice insisted.

"You're a cat. You can't talk."

"*And yet, Sheepherder, you hear me.*"

Nothing about the cat moved, and still the voice entered Howard's head just as if the words were spoken aloud.

"What's happening?" Howard asked Cate.

"*It's simply one more impossible thing, Sheepherder,*" the voice said.

"Stop calling me Sheepherder." He looked pleadingly at Cate.

"Heimao is not exactly what she seems," Cate explained. "She has been my companion for years and has helped me many times. She's very good at interpreting dreams."

"She's a cat!"

"*And you are merely a sheepherder,*" the voice said as Heimao hopped off Howard's lap and returned to her cushion.

"You must forgive her," Cate said. "She sometimes has a bit of an attitude."

"A talking cat with an attitude. Am I suddenly in a Disney movie?"

"Yesterday you accepted that I was a witch and that there are things in the world you don't understand. Why can't you accept that Heimao has her share of talents?"

Howard held his head in his hands and closed his eyes. He concentrated on his breathing until he had calmed down. After everything he had been forced to believe over the past twenty-four hours, what difference could a talking cat make? Either at least some of what Cate—and Heimao—had told him was true or…well, he didn't want to think about the alternative. That led to a room in the AIPC.

He raised his head and opened his eyes. "Okay, I'm calm." He glanced at Heimao, who appeared to be asleep. "Let's say I agree that the book gives us background. How does that help us? It doesn't tell us what to do now."

"Oh, but we *do* know what to do now. We must go to Leon's party. Everything points to that."

"And what then?"

"At the beginning of the book, the only bit of the ancient prophecy that Jingshen doesn't understand is the reference to the Ivory Ark. What does that remind you of?"

"I don't—" Howard began to say, but then it suddenly came to him. "The white ship that I keep seeing."

"It must be important. And it's closer to the beach every time you dream of it."

"And you think we can somehow get to it from Leon's?"

Cate shrugged. "It worked for Madison."

Howard couldn't think of an argument against that, but he wasn't thrilled by the idea of deliberately trying to get back to the beach with the creatures that had terrified him so much. "Assuming we get to the white ship, what do we do then?"

"Madison gave us the answer to that as well."

Howard ran through the things Madison had told him. "No way," he said finally. "She told me to go through the arch. I can't do that. That's worse than going back to the beach. I was terrified just looking at it."

"Maybe we won't have to go through it. But we have to do something, and the only place we can start is at Leon's party." Cate retrieved a folded sheet of paper from her pocket. "Maybe this will help. It was inside the back cover of the book."

Carefully she unfolded it. Curved black lines and odd geometric shapes almost filled the yellowed page. "I think it's a map."

"It's not a map to anywhere I've ever been."

Cate raised her eyebrows.

"Okay, okay," Howard held up his hands in mock surrender. "I know that's not saying much, and there are entire dimensions that I've never seen, but what *is* it a map of, and how will it help us?"

"I don't know," she admitted, "but I think it's important, just like the book. We have to get to the white ship."

"Okay. Let's go crash the party of the year."

AYLFORD

Moving Up the Social Ladder

"It's too early to go there yet," Howard said. He, Cate and Heimao were climbing Hangman's Hill, and the houses around them were growing larger and fancier. "I mean, I assume they were partying hard last night and it's only late morning now. Most people will still be asleep, and we'll really stand out among those who are up." As much as anything, Howard was looking for an excuse to turn around and go back to somewhere safe and comfortable. The trouble was, he wasn't sure there was *anywhere* safe and comfortable anymore.

Cate ignored the worry in her friend's voice. She was setting a blistering pace up the hill, and Howard was already breathing heavily.

"We need to talk to Madison," she said over her shoulder. "Do you know which one is her house?"

"Somewhere along here," Howard replied, unwilling to admit that he had memorized Madison's address long ago in case she ever asked him over. "Why do we need to talk to her?"

Cate didn't slow down as she answered. "When you met Madison on the beach, she said she thought Leon had spiked her drink—I doubt it. Some shamans use drugs to see other dimensions, but I don't think they have much control over where they go or what they see. I'm pretty sure that on some level, Madison knew how she got there and how she could get back. We need to ask her how she knew that."

"But what if she's still asleep?"

"Then we'll wake her up."

As they continued up the hill, Howard began to feel slightly nauseated. He couldn't believe they were on their way to wake up the girl he'd had a crush on since eighth grade—not to mention that lately he and that girl had been sharing dreams.

"Wait!" Howard made a grab for Cate's arm but missed. "Will Madison remember last night's dream?"

"I have no idea." There was a trace of impatience in her voice. "That's something else we'll find out."

The houses now were all two or three stories tall. Many were built of brick, and a few were decorated with turrets. The yards were immaculate, and Howard spotted a gardener hunched among some rosebushes outside one place.

"I think this is where Madison lives," he said.

"*As if you didn't have it memorized, Sheepherder.*"

"Don't call me Sheepherder!" Howard exclaimed.

"Is Heimao talking to you again?" Cate asked.

"Yes. Can't you hear her?"

"She chooses who she talks to."

"*That's a bit of luck, Shee—*"

"Don't," Howard warned.

Madison's house was modest compared to some of the others on the hill, but it was still three times the size of Howard's. It was of a traditional design, with lots of fancy carved wood and a deep verandah stretching the full width of the front and disappearing around both sides.

"Are you sure this is a good idea?" Howard asked, hoping Cate had changed her mind.

Without even hesitating, Cate pushed open the gate and strode up the path with Heimao. Howard followed, nervously scanning the surrounding bushes for armed security guards or a large vicious dog.

A bell echoed deep within the house. This was Howard's last chance to flee the inevitable embarrassment, but he held his ground.

Steps echoed, and the door opened to reveal a well-dressed woman. She smiled at them woodenly. "Can I help you?"

"Good morning, Mrs. Danforth," Cate said cheerfully. "Terribly sorry to bother you, but we're friends of Madison's from school, and we're wondering if she's home. We saw her last night at Leon's, and she asked if we wanted to drop by and hang out today."

There were so many lies in this little speech, but it seemed to work. Mrs. Danforth's smile softened.

"It's so nice to meet Madison's friends." She held out her hand. "What did you say your name was?"

"Cate."

Mrs. Danforth shook hands with Cate, then turned to Howard and frowned.

Once again, Howard's lack of fashion sense was putting him at a disadvantage. "I'm Howard," he said, putting on his most winning smile.

Madison's mom shook his hand with considerably less enthusiasm. "Madison's just in the shower. Perhaps you could—"

"We'd be happy to wait," Cate interrupted, not giving Mrs. Danforth a chance to suggest they come back later.

"Well…" Mrs. Danforth said reluctantly. "I suppose that would be all right. But not the cat. I can't have it leaving hair everywhere."

For an instant Howard had a strong feeling that Heimao was about to leap at Mrs. Danforth's throat, but then Cate said, "Not a problem. Heimao will be happy to stay out here in your lovely garden."

"*I'll just go and slaughter a few small mammals and birds,*" said Heimao sarcastically inside Howard's head.

Mrs. Danforth led Cate and Howard led into a huge formal drawing room and invited them to sit down on an antique couch with ornately carved legs. "I'll tell Madison you're here," she said as she left.

Howard sat gingerly on the edge of the couch, worried that the thing would break and he'd have to spend the rest of his life working to pay off the repair bill. Cate had no such qualms and bounced to her feet the moment the door closed. Howard watched nervously as she picked up elegant ornaments from the mantel and tilted them to look at their bases.

"Wow!" she said, examining a pale vase covered in an intricate honeycomb pattern. "This is a Royal Worcester by George Owen. It must be worth twenty or thirty thousand dollars." She replaced it, a bit too close to the edge for Howard's comfort, and turned to a pair of ornate vases sitting on the floor, one on each side of the fireplace. "These are Han dynasty *hunping* soul vases. They must be close to two thousand years old."

Howard wanted to ask Cate how she knew all this, but he didn't want to distract her, so he remained silent and prayed she would leave everything alone and sit back down safely beside him. She did, but only after she'd checked out everything in the room.

"This place is like a museum," she said, plopping down so hard that Howard glanced at the couch legs to see if they'd cracked.

"Houses should be for living in," he said, "not for storing expensive stuff to look at. I could never relax in this place."

"It's all a question of perspective. You'd be quite happy here if you had enough money to easily replace anything that got broken."

Howard doubted it, but he didn't argue. "What if Madison doesn't want to see us?" he asked.

"No problem," Cate said. "We'll simply take that Royal Worcester vase and leave."

"No way!"

They both jumped to their feet as Madison appeared by the sliding doors leading to the dining room. "That vase is worth more than both your families earn in a year," she said.

Howard felt Cate tense beside him and hoped she wasn't about to say something that would get them thrown out on the street. To his relief, she just smiled and said, "I know, right? You're so lucky to have so much cool, expensive stuff. I was just joking."

Madison sauntered across the room and struck a model pose on the arm of a chair that matched the couch. She was wearing skintight pink jeans, leather ankle boots and a loose crocheted top over a white T-shirt, and she carried a brightly colored clutch bag. Her face was made up, and every hair was in place. Howard tried unsuccessfully not to stare.

"It's good of you to see us," Cate said, as if they'd been granted an audience with the queen.

Howard detected a note of sarcasm and silently gave thanks that Heimao hadn't been allowed in. Madison noticed nothing.

"Yeah. Whatever," she said. An annoyingly cheerful jingle echoed from her bag, and she pulled out a pink cell phone and examined the screen briefly. "Okay," she said, "I've got to get back over to Leon's. Why are you here?"

"We wanted to ask you something about the party last night," Cate said.

Madison looked confused. Howard got the feeling it wasn't that hard to confuse Madison.

"Yeah, well, like, I'm sorry you weren't there, but what do you want? A class report?"

"We were wondering about your dream." Cate spoke slowly and calmly.

Madison looked as if she was about to fall off the chair. "How do you know about my dream?" she finally managed to squeak out.

"So you remember it then," Cate said. "Do you remember Howard being in it?"

Madison looked like a frightened rabbit, and Howard worried that she was about to flee the room.

"How...?" she began again, but she ran out of words.

"You and Howard had the same dream," Cate offered helpfully.

"What? Howard? But why? That's just too creepy." Madison stood up.

"It's true," Howard said. "We were on a dark beach. There were creatures coming out of the water, but you scared them away with the flashlight on your cell phone, and then you went through a portal and back to the party. You thought Leon had spiked your drink."

Madison stared at Howard with eyes like saucers. There was a time when that look would have made his knees go weak, but now he just wanted information.

"How did the dream begin?" he said curtly.

Madison frowned as she struggled to remember. "I'd had a bit too much to drink. Leon was being a jerk, wandering around mumbling some stupid words. I was the reason this party was going to be such a huge hit, and he kept ignoring me. That's not fair, right?" Madison looked as if she wanted Howard's approval.

He nodded agreement and asked, "What was he mumbling?"

"How should I know? It was nonsense."

"Was it Chinese?" Cate asked.

"Don't be stupid. Leon has enough trouble with English. He can't speak Chinese."

"Then what happened?" Howard asked.

"Leon came up behind me, mumbling his nonsense. I guess he was more drunk than I was. Anyway, I must have fallen asleep. Next thing I knew, I was waking up and feeling angry at Leon. I went looking for him, but he was sober enough to know to keep out of my way, so I just left and came home early. Last night was a bust. I hope tonight will be better. I'm going over there soon to warn Leon not to be such a jerk again."

"So," Cate kept pushing, "you think Leon spiked your drink? And then you passed out and had your weird dream?"

Madison nodded. "Something like that."

"Were you scared in the dream?"

"Scared? Of what? Howard?"

Howard had no desire to scare Madison, but he was disappointed that she had dismissed the possibility so easily. "What about those crawling creatures?" he asked.

"They were gross," Madison acknowledged, "and a bit creepy, but dreams are like that, you know. Weird." Her phone jingled again, and she read her latest text. "I've gotta go now," she said, replacing the phone in her bag. "Leon wants to talk. Probably ready to apologize."

"Why did you and Howard have the same dream?" Cate asked.

Madison shrugged. "He probably dreams about me all the time. Sooner or later he was bound to have the same dream as me. Kind of like winning the lottery." She flounced toward the door. "Don't steal anything," she said as she left.

They let themselves out. "Well, that was a bust," Howard said when they were back on the street.

"*Have fun with the rich and famous?*" Heimao asked.

Howard ignored her. "We didn't learn anything," he said.

"On the contrary, we confirmed that the portal's in the Whateley house and that Leon knows about it. What we don't know is why he sent Madison through it."

"He *sent* Madison through it?"

"I doubt she could do it herself. I think we should pay Leon a visit."

"How? We'll never get away with the 'friends from school' routine at Leon's place. Besides, Madison will be there now." Another thought struck Howard. "If Leon's an Adept and really did send Madison through the portal, do we want to mess with him?"

"I doubt Leon's that powerful. Madison's so suggestible that *I* could probably send her somewhere. But I wasn't suggesting we break in just yet. We'll simply stroll past and see what's going on."

"Okay," Howard agreed. Then he realized what Cate had just said. "Wait! *Break in?* You're suggesting we break into Leon's house? We can't do that—now or ever. It's illegal. And besides, rich people have security cameras and alarm systems."

"Perhaps *break in* was too strong," Cate said, setting off toward the top of Hangman's Hill. "Let's just walk past Leon's house and see what we can see."

Howard wasn't comforted, but he followed Cate anyway. "And when we get there, what do we do?"

"Save the world," Cate threw back over her shoulder.

THE PARTY

As they approached the top of Hangman's Hill, dark tendrils flickered at the edges of Howard's vision, and his worry level soared. Would Cate stand and stare at Leon's house or start crawling around the grounds? He had visions of his mom having to bail out her stalker son and his weird friend.

Barely breaking stride, Cate walked through the gate and up the steps of the largest house on Hangman's Hill. She turned the handle of the ornately carved front door and marched inside. Howard froze on the porch, but an arm extended out the door beckoned him in. Heimao slipped past his feet and disappeared inside.

"We shouldn't be doing this," Howard whispered as he closed the door behind him. The blackness around his view was slowly solidifying, and his fear of being plunged back into the tunnel was growing.

Cate seemed oblivious to his concerns. "Why not? There's a party on, and Leon simply forgot to invite us. Besides, look at this place. There's real money in selling old books."

The two stood in the hallway and stared. The Whateley house was even bigger and more ornate than Madison's. The floor of the entrance hallway was marble, and there was dark wood paneling everywhere. In front of them a wide staircase rose to a landing, where it split in two to give access to both sides of the floor above. Overhead, a domed stained-glass window let in subtle colored light.

Open doors on either side of the hallway showed well-appointed and expensively decorated rooms. The effect was spoiled, however, by the empty bottles and cans littering every flat surface, and the bodies asleep on every couch and chair. As Howard and Cate looked around, Brad Forman, the captain of the school football team, stumbled through one of the doors, wearing only boxers. For a moment he stared through bleary eyes, and then he grunted something that might have been "coffee" and headed toward the back of the house.

"Brad seems to be enjoying the party," Cate commented.

"*A wonderful example of human superiority,*" Heimao observed.

"So now that we're in, what do we do?" Howard asked.

"Good question. We need a plan." Cate headed for the grand staircase, climbed a few steps and sat. Heimao jumped onto one of the newel posts and positioned herself like an ornamental statue.

Howard took two steps toward Cate before the blackness rushed into his vision and the stairs melted away. He stumbled forward and fell to his knees on the bottom step, terrified that he was about to be plunged back into the horrors of the beach. But almost immediately the world solidified again, leaving him confused and dizzy.

"Are you okay?" Cate asked, taking his arm.

"Everything seemed to melt for a moment. It was just like that lightning strike outside the AIPC." He took a deep breath and sat beside Cate.

"Seems as if we've come to the right place," she said.

"What do you mean?"

"Aylford is a place of power, which is why Adepts are drawn here. But the power isn't uniformly distributed across town. There are nodes or vortices where the power is concentrated. The AIPC is one such place, and the Whateley house is obviously another. You're very sensitive to these places."

"So I can expect to have another attack here?"

"Maybe," Cate said unhelpfully.

"But if I do, you can say the words and bring me back, right?"

"Maybe."

Howard wasn't thrilled by the idea of being hurled into the horrifying world he had visited before. "What about the book?" he suggested. "You told me that words were important, and that what Kun said in the book told us about the white ship and led us here. Maybe there's also something in the book that will tell us what to do next."

"Maybe." Cate shrugged. "But we don't know what we'd be looking for."

"Will you stop saying *maybe*? I've had no idea what to do since all of this began. We're just stumbling around and hoping for the best."

"Okay," Cate said, taking the book out of her satchel. "Let's give it a try."

She and Howard starting flipping through the pages while Heimao occupied herself cleaning her fur. They tried reciting bits and pieces of the story, but nothing happened—until a loud, booming thump came from somewhere below them, sending vibrations up through the stairs.

"Did we do that?" Howard asked.

"I don't think so," Cate replied.

There was another thump, followed by several loud crashing sounds. The whole house shuddered so violently that Howard grabbed the banister. The thumps came more frequently, until they had merged into a deep, continuous roar. It sounded like a powerful waterfall.

A cold drip landed on Howard's head. He looked up to see a crack spreading across the glass dome. It had gone very dark outside.

"What's going on?" He turned to Cate and noticed a trickle of water running down the stairs beside her. The wall behind the landing had become a steadily growing waterfall. Water splashed onto Howard's face. "It's salty," he said. "It's seawater."

"I think a portal is opening," Cate said. "I think this is the ocean from the other dimension leaking through."

"It's bringing stuff with it," Howard added as something that resembled a cross between a squid and a sea star flopped about on the top step. Heimao watched disapprovingly as the water poured down the stairs below her. When a drop hit her from above, she shook herself angrily.

Cate kept flipping through the pages of the book. "There has to be something in here," she said under her breath.

Just then a wall of water collapsed out of the doorway to Howard's right, flooding the hallway. The water running down the stairs had become a torrent, and now it was swirling around his legs and Cate's hunched back, threatening to sweep them off the stairs. Pieces of furniture were beginning to float out of the rooms on each side of the hallway.

"Find something!" Howard urged. "How about that thing Jingshen recited when she and Kun were talking about Sanxingdui being destroyed?"

Cate flipped to that page and recited, "*When that which is far comes near...*" But nothing happened, and the water kept swirling around them.

Howard looked over the banister and screamed. Twisting along the corridor was a large gray tentacle. "It's not working!" he shrieked.

Cate said, "Something's missing."

"You don't say."

"Ugh! What's going on?" said someone from the landing above.

Howard looked up to see Madison, water swirling around her ankles.

"I couldn't find Leon, so I was having a nap upstairs when I felt this bump. Was it, like, an earthquake or something? There's water everywhere. Has anyone, like, called a plumber or something?"

"That's what we need!" Howard shouted hysterically. "A plumber!" The tentacle was now creeping up the stairs toward his feet.

"Well, I'll call one," Madison said, lifting her pink cell phone and dialing.

Howard was wondering vaguely why Madison had a plumber's number on her cell phone when his own phone rang.

"When that which is far comes near. Read the book," a voice said when he answered.

"What? Who is this?"

"When that which is far comes near. Read the book," the voice repeated. It sounded familiar. "Now!"

Howard looked down at the page Cate was studying. The poem Jingshen had recited was in the middle of it. Desperately he began to read:

> When that which is far comes near,
> That which is closed may open.
> When worlds bleed one through the other,
> That which cannot is.
> Doors that the power of the moon may open,
> The power of the sun shall close.

The words blurred on the page. The book vibrated, and a shimmering wave moved out from it in all directions. Howard's body tingled as the wave passed through it, but the water retreated. The tentacle slithered back down the hall. Cate, Madison and Howard were standing in the center of an expanding, glimmering globe. As the surface of the globe sped outward, passing effortlessly through banisters, stairs, walls and Heimao, the water receded before it. Within moments everything was back as it had been—the floor and the walls were dry, the cracks in the dome were mended, and there were no sea creatures flopping on the stairs or moving along the halls.

"Oh," Madison said, "I guess we don't need the plumber now. I'm going back to bed." She climbed the stairs as if nothing had happened.

Cate and Howard gasped with relief and slumped down onto the stairs.

"*I* had to recite the incantation," Howard said, feeling a touch of pride.

"*Yes. Surprising,*" Heimao said.

"What do you mean? Just because you're a talking cat, that doesn't mean you're the only one with powers."

"*Obviously not,*" Heimao replied, licking her paws. "*It may have escaped your attention, but you read the poem in ancient Chinese.*"

Howard looked down at the book. The page was covered in strange characters that meant nothing to him.

"What did Madison say when she called you on the phone?" Cate asked.

"It wasn't Madison. It was Aileen from the library at the AIPC. She recited the first line and told me to read the book."

"Aileen!" Cate rubbed her chin. "Now it's beginning to make sense,"

"No, it's not," Howard insisted. "It's getting more complicated. What does Aileen have to do with anything, and why did she call me? How does she even know my number? And how can I read Chinese?"

"Madison told Aileen your number."

"What? But she doesn't even know Aileen. And she's too clueless to be behind all of this."

"Intelligence has nothing to do with whether a person's an Adept. But you were right when you said that Madison is too much of an airhead to do the things she's been doing. Somebody is guiding her."

"Aileen?"

"Yes. Most Adepts are passive. Think of it this way. Some people have better hearing or sight than others, but that doesn't mean they can affect what they hear or see. It's very rare for Adepts to be able to influence the dreams they experience. They need help. Madison wasn't calling a plumber—she was calling Aileen."

"And somehow Aileen helped me read the Chinese words?"

"It looks like it."

"So what's Aileen?"

"That's the key question. Do you remember the story Jingshen told at the beginning of *The Golden Mask*?"

"The creation story about the struggle between good and bad?"

"Yeah. Guang and Heian in the original story, then Jingshen herself and Shenxian in Sanxingdui."

"And Amshu and Claec in Atlantis in Mom's story."

"Exactly. It's an eternal struggle that is fought over and over again, whenever the dimensions swirl together. I don't think it's a coincidence that she looks very much like the description of Jingshen in the book. Aileen is Guang, Jingshen *and* Amshu in our world."

"So who is Heian, Shenxian and Claec?"

"The Chinese guy in the basement of the AIPC."

"Leon's chauffeur!"

Cate nodded. "And probably Wat Heely's servant, Hei."

Howard realized that meant Wat Heely's servant had been alive for well over a hundred years.

"Guang and Heian may have been the very first Adepts, but their origins are so far in the past that it's impossible to know for sure," Cate continued. "Both are immensely powerful, but as long as their powers are in balance, like yin and yang, everything will be fine. There is danger only when that balance is disturbed."

"Like when Shenxian tried to take the mask and open the portal to the Realm of the Elder Gods."

"Or when Claec tried something similar in Atlantis. And I think Hei may have tried something at Wat Heely's mansion. Remember when Aileen told us about the walls bleeding water? For some reason it didn't work. Maybe the timing was wrong."

"Does Aileen control Madison?"

"Control's too strong a word. She tries to help when she can."

"So when Madison goes all weird and tells me to read the book or go through the arch, it's actually Aileen? Why doesn't she just do herself whatever it is she's trying to get me to do?"

"That's complicated."

"And monsters from other dimensions aren't! Maybe we should go back to the AIPC and talk to her." Howard had felt uncomfortable in Leon's house even before the walls started bleeding water from another dimension and a giant tentacle tried to grab him. He would be happy to leave now. "If Aileen's the manifestation of good, she can help us."

"I don't think that's what we should do," Cate said, crushing his hopes of escape. "The answer's here. The power's here. The portal's here. And I suspect that Hei, if that's what he still calls himself, is here as well."

"Hei is here?" Howard said. He had a horrible sinking feeling in his stomach.

"Well, someone or something here opened the portal to let the water through. That allowed things from the other dimension to enter ours. Your reading from the book closed the portal, but Hei is getting stronger. Next time the portal opens, we have to be in the right place to go through it in the opposite direction."

Howard really didn't want to go through the portal. His nightmares had taken him there already, and it hadn't been fun. "But we don't know how to do that," he pointed out.

"No," Cate agreed as Heimao jumped off the post, stretched and headed up the stairs. "But someone here does."

AYLFORD

The Basement

"Madison, wake up," Cate said, shaking the sleeping girl. Madison was lying fully clothed on top of a king-size bed in an extremely tidy room. Heimao was curled up beside her.

"Whaaa…?" Madison rolled over and blinked rapidly. She looked less attractive to Howard with drool running down her chin.

"Where was the last place you saw Leon mumbling things before you passed out last night?" Cate asked.

Madison rubbed her eyes, wiped her mouth and stared at them. "The basement," she said.

Cate's tone became urgent. "You need to come down there with us."

"Okay, you probably have some geeky reason to go to the basement," Madison said, as if she were talking to a five-year-old. "I get that. What *you* don't get is that cool people like me, who were partying late last night, want to sleep. My mom woke me up this morning, then the earthquake woke me here, and now you two want me to go to the basement.

Why don't you just go away and, like, learn something?" She rolled back over.

"It's important," Cate said, frustration creeping into her voice. "I can't explain, but there's something we have to do in the basement—and only you can help us do it."

Madison sighed loudly and said, "There is nothing I can— or want—to do with geeks in the basement or anywhere else. Now leave me alone. I have a history essay to do this weekend, and I have to sleep."

Howard didn't know how sleeping would magically get Madison's history essay done, but it might explain why she was only scraping by in the class. Then he had an idea. "I'll write your history essay for you," he said.

It looked like a win-win situation. Either Madison helped them go through the portal and save the world, in which case writing an essay was a small price to pay, or whatever was in the Realm of the Elder Gods escaped and destroyed this world, in which case Madison's essay would not be high on Howard's priority list for the next day.

His offer got her attention. Madison flipped over, almost squashing Heimao, and sat up. "Really?"

"Sure," Howard said. "I've written mine. I can do yours tomorrow."

"You're, like, getting As in history, right?"

Howard nodded.

Madison frowned, perhaps calculating how little she would have to work for the rest of the semester if she got an A on this one essay. Eventually she asked, "All I have to do is come to the basement?"

"That's all," Cate said.

"All right." Madison swung her legs off the bed and stood up. "But I need the essay by tomorrow night. Now give me a minute. And take that disgusting creature away."

Heimao gave Madison an evil look, jumped off the bed and disappeared out the door. Cate and Howard followed.

As they stood in the hallway, waiting for Madison to get ready, Brad dragged his way past them, a steaming mug of coffee in his hand.

"Good morning," Howard said. "I see that you've dried out."

He got a foul look in return. It was hard to believe that the hallway had been waist deep in water just a few minutes earlier and that nobody could remember it.

"This dimensional stuff can really mess with your mind," Howard said to Cate.

"No kidding. You can see why anything written down over the centuries has been so fragmentary."

"Okay. So if you're right, and Madison is able to somehow open the portal and let us through—then what?"

"We go to the white ship."

"Will it take us to the black arch?" Howard wasn't sure he wanted to know.

"The only thing I'm certain of," Cate said, "is that the answer must lie through the arch. Too many things point that way for it not to be important. After we go through, we'll just have to wing it."

Winging it didn't strike Howard as the best way to go about saving the world, but they had to do something, and he couldn't think of a better option.

A movement overhead made Howard look up. Madison was coming down the stairs—*descending* was a more accurate word. Even though her clothes were wrinkled and her hair was rumpled, she was stepping down in regal fashion, her hand delicately balanced on the banister.

"She thinks she's Vivien Leigh in *Gone with the Wind*," Cate whispered.

Howard almost choked trying to hide a laugh, but Madison didn't notice. She swept into the hallway and stopped in front of them. A puzzled look crossed her face.

"There's something I have to get…" she said. Her face brightened. "Oh, right. Back in a minute." She hurried down the hall to the kitchen.

Cate and Howard exchanged looks, but Madison was back before they could think of a comment to make. Her clutch purse was bulging.

"Okay," she said briskly as she headed down the corridor beside the stairs. "Let's get this done!"

She opened a small door behind the main staircase. A momentary shudder passed through Howard—the narrow stairs looked a lot like the slimy tunnel. Madison flipped a light switch, and the three headed down.

The basement was more modern and less luxurious than upstairs. "I thought basements were where parties happened," Howard commented. He was surprised there was no one sleeping off the revels of the night before, although he would be the first to admit that his experience of parties was seriously limited.

"Who would party down here when there's everything you need upstairs?" Madison said. "So we're here. Now what?"

Most of the basement was taken up by a large recreation room, filled with a collection of expensive fitness machines and a huge flat-screen TV. There were three doors leading from the room, two of which were open. Through one Howard could see a large wine cellar that had probably been raided during the night. The other was a furnace room.

"What's behind there?" Howard asked, pointing at the closed door. As he spoke, a wave of panic surged over him. He felt cold, but he was breaking out in sweat. The door was the most terrifying thing he had ever seen.

"It's what Leon calls the media room." Madison took a step toward it.

"Wait," Howard said, reaching for her arm. He felt a heavy sense of dread, and black shadows flickered around the edge of his vision. "Something's wrong."

"What?" Cate turned to look at him. "Do you feel something?"

"I'm not sure. I'm getting the black fringe around what I see."

"That idiot Leon's locked the door," Madison said, twisting the handle to no effect. "Okay, it's not my fault. You'll still write the essay for me, right?"

Howard didn't get a chance to answer. The blackness rushed in to form a tunnel with Madison at the end of it. She was still nagging him to write the essay for her when a piece of the blackness detached itself and leaped into her arms.

"What a beautiful cat," Madison said, cradling Heimao lovingly and stroking her fur.

The blackness faded, and Howard watched as Madison strolled across the room, mumbling sweet nothings to Heimao.

He and Cate stared after her for a moment. Then Cate stepped forward and grasped the door handle.

"It's locked."

She and Howard spun around. Leon was leaning casually against the wall at the bottom of the stairs.

"What are you doing?" Cate asked.

"Well, this is my house," Leon said smoothly. "And come to think of it, I don't recall inviting either of you to my party, so perhaps I should be the one asking that question. Never mind. You're here now. Have you enjoyed your tour?"

"It's a beautiful house," Cate said.

"It is," Leon agreed, "but you haven't seen the best room."

"Which one's that?" Howard asked, finally recovering his voice.

"The media room, of course." Leon stepped forward to stand beside them.

"Maybe we'll save that one for later," Howard suggested, the frightening blackness still hovering at the edges of his vision. "We just dropped by to say hello. We have to go to the library and do some homework now. We are geeks, after all."

"We'd love to see it," Cate said, turning the handle again. Nothing happened.

"I told you it's locked." Leon smiled coldly. "But there's someone inside who can open it."

As he spoke, the door handle turned and the door swung inward. In one smooth movement, Leon slipped his arms around Cate's and Howard's shoulders and ushered the surprised pair through the door.

Although the room was dark and Howard could make out only vague shadows, he had a sense of space. There was a damp chill in the air, and a cold draft was coming from somewhere.

"Not the most comfortable place to watch a movie," Cate commented as the door clicked shut behind them.

Leon hit the light switch.

Howard's jaw dropped open in shock.

The ceiling was not high, but the room was big in every other dimension. The floor was tiled, but the walls were rough and appeared to be carved from the rock of Hangman's Hill. Niches had been roughly dug into the rock face. Each contained a statue. Some had the heads of dogs and birds— these Howard recognized from pictures of ancient Egyptian deities. Others, more crudely carved, had an African or South American look to them. A few were like nothing he had ever seen, or even imagined, before. There were squat, formless creatures with no recognizable limbs but slavering mouths and too many eyes. Some had fins and tails suggesting an aquatic life. The worst were large tentacled beasts that, if they existed at all, could have moved only by undulations of their elongated sluglike bodies. All were unpleasant to look at and gave the room an overwhelming sense of threat and foreboding. But they were not what had caused Howard's jaw to drop. Standing in half shadow, at the farthest reaches of the light, was a tall, pale Chinese man.

"Say hello to Hei," Leon said with an unpleasant laugh.

Hei smiled, clasped his hands and bowed. "It seems we cannot help running into each other," he said. "Welcome."

Hei's voice was deep and resonant, but it was also soft, as if his vocal cords had been worn smooth with great age.

As he slowly walked toward them, Cate said, "I see you're still serving Wat Heely."

Hei's smile broadened. "I have served many over the years."

"Perhaps then we should call you Shenxian, Claec or even Heian."

Hei tilted his head in acknowledgment. "You may call me what you wish. I have many names."

"What do you want with us?" she asked.

Howard could hear that she was struggling to keep her voice calm.

"I don't want anything with you. It's young Howard I want. He's the one with the true power."

"What do you mean?" Howard asked in a panic. "I have no power."

"Just because you don't know you have it doesn't mean you don't."

Hei was close now, and black spots were racing wildly across Howard's vision.

"I can taste your power," Hei went on, licking his lips. "It runs off you like a falling tide off rocks."

Howard shuddered and struggled to keep his knees from giving way.

Cate began to speak. "Don't make the mistake of assuming that I have no power," she said. "Let us go or…"

Howard never found out what Cate's threat was. Without taking his eyes off Howard, Hei chanted something unintelligible. Cate's voice faded, and she slumped to the floor.

"Cate!" Howard crouched beside her.

"Your annoying partner is only sleeping," Hei said. "Leon, why don't you tell our young friend why we need him?"

Howard stood up and turned to Leon, who was lounging against the rock wall, idly caressing a tentacled idol.

"The goth geek," Leon began, waving casually at Cate on the floor, "told you some of it, and we've shown you some in your dreams, but there is more—much, much more.

"Long before you can imagine, when you were only a single cell floating on the ocean currents of this new world, the Elder Gods came here from the distant stars of a different dimension. They were the few surviving exiles fleeing from a great war that had destroyed entire galaxies. They found refuge here, hiding from the Ancient Ones who had defeated them in war."

Despite his terror and the swirling black spots, Howard felt himself strangely drawn to this bizarre tale of primordial aliens visiting Earth. He couldn't have pulled his gaze from Leon's wide, mesmeric eyes even had he wanted to.

"For countless millennia the Elder Gods hid, but eventually they were discovered. One of the Ancient Ones read the dimensions right and arrived on this world. He was greedy to destroy the Elder Gods, but he was careless, and his enemies had learned much during their long wait. He was too powerful to be killed, so they trapped him with knots of power in the empty expanses of nothingness between the dimensions of space and time. He lies there still, in R'lyeh—in a deathlike sleep, alive and yet not alive—and one day soon he will arise to take his rightful place as lord of all."

"This is insanity!" Howard shouted.

"No point in getting upset," Hei interjected smoothly. "You have no choice now, so just listen. All will become clear."

"After the Ancient One was trapped," Leon continued, "the Elder Gods felt safer. They built vast cities of stone in the remotest corners of the world. But they missed their home. As the puny life of this world struggled to pull itself out of the slime, the Elder Gods waited and planned. At length, they felt strong enough to return to their own dimension."

While Howard listened to Leon's ancient-history lesson, he managed to tear his eyes away for a second to look down at Cate. She was in the same position as before, breathing regularly. She opened one eye and winked at him.

"What does all this have to do with us?" Howard asked, returning his gaze to Leon. "The Ancient One is trapped, and the Elder Gods have returned to their dimension."

"Well, my geek friend," Leon said in an almost friendly voice, "setting aside the stories that some of the Elder Gods remained behind in lost and hidden corners of this world, we are concerned with the Ancient One. He sleeps in death and dreams. As you know, the Realm of the Elder Gods is sweeping closer. As it does, it squeezes the nothingness where the Ancient One sleeps. The void is being crushed closer to our own time, creating a congruence. We are closer to the Ancient One than we have ever been—he can hear us, and we can hear him."

"Why do you care?" Howard asked. "You're less than a backyard ant to these gods you're talking about. They won't even notice you."

"Those of us who worship the Ancient One," Hei cut in, "have been waiting for this moment of conjunction forever.

This is our chance to awaken our god so that he may bring death and destruction to all unbelievers."

Hei spoke with a chilling calm, but Leon chimed in with eager fanaticism. "He has promised that we'll be able to travel freely through the realms of time and space. Imagine the power! We will swim in the methane seas of Titan, surf the swirling rings of Saturn and more. We will watch suns explode off Orion's shoulder and understand Azathoth, the crawling chaos at the center of everything." Leon's eyes gleamed with a manic fervor as he described his mad dreams.

"All we need—all we have *ever* needed—is the key," Hei explained. "A key to usher in a golden age of belief and allow a select few to travel to places and times you cannot begin to imagine. You should be honored."

"Honored?"

"Yes, honored." Hei leaned forward, and Howard felt a wave of nausea sweep through him. "*You* are the key. You have been chosen to awaken the Ancient One from his dreaming death."

"What is the Ancient One called?" Cate asked, hauling herself off the floor and standing beside Howard.

"Threaten me again and I will return you to a less annoying state," said Hei. "The Ancient One is known by many names," he continued. "His true name can never be pronounced by human mouths, but he has been called Xieshen, or you may know him as Cthulhu."

"Cthulhu," Howard said, his tongue twisting around the odd syllables. "I've heard of that."

"As the dimensions have swirled closer," Hei said, "some of the Ancient One's dreams have leaked through to those who can hear them. I briefly thought we had found the chosen one in the writer H.P. Lovecraft, but the time was not right, and he was weak and merely used what he discovered to write stories. But enough of this idle chatter. The Ancient One has waited long enough. It is time."

SANXINGDUI

THE GOLDEN MASK

"Where is everyone?" Chen asked. He and Ting sat on their horses in front of Sanxingdui's open city gates. They looked up the wide boulevard that led directly to Emperor Kun's palace. Normally it was a thriving place, with market stalls lining both sides and the city's residents going about their daily business. Now it was deserted except for a flock of squabbling crows and a few skinny dogs scavenging for scraps among piles of garbage.

"The city's been abandoned," Ting whispered. It was obvious, but the sight was so shocking that she had to say it out loud.

"I can see that," Chen said, "but why? The flood is not too bad this far from the mountains."

After the landslide, Chen and Ting had worked their way down from the mountains, giving the destroyed army camp a wide berth. They had met only a few straggling survivors who paid them no attention. It had taken them most of the day, and as they traveled, they had felt four more powerful earthquakes and seen columns of dust rise from landslides in the mountains.

As they had neared the city, they'd moved closer to the river, which, fed by the water pouring out of Min Lake, had become a surging torrent. It had flooded fields and swept away dwellings built too close to the old riverbank. At Sanxingdui it had destroyed the docks by the river and washed away sections of the city walls. But everything else seemed intact, which made the total absence of people even stranger.

"Even if they had been escaping the flood," Ting pointed out, "they couldn't all have fled in the time since the landslide this morning. This has been planned. Look! The sacred masks have been removed from their pedestals on either side of the road."

"What should we do?"

"Let's go to the palace and see if we can find a clue there to tell us what happened."

Leaving the horses grazing on a patch of grass by the gate, Chen, Ting and Fu made their way through the eerily deserted streets. All the masks and the huge bronze trees that had decorated the city squares were gone. Even Fu seemed overwhelmed by the silence and stayed close to Ting.

Only when they reached the main square in front of the palace did they meet anyone—and it was someone they knew. Shenxian's assistant, Fan Tong, dressed in grubby workman's clothes, was hauling a large elephant tusk out of the palace and loading it onto a handcart.

"What are you doing?" Ting asked.

"What does it look like I'm doing? I'm taking this elephant tusk to the sacred pit. Nice of you to show up and offer to help, but I could have used the help this morning. I've moved sixty-seven of these things to the pit, and you show up when I'm on the last one."

"But the city looks abandoned. Why are you still here?" Chen asked.

"Because Shenxian left me here," Fan Tong said bitterly.

"Where is everyone else?"

"Packed up and moved to Jinsha." Fan Tong dropped the fat end of the tusk onto the cart with a thump.

"Why?"

"Because the end of the world's coming. If you ask me, it can't come soon enough. I've been Shenxian's loyal servant forever, and what do I get for it? I get abandoned in this collapsing dump to work for the emperor while Shenxian goes off to find an army. I should have gone to Jinsha like the rest of them, but what's the point of that? One place is as bad as another at the end of the world."

"The emperor is still here?" Chen asked.

"Of course. He and that sorceress woman are alone in the palace." Fan Tong shrugged wearily, lifted the handles of his cart and set off around the corner of the palace, leaving Chen and Ting staring after him.

"I almost feel sorry for him," Ting said.

"Not me. When he had Shenxian looking after him, he was unbearable. He deserves the job of filling in the sacred pits."

"We should go and find the emperor and Jingshen," Ting suggested. "They'll be able to tell us what happened."

As she led the way up the palace steps, Chen noticed that the huge statue of Emperor Kun holding an elephant tusk was gone, presumably into the sacred pit. As they reached the doors, a strong earthquake shook the building. It didn't last long, but cracks wide enough for Chen to put his hand in appeared on the mud walls.

When the shaking stopped they moved into the building, keeping close to the walls in case the ceiling collapsed. Fu scampered on ahead, checking out the rooms on either side. Eventually he disappeared into the tearoom.

"Even when my city is emptied, I cannot escape you."

Chen recognized the emperor's voice coming from the room. He and Ting hurried in to find Kun sitting at the tea table with Fu on his lap. He looked up as the two bowed.

"Dogs are very clever. For all my shouting at him, I could never hide the fact that I had a soft spot for this ugly beast." He happily scratched Fu behind the ears. "I see you made it back safely. Jingshen is making tea. Perhaps, Chen, you could honor us with one of your clever serving dances?"

"I would be glad to," he said.

"Sit and tell me of your journey across the mountains."

Before Chen could begin his story, Jingshen appeared in the doorway with a tray of tea. "I heard voices," she said, "so I brought cups for all."

With her encouragement, Chen served the tea. His body still hurt from the unaccustomed hours on horseback, but he struggled through.

Once they had settled, Chen and Ting told Kun and Jingshen about their adventures, the rescue, the journey across the mountains and the tribal army's destruction in the earthquake and its resulting landslide and flood.

"So," Chen concluded, "Shenxian's plan cannot work. Sanxingdui is safe. The people can return."

"I'm afraid it's not that simple," Jingshen said. "Shenxian's army is not the danger."

Chen was about to ask her what she meant, but a deep and all-too-familiar rumble came at them from the ground below. All four of them held on to their teacups as the room swayed and the table lurched wildly, throwing the teapot and its tray onto the floor.

When the movement had ceased, Kun said, "The tremors are getting stronger."

"And more frequent," Jingshen added.

"Is it time?" Kun asked.

"It is very close." Turning to Chen and Ting, she went on, "Come and look." She led them to the window that faced the Min Mountains.

The mountains still stood, but they were dwarfed by an immense cloud of dust. The cloud was round, but streamers of darker dust writhed out from it, and lightning flashed within it.

Chen found the red glow of the sun setting behind the cloud disturbing somehow. "It's much worse than this morning," he remarked. "The dust cloud is growing, and it almost seems alive."

He sensed Jingshen staring at him.

"Tell me what it looks like," she said.

"It looks like an overturned bowl with tendrils—no, tentacles—coming out from it. The lightning seems almost alive, and the sun, glowing red in the middle, looks like"—

Chen paused, searching for the right word—"it looks like an eye watching us."

"It's the eye of God," Jingshen said.

"What does it mean?"

"It means that Shenxian is still alive, and that we must go down to the Chamber of the Deep."

"Why?"

"Because," Jingshen answered, turning to look at Kun, "that is where the Golden Mask is, and it must be destroyed before Shenxian gets here."

The emperor regarded her calmly. "You have advised me long and well," he said at length, "but what you ask is hard. The Golden Mask is everything. It is our connection to the gods and the source of the power that has kept our city safe for centuries. Without it we are nothing. Are you certain?"

Jingshen nodded slowly. "There is no other way. The dimensions are opening, and already we have a glimpse of the ancient terrors hidden within them. Shenxian's power is growing by the minute. If we do not destroy the Golden Mask, he will put it on—and then nothing we can do will prevent the end of everything."

"If the Golden Mask is so powerful, can you not wear it and defeat Shenxian?" Ting asked.

"The power of the Golden Mask is far too great for any mortal to control. Putting it on will give the wearer access to all other dimensions and all times. What Shenxian's desire for power has blinded him to is that the mask works in two ways: it not only opens other dimensions to the wearer, but also opens our dimension to all others. There are beings in those other dimensions that would gleefully destroy everything in our world without a second thought.

"The time of the prophecy has come. The dimensions are close, and the magic holding the Golden Mask is weak. I fear it is already too late to save Sanxingdui, but if we fracture the mask's power and prevent Shenxian from wearing it, we will save the rest of the world. It must be done, and it must be done now. There is little time."

The emperor let out a sigh and nodded his head. "Of course you're right. This day has been long foreseen, but I had hoped…"

Kun lifted a heavy lantern from the wall, lit it with a flint and, with Jingshen beside him, set off to the stairs that led down to the Chamber of the Deep. Chen and Ting, their minds reeling with questions and worries, followed with Fu at their heels.

The stairs spiraled down around a vast bronze tree of life— taller than the highest building in the city, yet buried deep in the earth. Sacred ornaments, statues and masks hung from the tree's forged branches. Bells tinkled and the ornaments swayed as vibrations passed through the earth.

At last the stairs twisted in more tightly, ending in front of an arch formed by the tree's metal roots. A heavy door covered in fantastic carved faces sealed the arch. Jingshen passed the emperor a large key, and he handed her the lantern. He inserted the key in the door's lock and turned it three times. The door swung out, forcing the emperor to step back.

Chen stood in the fragile circle of light provided by the lantern and stared into the blackness through the door. Cold air wafted out of the arch, making them all shiver.

Chen suddenly had the odd feeling that the darkness beyond the door went on forever, and that if he stepped into it, he would be lost in infinity.

Jingshen stepped forward and held the lantern high. Something glittered in the depths of the darkness. "You must do it," she said.

Taking a deep breath, Kun moved through the door. Jingshen, Chen, Ting and Fu followed him, and as the light increased, they all saw the Golden Mask. It sat atop a roughly carved jade pillar. Kun and Jingshen had seen it many times before, but Chen and Ting were struck dumb by the mask's beauty and radiating sense of power.

The Golden Mask was a fraction of the size of the many sacred masks that had decorated the city's temples and public spaces, but it had an energy they lacked. In the flickering lantern light it seemed to move and change expression—one moment it was smiling, the next frowning. And always the large protruding eyes were watching. Chen felt they were searching deep into his soul. The three horizontal lines incised in the center of the mask's broad forehead seemed to be winking at him.

Jingshen tapped Kun on his shoulder and handed him a small bronze hammer.

"That's too small," Kun said. "It will never break the mask."

"Sometimes the power is concentrated in small things. Strike the mask three times," she ordered.

The emperor took the hammer. It felt stupidly light. This couldn't succeed in breaking the mask! Nevertheless, he stepped forward and held the lantern high.

Jingshen began intoning:

When that which is far comes near,
That which is closed may open.

Kun raised the hammer. The mask seemed to be grinning. Tentatively he brought the hammer down on the forehead. As far as Chen could see, nothing happened.

Jingshen's chanting became louder:

When worlds bleed one through the other,
That which cannot is.

Kun repeated the blow. Chen thought he felt a shudder run through the ground beneath him. Kun raised the hammer a third time.

Jingshen screamed. Kun, Chen and Ting turned to stare at her. Still uttering the unearthly scream from her gaping mouth, Jingshen closed her eyes and jerked her head back violently. She threw her arms wide. Her body stiffened, and she fell backward. Chen jumped to catch her, but all he managed to grab was the lantern. Jingshen's body stopped falling and hovered a good two feet off the stone floor. The scream faded into silence.

"You are too late."

Chen looked up to see Shenxian smiling in the doorway.

"The ritual is not complete and never will be. The Golden Mask is mine."

He stepped into the Chamber of the Deep and pointed at Kun, who collapsed in a heap, dropping the hammer. It clanged onto the stone floor.

Chen was about to assume his wushu attack stance when Shenxian glanced at him and said, "Stupid boy. It's your job to hold the lantern."

Chen froze with the lantern still in his hand. It was as if his body was no longer under his control. He could think. He could tell his muscles what to do. But they didn't respond.

Ting leaped forward, but Shenxian waved a hand dismissively, and she fell to the floor beside Kun.

Chen fought to move, but it was hopeless. It was a struggle against himself.

Shenxian moved farther into the chamber and reached for the Golden Mask. He smiled triumphantly. But he had little time to celebrate his victory.

Showing remarkable agility for such short legs, Fu sprang at Shenxian and fastened his teeth into the high priest's calf. Shenxian yelled and reached down to swat Fu away. In that instant, Chen felt the power that had immobilized him weaken. He dropped the lantern and launched himself into Scything the New Corn. Incredibly, this time it worked perfectly. His left leg swung around and caught Shenxian behind his knees. Chen twisted his body and aimed his right leg at Shenxian's stomach. Flinging his arms wide, the high priest catapulted backward and landed heavily on the floor.

Jingshen sat up and shouted, "Chen, hit the Golden Mask!"

Ting reached over, grabbed the hammer beside Kun and tossed it to Chen. He caught it and moved toward the mask.

He heard Jingshen recite:

Doors that the power of the moon may open,
The power of the sun shall close.

The Golden Mask was only a couple of steps away, but Shenxian was recovering quickly. Chen felt as if he were moving through molasses. Every movement he made was harder than the one before. He managed to raise the hammer, but he was too far away to strike the mask. Then a voice in his head said, *Do not fight yourself. Relax.*

Chen took a deep breath and exhaled. He concentrated on releasing all the tension in his body, from his toes and fingers, along his legs and arms, into his chest and out. He moved forward. His arm came down, and the hammer struck the Golden Mask for the third time.

It was only the merest of taps, but the results were spectacular. Two fractures spread down from the mask's forehead. They ran along either side of the nose and curved away across the cheeks, splitting the mask into three pieces that hovered above the jade pedestal.

Chen felt Jingshen move past him. He turned to see her embrace Shenxian. Their two bodies shimmered and seemed to melt into each other. They became hazy and morphed into a twisting, twirling column of gray smoke. The smoke rose and separated into three distinct clouds. The clouds moved away, and each one enveloped a piece of the broken mask. The three fragments began to glow faintly within the plumes of smoke.

As Chen watched, the glowing clouds moved off in different directions. They shrank and faded as they moved away and finally vanished into the darkness. He gasped and looked around. Emperor Kun was standing by the now bare jade pillar. Ting was getting to her feet, lifting the lantern. Fu was looking around and growling, as if searching for something else to attack. There was no sign of Jingshen or Shenxian.

A deep rumble shook the floor, causing Chen to stumble.

"You must flee," the emperor said.

"Where did the Golden Mask go?" Chen managed to ask.

"Places where it will not be found," Kun replied.

"And Jingshen and Shenxian?" Ting asked.

"They have gone to continue their eternal battle. Sanxingdui will be destroyed, but you have saved the world. Now you must go."

"What about you?" Chen asked.

"This is my place," Kun said with a smile. "I must remain here and wait. I'll be needed when the Ivory Ark arrives." An even stronger tremor ran though the ground. "The three of you have done well," Kun added. "Without you, all would have been lost. I see great things in your future—yes, even you, Fu. You must all go to Jinsha. You'll have dangers and struggles, but Jinsha will need leaders. And one far-off day, when the Ivory Ark sails through time and the world is once more threatened from beyond, the three shall return and I shall be waiting. But now it is time for you to go. Flee!"

Kun's voice was so commanding that Chen and Ting didn't even consider disobeying. They turned and ran up the spiral stairs. Every few steps, the stairs bucked so hard that they fell painfully to their knees, but they kept going. Fu leaped nimbly from step to step. Above the roar of the tortured earth, they could hear the bells on the great bronze tree clanging and the bronze branches breaking off and crashing down into the darkness.

After what felt like an eternity, they found themselves back in the palace. It was night, and the shaking was worse and made more unreal by the dancing shadows thrown by the wildly swinging lantern that Ting carried. The walls bulged and cracked, and large chunks fell from the ceiling as they raced through the corridors and out into the town. Moving in a staggering run through the cracked streets and between the collapsed buildings, they made it back to the city gates where their horses, although agitated, were waiting.

But the view of the mountains stopped them in their tracks. In the flashes of lightning that danced around the dust cloud above the mountains, they saw that it was still growing and struggling to take on a more concrete shape. At its base swirling images of massive ruins—shattered pillars, walls, streets and towers—formed and dissolved. None were illuminated long enough for Chen to get a good look at them, but he had the feeling that something was awfully wrong with what he could see. The geometry wasn't right. It wasn't...human.

Nor was the thing the dust cloud appeared to be forming. The tendrils of dust looked like tentacles. In one particularly bright lightning flash, Chen thought he could make out the rough shape of tattered wings. What really disturbed him, however, was that the red "eye" was still there, deep in the cloud, staring at him.

With shocking suddenness, the earth stopped its rumbling and shaking, and in the final flashes of lightning, the dust cloud collapsed in on itself and vanished. Chen felt his whole body sag as if something had released him. He was utterly drained, both physically and emotionally. "What was that?" he whispered to Ting.

"I don't know," she replied.

"Is it over?"

"It seems to be, but Kun said that Jingshen and Shenxian were fighting an eternal battle. I suspect they'll return."

"I hope not while I'm around," Chen said fervently. Fu nuzzled his leg, and he picked up the dog. "Fu, you were awesome! We couldn't have done anything if you hadn't bitten Shenxian on the leg."

"Or if you hadn't used your wushu on him and hit the Golden Mask the third time."

"Which I couldn't have done if you hadn't thrown me the hammer. Did we really save the world?"

Ting shrugged. "Maybe. But even if we did, no one will believe us."

"So what do we do now?"

"Go to Jinsha and start again."

"Nooooo!" Chen exclaimed. "That means I have to get back on that horse. I don't think my body can take it."

Ting laughed. "You'll get used to it. And anyway, it's much easier if there's no army chasing you."

The Moon

"Do we bring the witch?" Leon asked.

"Not a witch, Leon," Hei said in a fatherly voice. "I've told you—she's a wu. Yes, bring her. Great Cthulhu will be hungry when he arrives."

As the implication of that sank in, Howard screamed, "No! I don't understand what's going on. I don't know what Cthulhu is. I have no idea why I'm supposed to be the key or what you think I can do, but whatever insane cult this is, I'm not a part of it."

He kicked out wildly at Leon, catching him in the ribs and sending him flying. Then Howard lurched and made a grab for the door handle. It turned easily, but the door didn't move. He hauled on it, but it was solid. He beat on it with his fists, but the heavy door merely absorbed the pounding. He yelled and screamed for help, praying that Brad and the rest of the football team would burst through and rescue them.

"Locked," Hei said calmly as Leon struggled to his feet. "Your voice is no more than a whisper on the other side, so no one can hear you. There's no way out of the media room—at least, not in this world."

"Calling this the media room's my little joke," Leon explained as he pulled Howard away from the door. "People think of TV, movies and sound systems, but the media in here are different dimensions."

Hei started across the room, and Leon pushed Howard and Cate after him. Howard took Cate's hand and squeezed it. She squeezed back. Neither of them heard the door open behind them.

As they walked toward the far end of the room, the floor sloped gradually before them, but the end of the room got no closer. Impenetrable shadows hovered at the limits of vision, but a faint glow, just enough to see by, emanated from the walls.

"Are you okay?" Howard whispered to Cate. It was a stupid question. How could they be okay when they were being led to meet some ancient evil from another dimension? But what else was there to say?

"This wasn't what I had hoped would happen," she replied out of the side of her mouth. "I thought Madison would give us a clue and we would go through on our own, not as prisoners."

"Did you know all that stuff about Cthulhu?"

"Some. I don't think I've studied the Ancient One as well as Hei has."

"Is Hei controlling Leon?"

Before Cate had a chance to reply, Leon cut in and said sneeringly, "We've been waiting for you a long time."

"Why did Hei open the portal and let the ocean in?" Cate asked.

"That was a mistake," Leon admitted. "We thought your presence here would be enough for our purposes. My ancestor and Hei made a similar error in 1891, when they assumed that the storm and the location of Heely's house would be enough. Now we know better. We won't make the same mistake again. You must be part of the sacred ritual."

Howard didn't like the sound of that, but he and Cate walked on in silence. The room had become a sloping corridor. It was much wider than the tunnel Howard had gone to in the basement of the AIPC. Alcoves lined the walls and were filled with strange and disgusting statues and carvings. The air became colder and the smell of the sea stronger with every step. Howard could hear the rhythmic splash and rattle of waves on shingle.

At length the corridor opened up, and the group stepped out onto the beach. It was the beach from Howard's nightmare, yet it was different. A disturbingly large moon hung in a pitch-dark sky and cast a silvery glow across the undulating surface of the black water. The island was there, a darker shape on the horizon, and the peninsula stretched out to where the white ship glimmered in the unearthly light. Howard wondered how the day could have changed from afternoon to midnight in the short journey down the corridor from the media room.

The major difference from his previous visits to the beach was the circle of monolithic standing stones that rose to his left. The stones were a deep, almost phosphorescent green and looked as if they had just risen from the depths of the ocean.

Dripping strands of twisted seaweed hung from every cranny, and small crablike creatures skittered between the fronds.

The monoliths were crudely carved from a rock that contained the shadowy outlines of strange fossilized creatures. In the center of the stone circle stood a large flat-topped block of the same stone. The sides of this center block were covered with deep carvings of an astonishing array of tentacled creatures, some of which, Howard noticed, bore an alarming resemblance to the fossils in the monoliths.

About a dozen cowled figures stood around the center block, watching as Hei lead Cate and Howard across the beach. The heavy cowls and loose robes hid the creatures' true forms. Hei waved to the figures with an open-palmed gesture, which they returned in unison.

Howard was disturbed to see that their raised hands were clawed, and their fingers webbed. As Leon gently pushed Cate and Howard into the circle of monoliths, a whistling whisper ran through the gathered figures, and they drew back. Hei pulled Cate and Howard apart. Two of the cowled figures stepped forward, grabbed Cate, dragged her over to the altar and forced her to climb onto it.

Convinced they were about to cut her heart out in some ritual sacrifice, Howard lunged forward, yelling at the top of his voice, "Don't kill her!" Before he'd taken two steps, though, cold hands gripped his arms with surprising strength and held him firm.

"Calm down, Howie," Leon said smoothly as he moved in front of him. "We're not going to kill anyone. Think of your friend as more of a welcome present."

Cate seemed remarkably calm as she took up a position on the stone, standing and facing the sea. Even when her captors left her and jumped down to the shingle, she remained still, staring intently before her.

Hei and Leon began chanting, and soon their odd refrain was taken up by the others. Together, they circled Cate and the stone three times. Her eyes were closed, and her lips were moving, but no sound came out.

When the chanting stopped, Hei turned to Howard and said, "That should keep her in place. Now you must perform your role. Time draws on, and the Ancient One is impatient."

"Whatever it is you want me to do, I won't," Howard said as bravely as he could manage.

Leon laughed. "Howie, you don't understand. You don't have to *do* anything. Your power is enough. When the time is right, he'll taste it and come."

Leon and Hei led him out of the stone circle and down to the water's edge. The chanting devotees followed. Howard was guided into the icy water. The moon's reflection looked like a silver dagger pointed directly at him. At the tip of the dagger, as the water lapped above their knees, Hei and Leon dropped Howard's arms and led the followers into a chanting circle around him. The habits of the cowled figures floated out around them like halos of a deeper black than the water. As they circled, they waved their arms in mysterious rhythmic patterns. One by one, the figures threw back their cowls to reveal the faces of the creatures from Howard's dream. The gill slits on their necks pulsed rhythmically in time to the chanting.

Howard no longer felt any restraints, but his arms and legs wouldn't move. It was as if his entire body couldn't be bothered responding to the messages his brain was sending.

After a number of revolutions, Hei, Leon and their loathsome companions retreated to the shore. Howard couldn't turn to look, but he heard the stones rattle as they stamped back and forth in some arcane pattern. Their chanting was rising in volume, and there was an urgent expectancy to it that sent shivers down Howard's spine.

He was utterly helpless, and yet he felt almost serene. What was happening to him and Cate should have been sending his mind into screaming insanity, but he was oddly calm. He felt fear and dread at what the chanting might be summoning, but it was distant, like the memory of a weight he had carried and since put down.

As Howard stood in the water and stared at the sky, he wondered why the moon was so large. It was the same old friendly face, yet it loomed over him, threatening to crash down and crush him. He remembered learning in school that the moon's orbit was moving away from the earth, so the moon looked smaller over time. Did that mean that whatever dimension he was in was billions of years in the past? He wished he could talk to Cate about all this.

Howard snapped back to awareness when he realized that the chanting and rattling on the beach behind him had given way to an eerie silence. He felt something brush his leg. Unable to move his head, he swiveled his eyes down and stared at the water in front of him. There were flashes of silver beneath the surface. Small humped backs broke into the air all around him.

Some finned thing that looked like no fish Howard had ever seen emerged from the water and wriggled frantically for a second before flopping back beneath the surface. A large jellyfish-like animal, trailing bright red streamers, pulsed and wobbled past. The surface of the sea had become a roiling, seething mass of panicked marine life—all of it headed for the beach. Creatures brushed and bumped Howard's legs and crawled and slithered over his feet, completely heedless of him other than as an obstacle to their flight to the shore. Everything that could swim, crawl, wriggle or slide was escaping to the land.

Howard raised his eyes to the horizon. The island had grown. It was larger and nearer. In the middle distance, a vast whalelike creature with long toothy jaws breached, twisted in the air and crashed back down in a fountain of phosphorescent spray. For an instant Howard thought this forbidding predator was what all the other creatures were running from, but then he realized that it too was escaping in terror. From what? Howard had no idea. He knew only one thing, and that replaced his sense of calm rationality with a mind-numbing terror.

Whatever had been summoned was coming!

AYLFORD

The Island

Howard shuddered as larger creatures collided with him, and slimy things tried to crawl up his legs. Along the shore, some immense dweller of the deep beached itself in the shallow water in thrashing panic. The horizon was alive with bolts of lightning that flared down from cloudless skies and hissed in the churning water. Howard's mind screamed out for him to run, but Hei's magic had fixed him in place, a helpless spectator to the doom he was involuntarily summoning.

Howard watched in paralyzed fascination as the island grew, shedding water in falls that would have dwarfed Niagara. For the first time, he grasped the size of the island ruins being forced up from the ocean's depths. The scale was horrifying. Who raised single blocks the size of entire buildings? What required city streets wider than six-lane freeways? And the perspective was alarmingly wrong. A pillar became a street. A road bent back on itself in endless, impossible loops. A solid black block of stone was also a cold, dark cave. A three-dimensional shape projecting toward Howard one moment became a recess leading his eye into the far distance in the next. In the center of everything was the arch.

Howard blinked repeatedly to try to clear his overwhelmed brain. The ruined city had ceased rising, but the hill behind it continued to swell. In captive horror, he watched as the hill unfolded. A colossal fin expanded from the summit. Then two wings—ragged drapes hanging from skeletal arms—unfurled and swept wide until they cloaked the city below in shadow. The hill had become a head—although not like any head Howard had ever seen before or even imagined. A vast mass of writhing tentacles sprouted from where a neck should have been. They reached out over the city and into the surrounding ocean.

Howard couldn't look away. As the mountainous thing stood up, he saw a node at the base of the twisting tentacles. It was elongated and vaguely rounded. As he watched, slits on either side opened, and two malevolent blood-red eyes stared straight at him.

Even the power of Hei's magic could not prevent Howard's mouth from opening and his panicked scream from escaping. He wanted to close his eyes—to shut out what could not possibly be—but he had to watch. He had to because this gargantuan nightmare climbing from the primordial ruins was coming closer.

Howard's mind teetered on the cliff edge of madness. A part of him wanted to fall into the abyss, to find the blessed escape of a mindless insanity that could hide the horror before him.

Then he heard the voice inside his head. *"When that which is far comes near."*

"What?" he managed to croak out.

"*Say it, Sheepherder.*"

"When that which is far comes near."

In his panic, Howard couldn't remember the next line. The monster's bulk now completely blocked the moon, and there was a tentacle snaking through the water toward him.

"*That which is closed may open,*" said the voice in Howard's head.

"That which is closed may open," Howard repeated.

"*When worlds bleed one through the other.*"

"When worlds bleed one through the other."

"*That which cannot is.*"

"That which cannot is."

"*Doors that the power of the moon may open.*"

"Doors that the power of the moon may open."

"*The power of the sun shall close.*"

"The power of the sun shall close."

Around Howard a shimmering globe like the one that had forced the water out of Leon's house was slowly spreading. It flashed and glimmered uncertainly and seemed pitifully weak compared to the forces pushing against it, but Howard felt his body loosening. He could move.

"*Keep saying it,*" the voice in his head ordered as the gruesome tentacle smashed against the expanding globe, sending a shower of sparks down into the water.

Howard began again at the beginning. "When that which is far…" As he continued to intone, he turned and forced his way through the squirming ocean life that was clogging the water between him and the shore. Cate was standing at the edge of the stone circle, yelling at him to hurry. She had been replaced on the altar by Madison, who was holding Heimao in her arms.

Hei and Leon stood together at the water's edge. Next to them were the foul creatures, their arms spread wide and their cowls thrown back to show their disgusting heads. They were staring out to sea and chanting, "Cthulhu! Cthulhu! Cthulhu!"

They ignored Howard as he pushed past them and embraced Cate. "Thank you," he mumbled.

"We don't have time," she said, ignoring his gratitude. "Be angry."

"What?" he asked.

Cate's face twisted with rage, and she punched Howard hard on the chest. "For God's sake, why am I stuck with such a wimp?" She hit him again, even harder. "Your life's a mess, and I've made it worse. Why aren't you angry at me for bringing you here? Madison's right—you're such a dork. You deserve to have Leon make your life miserable. Your mom's a nutcase, and your dad went mad and left you. You're a pitiful excuse for a human being. I don't know why I ever thought I could rely on you for anything."

Howard stared at her openmouthed. "That's not fair!" he yelled.

"*Keep reciting,*" the voice ordered.

Howard glanced over Cate's shoulder and saw Heimao's green eyes blazing with light. He forced himself to say the words even while a different part of his brain realized that Cate was right. His life *was* miserable, and he should be angry at all the things that made it so—especially his dad for deserting him.

His fists clenched and unclenched with rage, and his voice rose as he repeated the stupid rhyme.

"You're right it's unfair!" Cate howled at him. She hit him again. "Why can't you get angry at all the people who have messed up your life? Any normal person would. They hate you. They despise you. They think you're a worthless geek. Fight back. Hate *them*."

Every muscle in Howard's body tensed. Wrath, rage, fury—all swirled through him. Cate was right. He wanted to hit something. He wanted to *kill* something. He had never been so angry in his life.

"Turn around," Cate ordered, roughly grabbing his shoulders and turning him back toward the ocean. He tried to resist, but she was surprisingly strong. He was about to lash out at her when he noticed the air. All movement in front of him had stopped. It was as if he were looking at a scene painted on glass. He could see everything, but it was two-dimensional. The horror on the island was motionless—but the glass was rippling in an odd way. Confusion edged into his brain, displacing some of his anger. The ripples became more intense.

"We're not strong enough to hold it," Cate said. "Run!" She grabbed Howard's arm and hauled him in a stumbling sprint toward the peninsula.

Howard shook off her grip, his anger still overwhelming him. "You're the one who got me into all this. You're the one who's crazy. Leave me alone. Why should I listen to you?"

"Because if you don't," Cate said calmly, "we're all going to die and the world will end."

Howard could see the creatures still chanting at the water's edge. Out on the sea, the image on the glass was twisting and rippling like crazy. He was distracted by Heimao rubbing against his ankle.

"*Keep reciting,*" the voice in his head insisted. "*And go to the ship.*"

The shimmering glass melted into a curtain of fire. Howard's anger was replaced by terror when he saw how close the monster and the island ruins were. The tattered wings formed an arch that reached almost over the beach, and the tentacles probed the water close to the shore. The chanting became ragged. One tentacle, as thick as a man's body, snaked out of the water, waved in the air as if sensing something and wrapped itself around three cowled creatures. The others screamed and scattered as the three victims were whipped effortlessly into the air and dragged out beneath the waves.

The scene gave Howard the push he needed, and he broke into a run. Heimao was out in front, Cate was by his side, and Madison was close behind. Trying desperately not to think about the tentacle or the screams, he ran as hard as the loose stones allowed.

As they turned onto the peninsula, the ground hardened and the running became easier, but Howard didn't think his body could hold out much longer. He was hauling great gasps of air into his tortured lungs, but it did little good. His legs were weakening, and he was wobbling from side to side. The white ship was very close, but did it matter? One of those tentacles could smash the ship to splinters in seconds. And even if they did escape, where could they go? Cthulhu was free.

Howard's legs gave way, and he collapsed onto the beach. "What's the point?" he asked when Cate tried to haul him to his feet.

"That's the point," she said, pointing to the island.

"It's the end of the world. I don't want to watch it."

Heimao jumped onto Howard's lap and flexed her claws. *"You just want to lie on the beach and feel sorry for yourself? Watch!"*

Reluctantly Howard lifted his head and peered out to sea. Then he jumped to his feet, his aching body forgotten. "The monster...it's smaller!"

"It's a matter of physics," Heimao said. *"Things farther away look smaller. I suspect even Madison knows that."*

"Why? What happened?" Even as Howard watched, the horrifying creature continued to shrink. Its tentacles barely reached a third of the way to shore now, its wings were folding up, and its head was shrinking back into the hill.

"Two things happened," a different voice said.

Howard turned to see Aileen standing next to the white ship.

"The ritual was not completed," she explained, "and you moved away from the power of the stone circle. That weakened the portal."

A slimy tentacle broke from the sea and crashed onto the shore three feet from Howard. It moved around as if searching for something to hold on to.

"Of course, the portal's not completely closed," Aileen added. "Perhaps we should get on board the ship."

Howard needed no more encouragement.

AYLFORD

The White Ship

Howard and Cate sat in the bow of the white ship as it sailed away from the peninsula. Both were relieved to see that they weren't heading for the island. There was no sign of the monster, but they could still see the ruins and the threatening black arch.

"I wonder where we're going," Howard mused.

"As long as it's away from Hei, Leon, the beach and whatever the thing that came out of the island was, it works for me," Cate said. She looked back over the deck of the ship, where Madison sat contentedly against the main mast, stroking Heimao. Aileen was standing near the stern, a thoughtful expression on her face.

Howard looked up. The sails were billowed and the ship was moving rapidly over the calm sea, yet there was no crew and he could feel no wind. It was one more inexplicable thing, but he was happy that it didn't seem dangerous. Safety was something to be treasured after what he had just been through.

"Did you mean those things you said on the beach?" he asked Cate.

She looked at him and smiled. "Of course not. I wanted to make you angry."

"Why?"

"To freeze what was happening and give us enough time to escape to the ship. Your power is always there, but it's like a pan of water simmering on the stove. It needs to boil to reach its full potential, and strong emotions are the way that happens. I'm really sorry—especially for the thing I said about your dad."

"Does that mean you don't think I'm a wimp?"

"No!" Cate's smile broadened, and she hugged him. "I think you're the most wonderful, balanced person I know."

"Strangely enough," he murmured to the top of Cate's head, "a lot of what you said was true. Deep inside, I know I should stand up to Leon more, and I do have unfinished business with my dad."

Cate lifted her head and looked at him.

"Okay," Howard said, taking a deep breath. "This probably isn't the best time for a therapy session. But I feel surprisingly calm, considering what just happened. It doesn't even bother me that I have no idea where we're going."

"Sanxingdui."

Howard and Cate turned to see Aileen standing behind them.

"That's in China!" Howard exclaimed. "It'll take us weeks in a sailing ship."

"If this were a sailing ship, yes. But do you see a crew? Do you feel a wind?"

Howard looked over the empty deck. "No to both questions. Why are we going to Sanxingdui?"

"So you can go through the arch."

"But wasn't the arch back on the island?"

"One of them, yes," Aileen said.

"Is there more than one arch?" Cate asked.

Aileen hesitated. "Not really. At any instant in time there is only one arch, but the arch has existed for millennia. That's a lot of instants. The arch on the island existed long, long ago."

Howard's head was beginning to hurt. "So does the arch appear on the island every few hundred years or something?"

"Not quite. You see, the arch is not always in the same place. In your world, it appears to move in time."

"So will it be somewhere else tomorrow?"

Aileen shook her head. "It doesn't move that fast. We're going to find the arch when it was accessible from Sanxingdui."

"You just said *when it* was *accessible from Sanxingdui*," Cate remarked.

Aileen's smile broadened. "I did say that." She looked at Howard. "I never said we were going to Sanxingdui in the future."

Howard's headache was getting worse. "The past? But time travel's impossible."

"There you go again, Sheepherder—calling something that is obviously happening impossible," Heimao projected from Madison's lap.

Howard ignored her.

Cate took his hand. "I thought we were past the stage of thinking things are impossible." She turned to Aileen. "Okay, you've told us where we're going—Sanxingdui. Next question. What time period are we going to?"

"Around four thousand years ago."

"That's imp—" Howard stopped himself before he received another reproof from Cate.

"*Better*," Heimao said.

"So if we can go through the arch in Sanxingdui four thousand years ago," Cate asked, "where and when does it lead?"

"It leads to R'lyeh, where time means nothing."

"Isn't that where Hei said the Ancient God lived?" Howard asked.

Aileen closed her eyes and recited:

The Ancient One in R'lyeh lies,
Shrouded in deathlike sleep.
If death shall die and
Baleful dreams awake,
Then sunlight, eon-aged and luminous,
Must bright the dreadful ink-dark streets,
B'yond eldritch vaults of time.
And one, from abyss black
And prehistoric depths, must call
The prime of three to bind once more
The sundered chains of sleep
Upon the ghastly Ancient One.

"What does that mean?" Howard asked.

"These words are instructions," Aileen said. "They tell you how to return Cthulhu to the state it was in before. It's not the

Elder Gods you need to fear. They are, as Cate so creatively put it, the humans coming out on the patio to thoughtlessly kill the ants. No, the Ancient One is what threatens the ants on the patio."

Howard's sense of calm safety was sliding away. "And this Ancient One sleeps in R'lyeh, and that's where we have to go?"

Aileen nodded.

"Is R'lyeh the ruined city on the island?"

"Part of it is," she said.

"What do we do when we get there?" Howard felt he had nothing to contribute but questions.

"I don't know." Aileen looked sad.

"You don't know! But you're coming with us, right?"

"I can't. The powers of light and dark must be in eternal balance. If one becomes too powerful, it feeds power to the other. If I take on your task and use what power I have, I will simply feed the power of dark. So I must be careful. All I can do is advise and point you in the right direction. Hei must guard against the same thing. When he opened the portal in Leon's house, he sapped his own strength and increased mine. That's why he stopped short of calling the Ancient One himself. If he had done so, he would have given me immense power. He had to use you to call the Ancient One."

"And you're going to use me to stop him?"

"I hope so."

"That doesn't sound very encouraging."

"I'm sorry, Howard. This is the best I can do."

Howard already felt defeated. "Why me? Why do I have to be the one to do this?"

"Because you always have been. You have no choice."

He watched Aileen head back to the stern of the ship, nodding to Madison and Heimao as she passed them.

"It's not fair," he said. "I never asked to become involved in all this. Why can't someone else be given the job of saving the world?"

"No, it's not fair," Cate agreed. "But that's the way it is. There is no one else."

"Will you be coming with me?"

"Of course. And"—Cate glanced over her shoulder—"I suspect Madison and Heimao will be there as well."

"*Wouldn't miss it for the world,*" Heimao said. "*Or should I say 'the dimension'?*"

Howard and Cate sat back and watched as the ship sped farther out to sea. It had sped up, but its movement remained smooth, and there was still no wind blowing. It seemed as if they were skimming across the tops of the waves rather than plowing through them. Only minutes earlier Howard would have thought this impossible. Now he simply accepted what was happening and pondered other things.

"The Golden Mask was broken thousands of years ago," he said eventually, "and the pieces were hidden somewhere, right?"

"Yes," Cate said.

"And you told me that if the mask was broken and lost, then the portal to the Realm of the Elder Gods was closed—meaning that none of these monsters could come through into our world."

"That's true."

"But we don't have the mask, and we have no idea where the pieces are, yet this Cthulhu thing sent a tentacle into Leon's house and rose up out of the island."

Cate rubbed her jaw. "Actually," she said, almost apologetically, "things aren't quite as simple as I told you."

"No kidding. You mean there's more to it than backyard ants?"

Cate smiled. "Much more, but it was still a good analogy. The trouble is that the edges of the dimensions are not like a solid wall. When they swirl close together, as they're doing now, one dimension can bleed into another. In our world, this usually causes dreams. There have been cases where Adepts around the world have had the same dream on the same night. At places of power, or when the edges of the dimensions are manipulated by someone with power, those dreams can become very strong."

"Like what happened to me in the basement of the AIPC, or with the water in Leon's house?"

"Yeah. Most people would call them hallucinations, and doctors would diagnose a mental illness of some sort. But sometimes those afflicted people are Adepts seeing a vivid glimpse of another world."

"Which would explain why Madison, you and I saw and felt the house filling up with water, yet the walls were dry when the water receded."

"Exactly. It also explains why Brad, making his coffee in the kitchen, had no idea what was going on."

"Okay, that fits, but what about the beach and the island, and where we are now?"

"This is where it gets a little more complicated."

Howard laughed. It felt good. "As opposed to how simple it's been up to now?"

Cate laughed too. "Point taken. The trouble is that the Ancient One is trapped between the dimensions. As they come together, the space between them becomes squashed, and it gets easier for the dimensions, and whatever lies between them, to bleed into each other. I think everywhere we've been is kind of like a no-man's-land between dimensions. Elements of both dimensions mix. Superficially it looks as if we are in our world, but sometimes that's because we can't comprehend what we see, so we project our world onto the unimaginable."

"But we're headed for Sanxingdui, a place that exists in our world."

"True, but not in our time."

"I guess," Howard said hesitantly. "I preferred the ant analogy. It was easier to follow."

"So how about this. We're surfers. We're between dimensions, but we're riding time waves on the surface of our familiar dimension. When we drop back down, we'll be in a different time and place."

"And the white ship's our surfboard?"

"Now you've got it."

"No, I haven't," Howard said. "I'm not even close to understanding what's going on, but I can focus on the ants on the patio and surfers." He pondered for a moment. "So how does the Golden Mask fit into all this?"

"When the mask is complete and secure back in the Chamber of the Dark beneath Sanxingdui, everything is fine.

Our world is safe. Or to put it another way, the edges of our dimension are solid and don't let anything through. The problem with restoring the mask is that if someone manages to put it on, that person will have unimaginable power—the power to move between dimensions and to allow the inhabitants of those other dimensions to enter ours. As the book told us, that was why Jingshen smashed the mask and hid the fragments. The fragmented mask is not as powerful as the complete mask. Normally that wouldn't be a problem, but with the Realm of the Elder Gods coming so close, and the Ancient One being trapped between the dimensions, the power of the mask is weakening even more."

"Sooo…?"

"So the three fragments must be retrieved and the mask rebuilt and replaced beneath Sanxingdui."

"And whose job would that be?" Howard asked, although he suspected he knew the answer.

"Everything points to you," Cate said, giving him what she hoped was an encouraging smile.

"I thought it might." He stared out at the ocean racing past for a minute and then said, "Oddly enough, I don't mind. I've been more scared in the past two days than I could have imagined possible, and the thought of traveling between dimensions populated by horrendous monsters so that the world can be saved doesn't worry me nearly as much as the thought of talking to Madison at school would have three days ago. Strange, huh?"

"Not really. You have a goal now."

"And I'm not alone." Howard glanced over his shoulder to where Heimao lay luxuriously on Madison's lap. "I have you and Heimao to help me, and Madison to keep us entertained."

"*Glad to be of service,*" Heimao said.

Cate put her arm around Howard and leaned into him. "Like, maybe when we've destroyed the monsters, we can visit the fashion and makeup dimensions," she said in a perfect imitation of Madison's airhead drawl.

As the two burst out laughing, a green landmass rose above the far horizon.

Meeting the Emperor

As the white ship approached land, it slowed to an almost possible speed and entered a wide river. Cate stared at the buildings along the bank. Howard was about to comment on the unusual lack of high-rises for a large city when an old-fashioned biplane roared by so low overhead that he instinctively ducked. He caught a glimpse of red circles on the wings before two small objects dropped into the city and exploded, sending up columns of smoke.

"Where are we?" he asked as he spotted other planes dropping bombs and saw more columns of smoke rise into the air. A different plane—this one stubby and with white suns painted on the wings—dove into the biplanes, sending one spiraling down in flames. "Is this Sanxingdui?"

"No," Cate answered, looking around. "I recognize it from old photographs. It's Shanghai. Those are Japanese planes bombing it, so this must be the battle for the city in 1937."

"Wow, 1937!" Howard had known that they were traveling back in time, but to actually see a scene that had happened more than eighty years back was a shock.

"So this is the Yangtze River we're entering," Cate explained. "We're heading west and going back in time."

Before Howard could fully take in the view it was gone, and they were passing through open countryside where farmers tended crops on both sides of the wide river. They passed a walled city even farther back in time. There were no paved roads or cars, just oxen hauling carts along dusty tracks.

"Nanjing," Cate said before they moved out into open country again.

As they wound along the river, it became narrower, although this didn't affect their speed. Along the bank, the villages became smaller, more scattered and more primitive. They caught a glimpse of thousands of soldiers engaged in a vast battle. For a while they passed through a rugged landscape of hills and ridges. As soon as they broke out into flat land once more, the ship swung up a narrow tributary that wound across the countryside like a tangle of fallen yarn. The land was cultivated close to the river. Small collections of mud-and-wattle huts were scattered along the banks. The people in the villages seemed oblivious to the white ship, and although time seemed to be passing, for Howard and Cate it remained late afternoon.

At last, in the distance they saw the land rise to green foothills in front of purple mountains topped with caps of gleaming ice and snow. The ship slowed beneath the high mud-brick walls surrounding a large city. As they pulled up to a wooden dock, Howard and Cate noticed an old man dressed in ornate flowing robes standing by a wooden gate and watching their approach.

"Sanxingdui," Aileen said. "You should go and meet the emperor."

"You're not coming?" Cate asked.

"My role is here, as I suspect Madison's is." She looked back over her shoulder. Heimao slid off the girl's lap and padded across the deck. Madison looked confused, shook her head and stood up. She took a spot beside Aileen, a puzzled frown on her face.

"Wait," Madison said, despite the fact that everyone was standing still and watching her. She opened her bulging clutch purse, rummaged through it and pulled out a forehead flashlight like the ones used by cavers. "You might need this," she said, handing it to Cate.

"You have a head lamp in your purse?" Howard said, astonished. "Where did you get it, and why are you giving it to us?"

Madison frowned as if she was thinking really hard. "It's from the drawer in Leon's kitchen. I sort of thought you might, like, need it," she finished weakly.

"Thanks," Cate said.

"Uh-huh," Madison grunted as she took some lip gloss out of her bag and began applying it.

"I'll look after Madison," Aileen said. "It's your journey from here. You must go now."

The instant Howard stepped off the ship and onto the dock, he was overwhelmed by a sense of sadness and loss. He had felt safe and secure on the white ship, and now he felt alone and anxious. He wanted nothing more than to go back on board and sit on the deck with Cate forever. As if she understood, Heimao rubbed against his ankle.

As they walked up the dock, the old man stepped forward. "I am Kun Zhuang, emperor of the City of Masks, and all the surrounding lands that can be reached on a galloping horse—" He stopped and appeared to reconsider. "But you are honored strangers from far off. My puny titles will mean little to you."

"You're in the book," Howard blurted out.

Kun merely smiled and bowed slightly. "Welcome to Sanxingdui, the City of Masks. Long have I waited for your arrival."

Howard was tempted to ask how long, but he suspected the answer would either baffle or scare him. Instead, although he wasn't exactly telling the truth, he said, "Thank you. We are pleased and honored to be here."

"I would very much enjoy showing you my city," Kun said, "introducing you to our culture and hearing about yours. Unfortunately, time is against us, and there is only one thing upon which we must focus our attention—the Golden Mask. Let us, therefore, go straight to the Chamber of the Deep."

Howard didn't much like the sound of that, and he didn't know why time would be a problem, since they had just traveled back through more than four thousand years, but he thought it best to remain silent. He, Cate and Heimao followed the emperor through the gates.

Most of the buildings on each side of the wide streets of Sanxingdui were built from pale-brown mud bricks and were small and square, with thatched roofs. Howard noticed larger ones with flat roofs as they moved deeper into the city. Outside staircases gave access to upper floors and roofs. People went about their daily business, moving in and out of buildings, talking in groups and carrying goods and produce back and forth. Kun, Howard and Cate moved through the streets like ghosts. The townspeople paid them no attention, even though it was their emperor leading the oddly dressed strangers past them.

Soon they were approaching the heart of Sanxingdui. The buildings became more impressive, and more were built of stone. Jade pedestals began to appear in open spaces, often supporting strange bronze heads topped with ornamental crowns and feathered headdresses. In the first open space they came to, a fountain was surmounted by a large bronze tree covered in tiny bells that tinkled in the breeze.

Howard was thrilled to be walking through the city he had read about in *Jinse de mianju*. He could almost imagine Chen, Ting and Fu running through the streets he was walking along. The buildings became even larger and more impressively decorated, and large bronze heads and masks stood outside some buildings. Howard was awestruck, but it was nothing compared to what he felt when he reached the square in front of the emperor's palace. Here the masks were brightly painted and the size of small cars. They were also like no human faces Howard had ever seen. The pointed and ornament-draped ears, bulbously curved noses and wide, almost smiling mouths were odd enough, but the dramatically protruding eyes really held his attention. It was almost as if the eyes were leaving the face to come out and look into his very soul.

The emperor led Howard and Cate, followed closely by Heimao, through the masks toward the palace steps. At the top, in front of a pair of large doors and just as the book had described, was a ten-foot-high statue of Kun dressed in ornate robes and holding a huge curved elephant tusk.

"The mightiest of beasts," Kun said as they passed the statue. Howard had no idea whether he was referring to himself or the owner of the impressive tusk.

Costumed servants opened the right-hand door, and Howard and Cate found themselves in a long corridor leading deep into the building. Ignoring the rooms on either side, Kun guided them down it at a brisk pace until they reached a wide staircase that led both up and down. Howard hoped they were headed up, but Kun steered them down without hesitation.

The staircase narrowed until it had become the one in the book—a spiral around a huge bronze tree covered with ornaments and tinkling bells. Howard wasn't surprised to see the bronze door set into the tree's base. The door opened with the merest touch of Kun's hand, leading them into the Chamber of the Deep.

The room was dark, but a single beam of light shone down from the ceiling, illuminating a rough jade pillar in the center of the floor. The emperor stepped forward and rested a hand on it. "For countless ages," he said, "the Golden Mask sat here. It must be returned if the world is to be saved."

"And we have to go through the arch to achieve that," Howard interjected, although he wasn't clear on how replacing the mask thousands of years before he was born would save his world.

"And there is not much time," Kun added.

"I thought time was what we had a lot of," Howard said.

No one even smiled.

"The arches are around here," Kun said, stepping behind the jade pillar.

"Arches? Plural?" Howard asked as he and Cate moved to stand beside Kun. Heimao came as well, but she stayed close to Cate. "I thought there was only one arch that moved around in time."

"Three arches were formed when the Golden Mask was broken," Kun explained. "Each leads to a fragment of the mask. They were created here, but they have been moving in separate directions through space and time. Because you were delayed on the beach, they have already begun to spread apart. Time is short."

Howard wondered how Kun knew about what had happened on the beach, but he decided there were more important things to worry about. "How do we know which one to go through? And where are they?" he asked, looking around. The curved wall at the back of the Chamber of the Deep was in profound shadow.

"Look hard," Kun instructed.

"There," Cate said, pointing to the wall on their left.

Howard squinted. He thought he could make out a darker area that might be the shape of an arch. "I think I see it." As he stared the shape became sharper. "Yes, it's definitely an arch." He scanned the rest of the wall, but even though his eyes were adjusting to the gloom, he could see nothing else. "I can only see one."

"You are looking in only one place," Kun said. "You must think of the world as more than just a wall that surrounds you."

Howard was wondering how to interpret Kun's philosophical message when Cate pointed up and said, "There."

Howard looked up. There was a darker patch on the ceiling. It could be an arch. He took a step forward to get a better look.

"Beware," Kun said.

Howard hesitated and looked down. The tip of his right foot was sticking into a patch of darkness. He tilted his foot forward and met no resistance. He was standing on the edge of a hole so black it didn't even look like a hole.

Hurriedly he stepped back beside Cate. "Okay," he said, feeling a bit shaken. "We have three arches. But I still don't know which one we should go through."

"You must decide."

"How?"

"Can you fly?"

"Only in my dreams," Howard said, and immediately he understood that the arch in the ceiling was not an option. He also had no desire to leap into the hole in the floor. "I guess it's the one in the wall," he concluded.

"Do not guess," Kun said. "Decide and do. Even if the only possible decision seems wrong, it may be the wrong decision at the right time."

"Or the right decision at the wrong time."

"True enough," Kun conceded. "Now, Howard and Cate, you must go. Good luck."

"I suppose we have to do this," Howard said, hoping Cate would come up with a reason why they didn't. When she said nothing, he added, "Can you at least give us a bit more advice about what we are to do?"

But Kun was gone.

"We really have no choice?" Howard still hesitated.

Heimao crept around the darkness on the floor and stood at the edge of the arch. She looked back. "*Enough questions, Sheepherder. It's time.*"

She disappeared.

"We have to go," Cate said as she carefully followed Heimao.

"I hope this is one of those right decisions at the right time," Howard said as he followed the pair into the darkness.

R'LYEH

THE RUINED CITY

As they stepped though the arch, the Chamber of the Deep seemed to expand and elongate into a wide tunnel. The darkness was a physical presence, as it had been during Howard's episode in the basement, but here the tunnel was wider and the walls were not draped in slime. An icy wind blew up from below, chilling them both.

"We could use some light," Howard said, proudly remembering the trick Madison had used on the beach. He pulled out his phone and tapped the flashlight app. It didn't illuminate more than a couple of feet in front of them, but it was better than nothing.

Without warning, a much brighter beam of light punched through the darkness from Cate's forehead.

"*Wow!*" Heimao said. "*That's a powerful lamp. Either Leon's a serious caver, or he's really scared of going to the washroom at night.*"

"Yeah," Howard agreed, putting his phone back in his pocket.

Holding hands for comfort, Howard and Cate edged forward down the gentle slope. Even with Cate wearing the head lamp and moving slowly, Howard became increasingly worried. What if this passage took them right to Cthulhu or some other equally hideous and dangerous creature from another dimension? What if they ended up on the beach, overwhelmed by the crawling horrors from the sea? What if they ended up under hundreds of feet of water in Atlantis? Why couldn't he just go home and let someone else save the world?

"Where are we going?" he asked, as much to break the oppressive silence as to get an answer.

"Wherever we're supposed to, I guess," said Cate. "I'm not certain of anything, but so far so good."

"That's what the guy who fell off a high-rise said as he passed each floor," replied Howard, remembering an old joke he had once heard.

Cate didn't laugh, but a chuckle echoed around his head from Heimao.

"But don't you get the feeling that this is somehow…I don't know…right?" Cate asked.

Howard took a deep breath and exhaled slowly, pushing his worries away as much as possible. This wasn't like the cramped, terrifying tunnel he had gone through in the AIPC basement. He had no idea where this tunnel led, but Cate *was* right. Deep down, Howard knew he was doing what he was meant to do.

Then black feathers edged in over his peripheral vision, and a cool breeze blew up the tunnel, making him shiver. Before he could say anything, a horrible nausea overwhelmed him. He felt as if he were spinning insanely fast through perfect emptiness. He couldn't see a thing, but somehow he knew with unquestionable certainty that there was nothing in any direction. Not the feeling of nothing he knew from looking down a deep well or off the edge of a high cliff, but a terrifying awareness of an absolute absence of everything—no ground, no planets, no stars, no air, not even a single atom of any substance—stretching off to infinity all around. Howard was floating in an overwhelming sense of aloneness.

Then his feet touched ground, and the beam from Cate's head lamp cut through the darkness. She was standing beside him.

"Did you feel that?" he asked as he fought to get his heart rate back under control.

"The loneliness?" Cate whispered, her voice breaking with emotion.

Howard put his arm around her shoulder and hugged her. She returned the gesture, and the pair stood for a moment, both overwhelmingly relieved that there was another human being nearby.

Cate stepped back. "That must be what it's like between the threads of dimensions."

"It was terrifying," Howard said. That didn't even come close to describing it, but there were no words for what he'd felt.

Cate swung her head lamp around. The beam illuminated fallen pillars and dark stone blocks covered in unreadable hieroglyphs. They were piled around a black arch.

"We're on the island!" Howard exclaimed, looking around to see if there were any sea creatures crawling over the stone. "And there's another arch."

"I don't think it's another arch. I think it's just the other end of the same arch. Nobody said how long the arch was going to be."

Cate shone her head lamp into the arch—it showed only blackness. The pair took a couple of faltering steps forward. With each step, Howard's agitation increased. His breathing became shallow and rapid, and it took Herculean effort to place one foot in front of the other. He forced his way forward until he was close enough to reach out and touch the stones on either side of the arch.

Cate's lamp still showed nothing. It was as if the darkness in the arch was thicker somehow—too thick to allow light to pass through. It was the blackness that had been affecting Howard's vision, but it was deeper and more frightful than anything he had ever experienced. His fists were clenched, and he was beginning to sweat profusely. He knew with absolute certainty that the blackness was hiding horrors he could not even imagine.

"I can't go in there," he managed to croak out.

"Me neither." Cate's voice sounded just as strained as Howard's.

"*I'm not keen on it myself,*" Heimao added.

Howard glanced at Cate and saw she was tense and sweating. The three stood paralyzed, staring into the utter black. It was Cate who moved first, lifting her head to sweep her light slowly around the edge of the arch. The narrow beam illuminated a series of geometric symbols, curling whorls and hieroglyphs representing no animals Howard had ever seen. They seemed random, but he had a strong sense that the symbols were writing in some unknown language.

"What does it mean?" he asked.

"It's an incantation," Cate replied.

"Can you read it? What's its purpose?"

She waited a long time before answering. "I can read it. It opens the portal."

"You mean it lets us out this end of the arch?"

Cate nodded. Her beam was fixed on a large hieroglyph at the center of the writing. It showed the globular mass of writhing tentacles, set around teeth-lined mouths and far too many eyes, that they had glimpsed as a statue in Leon's media room. It was crudely carved, but it radiated a primitive power that forced Howard to look away.

"What is that?"

"Yog-Sothoth," Cate said. She paused and then continued in a monotone, as if reciting something from memory. "The blind idiot god Azathoth, who gnaws hungrily in unlit chambers at the center of Ultimate Chaos, gave birth to Nyarlathotep, who lives at the center of the world and who in turn birthed Yog-Sothoth, the keeper of the gate."

"Those names don't sound Chinese," Howard said.

"These names are older than China. They are older than humanity itself."

"Okay," Howard said hesitantly. "Can this Yog-Sothoth open the portal for us?"

"He can."

"Then let's say the incantation and do whatever it is we have to do."

Cate turned to look at Howard. Her eyes were wide with fear. "There are two problems. First, although the words on the arch will open the gate for us, they are also an incantation to revive the dead. And second, Yog-Sothoth is the grand sire of Cthulhu."

"Sooooo, what else will happen if you say the incantation?"

"We'll go through the portal and then...I don't know."

"But we have no choice," Howard said, struggling to sound braver than he felt. "We have to say it. We've come too far to stop now. We must take the next step. It's either that or wait in terror for Hei and Leon to find another way to summon the horror back into our world. To never sleep because of the insanity of the dreams beckoning us. To be always looking over our shoulders, in whatever short time is left, for the wall that is leaking seawater or the disgusting tentacle reaching out of the nearest sewer."

Heimao surprised Howard by saying, *"That was awesome! Really well said."*

Despite his fear, Howard smiled. "Thank you. It just sort of popped into my head."

"You're right," Cate said. "We have no choice. Here goes."

As she started the incantation, her voice was deeper than normal and came from far back in her throat. It sounded as if she was almost choking at some parts. Howard stood beside her, looking around nervously and wondering if the world was about to end.

Cate intoned:

Y'ai'ng'ngah
Yog-Sothoth
H'ee-L'geb

F'ai Throdog
Uaaah.

She finished with a long-drawn-out wail, and they both looked expectantly at the arch, Howard silently praying that no huge, slimy tentacle was going to whip out and drag them both into whatever hellish dimension existed on the other side of the dark.

Nothing happened.

There was a long, soft sigh and a cool, gentle breeze that carried the faintest suggestion of piped music. The darkness thinned, and the light slowly revealed a titanic vista of shattered walls, crumbling towers and cracked streets running off as far as the head lamp's beam could discern.

Nervously the three edged forward. Nothing horrifying happened as they passed under the arch, and Cate and Howard both sighed with relief. As they took their first tentative steps along the street, they noticed that the sky was lightening. They looked up, but there was no obvious source. The light was flat and dull and seemed to be coming from everywhere at once, and it cast no shadows. It was as if there were high clouds diffusing the light, but there was no brighter spot where a sun or a full moon could have been. Cate switched off her head lamp.

The road that stretched before them was constructed from irregularly shaped slabs of dark, fine-grained greenish rock. There was a layer of gray dust on top that muffled the sound of their footsteps and preserved their prints as they progressed. As they proceeded cautiously forward, they had to weave between or clamber over huge stone blocks that had fallen from the surrounding walls. Heimao kept as close as possible.

"Where do we go?" Howard asked as he apprehensively checked the buildings on either side.

"The most powerful place in a city is usually at the center," Cate replied. "That's where most cultures build their important temples and cathedrals. I assume this road will lead there."

What Cate said made sense, but Howard also had an idea. There were towers rising from the ruins along the road. "If there's a way up one of these towers," he suggested, "we might be able to get a sense of where we are and how far we have to go."

Cate agreed, and they selected the least damaged nearby tower and entered by climbing over a pile of rubble in the doorway. The faint light illuminated a hollow space about the size of a regular house. The floor was littered with masonry blocks that had crashed down from above. The space narrowed gradually as the walls rose to a ragged circle of light at the top. There was a spiral ramp winding around the inside of the wall. It looked sturdy enough and was about the width of a normal corridor, but there was no guardrail, so if something went wrong, it was a straight drop to the ground.

"*If you have no objection,*" Heimao said to both of them, "*I'll wait here. Someone has to guard our rear.*"

As they started up the spiral ramp, Cate said, "Heimao doesn't have much of a head for heights."

"She's a cat," Howard pointed out. "They always land on their feet."

"As you may have noticed," Cate said, "she's not quite your ordinary household tabby."

They climbed slowly, one behind the other, keeping tight against the inside wall. Howard hadn't said anything, but he wasn't particularly keen on heights himself. A visit to Niagara Falls when he was eight had been a traumatic experience that had given him nightmares about falling for weeks afterward. But he forced himself to look at the wall and keep climbing. He even managed to negotiate a couple of places where stones falling from above had caught the edge, chipping off large chunks and narrowing the width. He prayed that he wouldn't have one of his nauseous spells up here. He was beginning to regret suggesting this.

After what felt like a week but couldn't have been more than half an hour, they reached a point where the tower was too damaged to allow them to go farther. The last solid piece of the ramp was complete enough for them both to crawl onto. Cate sat looking out over the edge, while Howard lay flat and peered around the corner. They were looking approximately in the direction they had been traveling, and the view, even through Howard's nervousness, was awe-inspiring.

The vast ruined city stretched away to a distant horizon where Howard could just make out a range of snow-capped mountains against the pale gray sky. The view looked a little like the old photos he had seen in history class of the bombed cities of the Second World War—Hamburg, Dresden or Berlin. The difference was that those destroyed German cities had been built and populated by humans. Whoever or whatever had built this place knew nothing about humans or the geometry Howard had learned in school.

The city was constructed of stone, yet it looked as if it had grown straight out of the ground—there was hardly a straight line or right angle anywhere. Roadways curved wildly in strange directions and suddenly disappeared below ground or soared into the air on impossibly thin supports. Some buildings resembled immense gnarled tree trunks at ground level but widened and branched into what looked like great organic inverted pyramids.

Jagged needles of stone jutted from high on the buildings, marking where walkways had once joined them together. Ramps wrapped themselves around some of the buildings. They twisted and turned so sharply that anything traveling along them would have had to defy gravity not to fall to its death.

The magnitude of the view, combined with a total lack of recognizable landmarks, made it impossible for them to understand the scale of what they were looking at. At times it seemed like a toy city, and Howard felt that he was hovering over it. At others, he felt like a tiny speck of dust falling forever through the vastness. He pressed himself against the solid stone of the ramp and tried to fight off the vertigo.

"It's incredible," Cate breathed.

The height and the strangeness didn't seem to bother her, and she was leaning perilously far out to get a better view. Howard wanted to grab her and drag her back to safety, but that would have meant moving, and he doubted he could let go of the piece of stone he was embracing. He grunted something he hoped sounded like agreement.

"Look," Cate said, leaning even farther out and causing Howard to whimper in fear, "the city's designed like some octopus creature. See? The arch we came through is at the end of one of the arms, and we *were* walking toward the center."

Howard took a deep breath and inched forward until he could see a bit more of what Cate was talking about. Only his head was sticking out the gap in the wall of the tower, but when he made the mistake of looking down, it felt as if his whole body was about to hurtle onto the stones below. He closed his eyes until the feeling passed.

Looking up, he could see that Cate was right. The road they had traveled on was the arm of an octopus—or rather, one of dozens of arms that twisted and intertwined as they wound toward the city center. Where they crossed, one sometimes descended to become a tunnel below the other. Elsewhere one arm would rise on thin trunk-like supports to fly over the other. Some of the arms were roads like the one they had walked along. Others had no obvious purpose. Buildings, towers and impossible upside-down pyramids lined both sides of all of them.

The spaces between the winding arms were mostly open. There were a few small buildings here and there, and some low mounds with what looked like entrances to caves, but most of these spaces were piled high with black cinders, like the aftermath of some great fire. As the arms came together, the spaces between them narrowed and became filled with buildings, until they formed a solid ring around the two biggest structures in the city. These were sharply curved on one side and almost flat on the other, and they faced each other like the open jaws of some unimaginable predator. Just looking at the two edifices made Howard feel a creeping sense of dread.

"Are we going there?" he asked weakly.

"That has to be the center," Cate said. She sounded distracted as she peered out over the city. "That's where the power must be. That's where we have to go."

"And what'll we do when we get there?"

"I don't know." She turned from the view to look at Howard. "Are you okay?" she asked, worry crossing her face.

"Heimao's not the only one who's not good with heights," he admitted.

"I'll help you," she offered, standing up.

Howard wanted to scream, "Get down! You'll fall!" but his throat seemed to be as paralyzed as the rest of him. He watched wide-eyed as Cate stepped past him, her feet on the very edge of the broken ramp. If she fell, he'd never be able to move again.

When she reached Howard's feet, she said, "Give me your hand."

Very slowly and carefully, he rolled over and took Cate's hand, trying not to crush it. Knowing what was outside the tower made the journey down much worse than the one coming up, and Howard didn't think he could have managed without Cate's encouragement. As it was, he was shaking like Jell-O by the time they were back on level ground.

"*Nice view?*" Heimao asked.

Howard would have said something rude if he hadn't been so relieved to be back on the ground.

"Did the city remind you of anything?" Cate asked as they returned to the road.

"Apart from my worst nightmare?" he said. "No, not really."

She reached into her satchel and pulled out a piece of yellowed paper.

"That's the map that was folded in the back of the book."

"Yeah. I thought it might be important, so I brought it along."

"What's it a map of?"

"I think it's this city." Cate held the paper up for Howard to see. It did look a bit like the city they were in. It was roughly circular, and there were roads crossing and recrossing each other. But it wasn't exactly the same.

"It's much more complex than the arms we saw from the tower," Howard said after a long look, "and there doesn't seem to be any sign of the buildings we saw at the city center."

"I know," Cate agreed. "It's not quite right. There are no buildings marked at all."

"What's that?" Howard pointed at a bright spot between two of the arms.

Cate shrugged. "I'll keep looking at it as we go. Maybe it will make more sense as we get closer to the center."

As they set off again, Howard looked back up at the tower they had climbed. It didn't look nearly as high from below as it had from the top. A thought struck him. "If this is R'lyeh," he asked, "won't Cthulhu be sleeping here somewhere?"

"Yes. But I don't think we'll wake him."

"As long as we don't stumble into his bedroom."

Cate laughed, and for a moment Howard felt wonderful. Then she said, "Remember the poem that Aileen recited?"

"Bits of it."

Cate stopped and closed her eyes and began to recite it:

The Ancient One in R'lyeh lies,
Shrouded in deathlike sleep.
If death shall die and
Baleful dreams awake,
Then sunlight, eon-aged and luminous,
Must bright the dreadful ink-dark streets,
B'yond eldritch vaults of time.
And one from abyss black
And prehistoric depths must call,
The prime of three to bind once more
The sundered chains of sleep
Upon the ghastly Ancient One.

"The first two lines tell us that the Ancient One is in death-like sleep in R'lyeh," she explained.

"Okay, I get that. But what about death dying and baleful dreams?"

"I think that's Hei and Leon waking Cthulhu and your dreams. They're obviously related. The aged and luminous sunlight illuminating dark streets does sound like here."

"That makes sense, I guess, but then what's the abyss? And what does the bit about three broken chains mean?"

"That might be a reference to the three pieces of the Golden Mask, but I'm not sure about that," Cate admitted. "Hopefully, we'll be able to work it out."

Howard had been hoping a lot of things recently, and it hadn't done much good. But he pushed back the thought of what it might mean if they couldn't work it out.

As they progressed, the buildings got larger. The towers were taller—some two or three times the height of the one they had climbed. Most were broken, but a couple tapered to narrow pinnacles. There were archways in impossible places, stairs that led nowhere and roofs where floors should have been. The remains of narrow walkways projected from some of the towers and pyramids. Most ended in jagged broken blocks, but a few spanned incredible distances to join with other buildings. It made his heart race just to think about crossing these soaring, unprotected pathways. One of the inverted pyramids loomed over them threateningly. Howard looked up as they passed, but he couldn't shake the feeling that he was looking down.

"It's us!" Cate exclaimed, stopping in midstride.

"What is?"

"Well, not us exactly," she corrected, showing Howard the map she had been looking at. "I think it's the position of the map." She pointed to the bright spot. "The point moves when we do. It seems to know where it is."

"A GPS system," Howard said. "But it's not accurate. We're obviously on a road, but the bright spot is in the middle of a space between the arms."

"I know. The spot moves when we move, turns in the right direction when we turn corners, but the route we're on bears no relation to any of the arms marked on the map. I don't understand it."

"I don't have a clue how it works either," Howard said, "so I guess all we can do is keep watching, and maybe it'll make sense eventually."

Cate didn't seem convinced, but they continued their journey.

They walked on for a couple of hours, climbing and descending a huge overpass when the road they were on crossed one running at a different angle.

"How much time do you think has passed back in our world?" Howard asked once they were back on a flat road.

"Impossible to say. Time moves at different rates in different dimensions, but I have no idea of the relationship between two specific dimensions. It might even be possible for time to move backward in one dimension relative to another."

Howard walked on in silence, trying to get his head around the idea that what seemed to be a few hours here could conceivably be only seconds in Aylford. Possibly several days had flown past, and his mom was having a fit, wondering where he'd gone. Whatever speed time was moving at in Aylford, it was a good thing his mom didn't know where he was. He thought of asking Cate what would happen if time in Aylford was moving backward and they arrived home the previous Wednesday and met themselves, but he decided against it.

Beside him, she switched the head lamp on. As soon as she did, Howard realized that it was getting darker everywhere at once, as if someone were slowly turning a dimmer switch. Was it night in this strange world? The thought terrified him.

Daytime, when he could see as far as he wanted, was bad enough. What would darkness be like with only Cate's head lamp and his cell phone to show the way? He was in the middle of working up a good worry when they turned a corner and arrived at the center of the city.

The central square was even more vast than it had looked from the ruined tower. The paved open area was easily large enough to hold most of Aylford, and the two jawlike buildings in the middle were like two cruise ships sitting on their sterns.

Awed by the scale, Howard and Cate walked forward. It was still light enough to see across the square, but details on the buildings were vague. As they progressed, they passed scattered stone pedestals covered in the same hieroglyphic writing they had seen on the archway, but a lot of it looked as if it had been deliberately chiseled out to make it unreadable.

"Can you make out anything it says?" Howard asked.

"Not much. It was probably about whatever once stood on top of each plinth. And whatever those things were, it looks as if they were torn down and broken up," she said, pointing to the piles of rubble around the bases of each pedestal.

Howard was relieved that the statues had been destroyed. Some of the fragments were large enough to suggest things that couldn't possibly have existed in any world he was familiar with.

As they approached the central buildings in the fading light, Howard noticed black patches on the walls that faced each other. He pointed them out to Cate, who aimed her head lamp at one. It looked like a package wrapped in old paper or torn parchment and stuck to the otherwise smooth surface.

Howard was about to mention the rustling noise he could hear when the package they were looking at unwrapped itself. With a sickening, high-pitched scream, something hideous— an incubus of scales, horns and claws—spread a pair of tattered, leathery wings and dropped toward them.

R'LYEH

THE ABYSS

"Run!"

Cate's advice was hardly necessary. They had barely taken three steps when Howard heard the scrabble of the creature's claws on the stone behind them. Cate abruptly changed direction, and he followed. Heimao kept straight on and disappeared behind a pile of rubble. There were more ruined statues and fallen rubble between the two monstrous buildings, and the pair struggled to find their way in the fading light. At last they stopped, breathing heavily. Cate turned off her head lamp, and they slumped down behind a carved plinth.

The horrific creature advanced slowly, checking every fragment of darker shadow as it went. It didn't move very efficiently on the ground, and they had left it some distance behind. But they could hear it calling a thin, childlike scream as it searched for them.

"What is that thing?" Howard whispered.

Quietly Cate replied, "It's said that the Elder Gods were expert at manipulating the creatures they found, turning them into whatever they needed. I think what attacked us was a night-gaunt, a vicious creature designed to protect the city."

"You know a lot," Howard said in awe.

"I read too much."

"Do you think Heimao will be all right?"

A voice echoed from far away. *"I'm a black cat on a dark night. What do you think?"*

"Could we have been wrong about coming through the arch?" Howard asked Cate.

"Not that, no. But perhaps we weren't supposed to come exactly here. There's nothing but ruins and night-gaunts."

Howard risked a look around the plinth to see if he could spot the one that was chasing them. The darkness was thickening, and at first he saw nothing but shadow. Then a piece of the shadow moved. With a loud screech the night-gaunt hopped onto a pedestal not more than thirty feet away and cocked its head as if listening.

Howard got his first good look at the creature, and it was not encouraging. The beast was about the size of a grown man and lightly built. Its fingers and toes ended in viciously curved claws, as did the bones supporting the wings that grew from behind its shoulders. Two curving horns sprouted from its head, and, most disturbing of all, it had no face. As Howard watched, its wings spread and, with a couple of ponderous beats, launched the creature into the air.

"It's searching for us," he said, pulling back out of sight.

"And it's not alone," Cate added, pointing up.

All across the faces of the two buildings, night-gaunts were waking up, stretching their wings and dropping into the air. Most were spiraling aimlessly, but several were coming closer.

"We have to move," she said.

"Where?" Howard asked. Nowhere he could see was any better than where they were.

"Maybe we can get inside." Cate pointed to the closer of the two buildings. "We can't stay out in the open. Once it's completely dark, we'll be at the mercy of those things."

"Okay, let's go." Howard forced himself to his feet.

The first night-gaunt hit them before they'd run five steps. Howard felt a searing pain as its talons ripped long gouges across his shoulders. He managed to keep his feet and lunge sideways. They evaded the second attack, but the wing of the third night-gaunt caught Cate on the cheek, leaving a nasty cut.

They darted, lunged, leaped and stumbled, desperately trying to make their movement as unpredictable as possible. The night-gaunts were blind, but they clearly had some other form of navigation, like a bat's sonar. Howard and Cate had an advantage as long as the light lasted, but it was getting darker by the minute. Then it would all be over. The night-gaunts would continue to slash, cut and tear until they hit something vital or until Howard and Cate were so weakened by loss of blood that they couldn't go on.

The pair staggered over increasing amounts of rubble, trying to keep as close as possible to the plinths, where the night-gaunts had more trouble swooping in on them. Even so, they were exhausted and bleeding from a dozen slashes by the time they heard a familiar voice say, "This way."

Cate stopped so suddenly that Howard steamrolled into her back, and they both fell just as a huge night-gaunt swept its dagger-claws through the air above them.

"Over here! This way!" Aileen's voice urged.

Howard squinted into the darkness and saw an arm beckoning from a patch of deep shadow at the base of the closest building. "Come on," he said to Cate.

It was not far to run, but both got hit once more before they arrived at a narrow doorway in the ground.

"One at a time." Aileen's voice came from the blackness. "Feet first."

Howard ushered Cate in and saw her disappear. Just as he was sitting down to go next, a night-gaunt made a final attack, and the tip of a claw raked across his forehead. Then he was in a tunnel, sliding painfully down a sloping, narrow ramp into total darkness. It was a short slide, and he was soon beside Cate on level ground.

"Are you okay?" he asked.

"I think so," Cate replied.

"You can stand up," Aileen said. "There's room, and the night-gaunts can't get down the tunnel."

"*So you made it.*" Heimao's voice came from the same place as Aileen's.

"No thanks to you," Howard said.

"*And I was supposed to do what? Sacrifice myself? I hardly think that would have stopped them for long.*"

Choosing not to reply, Howard stood up and helped Cate to her feet. She switched on her head lamp and turned to their rescuer. Howard almost collapsed in shock.

"Hello," Madison said in Aileen's voice. "You seem to have had a rough time with the night-gaunts."

"Madison—is that you?" he stuttered.

"In a way," she said with a puzzled frown. "I think I'm also asleep on the white ship. Maybe I'm having a dream."

"Dreaming this?"

Madison shook her head. "A much more pleasing dream. But we have to go. We don't have much time, and you must reach the Abyss." She turned away.

Howard looked at Cate, who simply shrugged as she and Heimao followed Madison. He was left to trudge behind, dragging the weight of a million more questions with him.

The group wended their way through twisting tunnels and corridors. Occasionally they crossed larger chambers, one of which was filled with the crawling sea creatures from the beach. But when the creatures approached, Madison intoned something, and they slunk off into the darkness.

Eventually they entered a chamber so vast that Cate's head lamp could not pick out the walls or roof—but it did pick out the sharp edge of a hole in the floor. There was no sign of the far edge. The nearer they got to the precipice, the more nervous Howard became. A cold wind blew out of the pit, and it carried faint sounds of waves and a musical whistling. The aching loneliness of the journey between dimensions returned.

"The Abyss," Madison said as she beckoned them forward.

To Howard's great relief, she indicated that they should lie down. They did, then peered over the edge.

Howard could see nothing but blackness. The wind was icy on his face, and the unearthly music chilled his soul. He could distinctly hear waves crashing on a shingle beach and wondered if this was a link to the dimension Hei and Leon had taken them to. He prayed it wasn't, because it was where Cthulhu was, and he really didn't want to be close to that monstrosity ever again.

"Do you hear it?" Madison said. "It's the music of infinity."

"Yes," Howard said.

"No," Cate said.

He twisted his head to look at her. How could she not hear it? He pushed back from the edge and sat up. Cate joined him.

"The music of infinity was played by the Elder Gods to trap and hold Cthulhu," Madison explained. "Only a few with great power can hear it."

"If the music's still playing," he asked, "why is Cthulhu waking up?"

"Because someone has found a way to weaken the sound."

Howard thought for a moment. "It's me, isn't it? I have the power to weaken the hold of the music and release that horror we saw. That's why Hei and Leon were using me."

Madison nodded sadly. "With great power comes great responsibility, but the responsibility cannot be learned if the bearer of the power doesn't realize he has it. You are an innocent with a gift—or a curse—that you don't understand. You don't have time to learn, and that leaves your power open to be used by others. When you were by the ocean, you were scared, yes?"

"I was terrified," Howard said.

"And your fear increased?"

"Of course it did. When that thing rose from the island, I was scared witless."

"You haven't learned the discipline to control your power, so it feeds on your emotion. When you're worried or angry or scared, the power surges. When you're calm, it lies dormant. That's why Leon took you to the ocean shore. He terrified you to make the power work for his dark purposes, just as Cate made you angry to escape the stone circle."

"So I'm the cause of all this chaos? I'm bringing on the end of the world?"

"Unwittingly, yes."

Howard felt crushed by the responsibility and by what he was. He looked over at Cate, but she was staring at the ground, her expression grim. Even Heimao had her back turned.

"What can I do to make it right?" he asked miserably.

There was a long pause, during which the alien music from the Abyss got louder, swelling to drown out Howard's thoughts.

"There's only one thing you can do," Madison said. Her voice was soft and filled with an almost unbearable sadness.

"What is it?" he asked. "I'll do anything."

Cate looked up, took a deep breath and said, "You have to die."

R'LYEH

THE GOLDEN MASK

The music was too loud. Howard had misheard. She must have said "try" and not "die."

"What do I have to try?" he asked.

As soon as he saw the desolation in Cate's eyes, he knew he hadn't misheard. "It's impossible," he said, knowing full well that, like all the other times he'd said something was impossible, he was wrong.

Slowly he got to his feet. "This can't be the only way. There must be something else. You're an Adept, Cate." He turned to Madison. "And you're a sorceress who can travel through time and between dimensions. It can't all depend on me dying."

Madison's face became hard, and she stared at Howard with a coldness that made him tremble with fright. Cate let out a series of shuddering sobs.

It was true? This strange being who had taken over Madison and the girl he thought was his best friend were going to kill him?

"Cate," he pleaded.

Her eyes were wide beneath her dark fringe, and tears streamed down her cheeks. She looked helpless and…beautiful. Then she closed her eyes, gave a single choking sob and lowered her head.

"I won't let this happen!" Howard felt anger surge through him, overwhelming the fear. Darkness edged into his vision, forming a tunnel. At the center of the tunnel stood Madison, cold and uncaring. Howard took a step forward. He saw Madison's lips move and felt his muscles seize in midstride. He was paralyzed, just as he had been at the beach, but this time no one was going to rescue him. All Madison needed to do was push him over the edge of the Abyss and leave him to die in a broken heap at the bottom—or, worse, to fall forever in an eternity of frightful, monstrous loneliness in the sickening emptiness of nowhere.

Rage overwhelmed him. Darkness blinded him. He forced his lips to move and screamed into the darkness, "No! I won't let you do this! I'll fight to my very last breath!" He was grinding his teeth, and his arms and legs shook with the effort of trying to move.

"Leave him alone!"

The shock of hearing the familiar voice cut through Howard's rage. The blackness retreated. Five minutes earlier Leon would have been the last person Howard wanted to see stepping forward out of the darkness. Now he wasn't so sure.

"Leave him alone," Leon repeated. "I need him."

His voice was recognizably Leon's, yet it was different. It was flat and emotionless, like Hei's. He was Hei and Leon in the same way that Madison was Aileen and Madison.

"Hello, Aileen," he said. "Or should I call you Guang? Madison was a good disguise. I wasn't expecting you here, but your presence explains why things have not gone as I planned."

"Hello, Heian," Madison replied, turning to face the newcomer. "It's good to see you after all this time."

"I doubt that," Leon said with a sneer. "Especially since you're too late. You should have thrown these two into the Abyss as soon as you got here. I couldn't have stopped you. But you didn't have the strength. You had to have the emotional farewell scene. You were always too soft. That's why you'll always lose and I'll always have power."

"You think that awakening Cthulhu will give you power?"

Madison and Leon were standing an arm's length apart, staring intently into each other's eyes. Howard sensed there was a struggle going on that had nothing to do with what they were saying.

"Cthulhu will thank me for freeing him. In my dreams he has promised that once he returns, the remotest corner of the universe will be mine to explore. I'll be able to leave this puny world that has trapped me for so long and voyage to planets you cannot even imagine. I will move in time like a bird through the air. I'll see the beginning and the ending of everything. I will feel the heat of exploding suns and the icy electric wind from galaxies where a billion stars are born and die. I will touch absolute cold and taste the metallic tang of radiation. I will talk with the chaos of Azathoth at the center of creation."

Leon was enjoying his moment. He was relaxed, smiling—gloating. Howard wondered what he had in store for him.

Not a fall into the Abyss, that much was clear. But what was the alternative? Was he to be returned to the ocean shore and given over to the horror that he had been a part of summoning? Perhaps the Abyss would be preferable.

"You could have come with me, Madison," Leon said. "We would have made quite a couple, wouldn't we? The moon and the sun together. We would have illuminated the universe with our power. But no, you had to have this stupid sentimental attachment to these insignificant creatures. One"—he pointed contemptuously at Cate—"a pitiful Adept who imagines she can see what she cannot even understand. And the other"—he looked at Howard, and his sneer broadened—"a fool who has no concept of the power he's been blessed with."

"You're the fool." Madison seemed remarkably calm given the circumstances. "Do you honestly believe that Cthulhu will care about you? You call these two insignificant. How much more of a trifling nothing must you seem to Cthulhu, a being to whom eons of time are but seconds, and the infinities of space mere gardens to play within? To Cthulhu you are but an inconsequential, worthless spot. It will not even do you the honor of killing you. It will ignore you—leave you to scream your loneliness for eternity in nowhere."

For an instant Leon's arrogant sneer slipped to reveal a flash of anger. Then it was back in place. "You've always talked too much. I think it's time to end this."

"I have one more thing to say." Madison leaned toward Leon as if she was about to confide a secret. "I *am* emotional, and I *am* attached to these puny creatures, but had I not organized the emotional farewell scene you so despised, my friend Howard would not have become frightened and enraged. He wouldn't have radiated the power he doesn't know he has. He would not have called you here."

A frown crossed Leon's face. "What?" he asked.

Madison moved with lightning speed, lunging forward and wrapping her arms around Leon's waist. Unbalanced, he toppled. Madison took two steps and launched them both out over the Abyss. Locked together, they hung for an impossibly long time over the blackness. Madison began to glow and change shape. She brightened to an intense light that hurt Howard's eyes, but he couldn't look away. Leon was engulfed by the light, and Howard could just barely make out his form—but his piercing shriek stabbed his ears. The light began to spin, and with unbelievable speed, it fell.

Howard strained to follow the light, until it was no more than a bright star in the endless darkness. Leon's scream was lost to the unearthly piping music, which grew so loud that it became a physical thing, pounding Howard's body inside and out. He groaned, clamped his hands over his ears, closed his eyes and collapsed onto the ground. He felt as if there were a huge weight pressing on every inch of his body. At the instant he couldn't take any more pressure, it stopped. It was as if someone had flipped a switch. The piping sound stopped and an eerie quiet descended.

Utterly drained, Howard drew in a shuddering breath and hauled himself into a sitting position.

Cate was beside him, arm around his shoulder. "I'm sorry. I'm sorry. I'm sorry," she repeated over and over again.

"Sorry?" Howard breathed deeply, trying to calm himself enough to work things out. "For what?"

"I had to do it. It was the only way."

"Do what?"

"Help Aileen convince you that we were about to throw you into the Abyss."

"You weren't really going to kill me?"

"Of course not." Cate hugged Howard harder and put her head on his shoulder. He buried his face in her neck. "Don't ever think that again. Aileen knew that the only sure way of stopping Hei from using your power to call Cthulhu was to cast him into the Abyss. We had to lure him here—and to do that, we had to let him sense your power. You had to be scared or angry or both. I'm sorry. That's twice I've used you shamelessly."

"It's okay." Howard stroked Cate's hair. She looked up, and the two stared into each other's eyes. Then he said, "But Madison or Aileen—or whoever she was—went into the Abyss as well."

"The real Madison and Leon are just as dumb and obnoxious as they ever were. Aileen and Hei used their forms alone. Light and dark are two parts of the same thing—two sides of the same coin. They always will be."

"Is Aileen dead?"

Cate laughed. "I thought by now you would have worked out that death is not as simple as you believed. The Adept H.P. Lovecraft understood. He said, *In his house at R'lyeh dead Cthulhu waits dreaming.* What is dead in one dimension isn't necessarily dead in another."

"Is Cthulhu still awake?"

"Probably, but not fully. The ceremonies on the shore weren't completed, so a large part of what the Elder Gods put in place still holds. Cthulhu is more aware than it was, but it's still trapped between dimensions, and its power is only a tiny fraction of what it's capable of."

"It seemed powerful to me, coming out of the sea like that."

Cate nodded. "And that gives you a minute suggestion of what it would be like if it was fully awake and free to travel between dimensions."

The pair sat quietly for a moment. Then Cate said, "There's just one more thing you have to do."

"No," Howard groaned. "Haven't I done enough?"

"Almost." She smiled. "But you were brought here for two reasons—to tempt Hei to come here and…"

"And?" Howard prompted.

Cate raised her arm and pointed over the Abyss. "To get that."

Howard looked to where she was pointing and gasped. On the spot where Madison and Leon had disappeared there now hovered a slender green-jade pillar. On its top, gleaming in the beam of Cate's head lamp, was a fragment of a golden face. It was part of the top of a rounded head, an eye, an ear and most of a cheek.

"The Golden Mask," Howard whispered in awe.

"A fragment of it," Cate agreed.

"It's beautiful."

"It's even more spectacular close up."

"What do you mean?" Howard tore his eyes away from the mask and looked at Cate.

"You have to go and get it."

"What? That really *is* impossible. It's in the middle of a bottomless pit, balanced on a hovering pillar of stone. There's no way to reach it."

Cate smiled again. "Heimao will show you the way."

Howard had almost forgotten that the cat was with them. Now she strode out from behind Cate and, with a glance at Howard, strolled over to the Abyss and stepped off the edge.

Heimao took a few steps over nothing and turned to look back. *"There is a path through the darkness,"* she said, *"but I'm not going to wait here forever."*

"There's no path out there," Howard said in a panic. "There's nothing there. I'll fall."

"Am I falling?" Heimao sat and casually began cleaning her face.

"No," he admitted, "but you're a familiar. You can do magic."

"So can you. Come on, Sheepherder. Time is short. Trust me."

"Don't call me that," Howard said as he nervously approached the edge and peered over. There was no sign of a solid path, just blackness. Oddly, this made it less scary. There was no dizzying drop to imagine himself falling down, just blackness.

Tentatively he extended his right foot. Instead of going down, it met a solid surface.

"That's the way," Heimao encouraged. *"Now the other foot."*

Very slowly, Howard transferred his weight to his right foot. It felt solid. He lifted his left foot and gingerly placed it in front of his right. It too found solidity.

"*Well done,*" Heimao said sarcastically. "*But try a little faster. I know you have only two feet, but it's not hard, and you have been practicing walking for years.*"

The cat stood up and continued strolling toward the shimmering mask. Howard followed, concentrating on his goal and placing his feet exactly where Heimao had stepped. He had no idea how wide the invisible path was—and no desire to find out.

After what seemed like an eternity, they reached the green pillar. Howard found it more frightening here because he could see the pillar receding into the blackness below, and that gave him a sense of how far he could fall. To calm himself, he focused on the mask. Heimao jumped calmly to the top of the pillar and sat beside it.

"What do I do now?" Howard asked.

He heard a sigh inside his head. "*I have never met anyone who asked as many pointless questions as you,*" Heimao said. "*Do you think I brought you out here to look at the view? Pick up the mask.*"

Carefully Howard leaned forward and lifted the fragment of the mask off the pillar. It was surprisingly heavy.

"*Well done,*" Heimao said. "*Now take it back to Cate.*"

"Aren't you going to lead the way?"

"*You've done it once. How hard can the second time be? Just walk toward Cate.*"

The journey back was more nerve-racking than the one out, but at last Howard stood beside Cate. She paid no attention to either him or the mask but instead gazed out at Heimao, still perched on top of the pillar.

"Now," Cate said under her breath. "Come on."

Howard saw that the pillar was beginning to drop. Heimao stretched and leaped off the pillar, which began to sink faster. The cat was running toward them as fast as she could, but the invisible path was now sloping—and getting steeper. It was as if it was attached to the pillar and was being dragged down with it.

"Come on. Come on!" Cate encouraged as Heimao struggled toward them. The slope was very steep now, and Heimao was moving more slowly. "She's not going to make it."

Howard thrust the mask into Cate's arms. "Hold this," he said and lay down on the edge of the Abyss. Leaning out as far as he dared, he stretched his hands toward Heimao. "Come on," he said. "I thought cats were supposed to be agile."

Heimao leaped. It was not elegant, and Howard felt a searing pain as her claws dug through his shirt and gripped his arm. He pulled his arm back, and Heimao landed in a graceless heap on the ground at Cate's feet.

"*Did you have to be so violent?*" came the voice in Howard's head.

"Did you have to dig your claws in so hard?" Howard replied, examining the scratches on his forearm.

"Stop squabbling, you two, and listen," Cate said.

"What? I can't hear anything."

"Exactly. Listen to the silence. There's no music coming from the Abyss and no sound of waves. Aileen was successful. That portal's closed."

"And we've got a piece of the mask!" Howard said.

Cate handed it back to him. "It was your task to retrieve it, so you'd better hold it while we take it back."

"How do we get back from here?" Unpleasant thoughts of black tunnels, crawling beasts and faceless night-gaunts dragged themselves into Howard's mind.

"Easy!" Cate said. "All we need to do is close our eyes, tap our heels together three times and say, *There's no place like home.*"

For a moment Howard thought she had gone crazy. Then he blurted, "*The Wizard of Oz!*"

"Yes. Dorothy was one of the best Adepts ever."

"You're joking, right?" He hesitated, unsure. "Aren't you?"

Cate gave him an exaggerated wink. Then she pulled the map from her satchel and unfolded it for Howard to see. The bright spot was exactly in the center.

"Probably easier if we use this. I was watching it on the way here. It's a map not of the surface of the city but of these underground tunnels we came through. It should be simple enough to find our way back to the arch. With luck, we should be able to avoid the main square and the night-gaunts, but we should get going or your mom will start worrying about you."

"I don't suppose we can ever tell anyone about all this?" Howard said as they set off, arm in arm.

"Oh, I don't know," she responded with a laugh. "Don't you think your mom would want to know we met Amshu and Claec from Atlantis?"

BACK HOME

Using the map, Howard, Cate and Heimao easily navigated through the undercity without meeting the night-gaunts again. They came out at the lower entrance to the arch and walked up to the Chamber of the Deep, where Kun was waiting for them.

"Welcome back," he said with a smile. "I see you have been successful."

Howard handed him the piece of the Golden Mask. "I think this is for you."

Kun took the fragment and stared at it. "I knew this day would come, but I still cannot believe it."

He gently placed the piece on top of the jade column in the middle of the room. He stepped back and recited a few incomprehensible words. The top of the jade pillar wavered. It became almost liquid and then solidified with the fragment of the Golden Mask sitting upright on top.

"That is safe for now," Kun said.

"I thought it took two of the three fragments to work the spells in the Chamber of the Deep," Cate said.

"To unlock the mask, yes, but closing is often much easier than opening. Now, may I offer you some tea before you go back?"

"We'd love to, but we have to hurry," Cate apologized. "It's been a long journey, and we must rest and recover. Perhaps some other time."

"Of course," Kun said. Howard thought he detected a twinge of sadness in the emperor's voice. "Some other time then. Allow me to lead you back to your ship."

As they followed Kun through the streets of Sanxingdui, Howard whispered to Cate, "Why couldn't we stay for the tea ceremony? From the description in the book, it sounds as if it could be interesting, and maybe Chen would perform it."

"It's best not to stay too long in another time," Cate whispered back. "Strange things can happen."

"*And Chen's friend Ting might bring that annoying, ugly canine, Fu,*" said the voice in Howard's head. "*I cannot stand that beast—far too arrogant and sarcastic.*"

Howard and Cate were still chuckling quietly to themselves when they reached the city gate and emerged onto the dock. The white ship was docked just where they'd left it, but it was deserted.

"Where's Aileen?" Howard asked.

"She had business elsewhere," Kun said. "Do not worry—the ship will take you back home." He took Howard's and Cate's hands in his and said, "I cannot thank you enough for what you have done. You are welcome in Sanxingdui any time and any when."

"Thank you," Cate and Howard said together.

The emperor released their hands, and they boarded the ship. Immediately it moved away from the dock and began traveling rapidly down the river. Howard watched as the tiny figure of Kun shrank until he and the walled city were invisible.

Once at sea, Howard again felt relaxed and calm and barely noticed the time passing. Much to his relief, instead of returning them to the peninsula by the beach, the ship moved up the Bane River and docked by the old wharves in downtown Aylford. As soon as they stepped ashore, the ship left the dock and shot off down the river. Oddly, none of the people strolling on the riverfront paid it or them any attention.

"What time is it?" Cate asked as they stood on the dock.

"Three thirty," Howard said, checking his cell phone. "We've only been gone for an hour."

"Or a day. How do we know it's still Saturday?"

"It must be," he said with more confidence than he felt. "If it was Sunday, Mom would have everyone in Aylford out searching for me by now."

Cate laughed. Neither of them said anything about the possibility that years had passed—forward or back.

"I guess we should head home," she said.

Howard glanced at her. "I'm not going anywhere with you until you take off that silly head lamp. That's too much, even for a geek."

Cate slid the lamp into her satchel. "You don't look too hot yourself," she said, pointing out the rips in his sweatshirt and the cut on his forehead. "We'd better swing by Crowninshield House and tidy you up before your mom sees you. That cut looks nasty."

"I'll say I walked into something," Howard replied as they headed out onto Arcton Street. "The gash on your cheek looks painful."

"It stings a bit," Cate acknowledged, gently touching the dried blood below the cut.

Howard looked around. Everything seemed shockingly normal. The residents of Aylford were going about their business, totally unaware that the grubby kids and the scruffy cat in their midst had just saved them from unimaginable horror.

"Did it all really happen?" Howard asked as they headed up the hill.

"Well," Cate said, "if it didn't happen, we've spent a lot of the day beating each other up."

"Yeah, I know it happened," he said with conviction. "It felt far too real to be anything else, but it still seems unbelievable. It's going to be tough to worry about school next week."

"It's been quite the day," Cate agreed.

"Is it over?"

She took a long time to answer. "For now," she said finally. "But things we can't even guess at have been set in motion."

"Things that will involve us?"

She shrugged. "Who knows? They might. Aylford has a lot of power."

A worrying thought pushed its way into Howard's brain. "You came to Aylford because of your dreams about my dad and me. Will you stay here now that things have settled down?"

"I think I'll hang around for a while," Cate said. "I'm not sure you're ready to look after yourself yet."

"Thanks," he said with exaggerated annoyance.

"*She's right, you know, Sheepherder.*"

"You be quiet," he said to Heimao. "I'm done talking to you."

Heimao arched her back and strode huffily up the hill.

"Just don't try to get me angry or threaten to throw me into any abysses," Howard said to Cate.

"I promise."

He was enjoying being back in the normal world so much that he hardly noticed when Leon and Madison swung around a corner and almost bumped into him.

"Geeks out for a stroll," Leon said nastily. "And they've been fighting too, by the looks of it."

"Walking helps the blood circulate to the brain," Cate replied without missing a beat. "The peripatetic Greek philosophers used to walk along the agora in Athens as they discussed their theories."

Leon and Madison both looked at them blankly.

"Doesn't work in every case," Howard said. It felt good to put Leon down, even if he didn't realize it was being done. The truth was, Leon still scared him. It was hard to get over the memory of being forced out into the water to summon a horror that could destroy the world.

Cate, however, seemed perfectly at ease. "How's Hei?" she asked.

Leon looked confused. "What do you care how our servant's doing? Besides, it's his weekend off."

"Oh, that would explain why I bumped into him down at the beach."

"Beach?" Leon said. "Hei doesn't go to the beach."

"Maybe I was mistaken," she said blithely. She turned to Madison. "Had any good dreams lately?"

Madison shook her head. "You geeks are really beginning to creep me out. Come on, babe," she said to Leon, linking her arm with his. "Let's go."

Howard realized that Cate had been pushing to see if anything was left of Aileen or Hei. "Have you done the history essay for Monday?" he asked Madison.

"It's Saturday," she said, looking at him as if he was stupid. "I've got plenty of time. I bet you rushed home and wrote it the day Campbell handed it out."

Howard couldn't help smiling.

Cate reached into her satchel and pulled out the head lamp. "Thanks for lending me this," she said, offering it to Madison. "It was very useful."

Madison looked totally stunned.

"Hey, that's from my kitchen," Leon said, grabbing the light. "How did *you* get it? You're in big trouble if you tried to crash the party last night. I'd better not see you trying anything like that tonight."

Howard smiled harder as Leon led Madison past them, but Cate had one last creep-out in store.

"Madison!" she shouted after them. "Check out the photos on your phone and tell Leon where you took that cool shot of the creatures on the beach."

Author's Note

The Ruined City is a fantasy novel, but some of it is true. Sanxingdui is, and was, a real place. It lies some fifty kilometers north of Chengdu in China's Sichuan Province. During the Bronze Age (between three and five thousand years ago), it was a thriving walled city. At some point, the city was abandoned, and a vast quantity of elephant tusks, jade artifacts and the incredible masks that the city is famous for were buried in a series of pits. Today a superb modern museum is located within the ancient city walls. There you can find displays of the remarkable finds, including several golden masks, from the ongoing archaeological research.

Aylford, on the other hand, is a fictitious place based loosely upon another fictitious place, Arkham. The adventures that Howard, Cate and Heimao have are inspired by the stories of Cthulhu and the Elder Gods written by a real author, Howard Phillips Lovecraft, whose short stories from the 1920s and '30s influenced such modern writers as Stephen King, Neil Gaiman and Guillermo Del Toro. Cthulhu makes an appearance in the music of Metallica, Arctic Monkeys and the psychedelic rock band H.P. Lovecraft, which recorded a song based on Lovecraft's story "The White Ship."

Of course, there are no other dimensions inhabited by unimaginable, all-powerful monsters—I hope.

Gratitude must be expressed to Lovecraft and all those who have played with his ideas and images and made Cthulhu a part of our modern culture. Thanks are also due to Gordon Mcghie and Calvin Yao for their support and ideas, and for making it possible for me to visit the astonishing artifacts on display in the museum at Sanxingdui. Without the ever precise and thoughtful editing of Janice Weaver, the story of the Golden Mask would not be what it is.

JOHN WILSON is the author of almost fifty novels and nonfiction books for kids, teens and adults, including *Lost Cause* from Seven (the Series). History inspires everything John writes—from stories about dinosaurs and kids caught up in the chaos of war to contemporary characters discovering forgotten family journals and trying to solve mysteries and recover stolen artifacts. He was a finalist for the Governor General's Literary Award, and his books have won or been short-listed for most Canadian children's-literature prizes. John lives in Lantzville, British Columbia. For more information, please visit johnwilsonauthor.com.